As an author, there's nothing I like more than hearing how people enjoy my books. Your reviews are not only welcome but also really helpful to others who are seeking good books to read. Please consider taking just a few minutes to leave a brief review.

Further reading

Eli Ross series

Dark Matter
Final Act
Tears of Joy

Crime thriller with a supernatural twist

Seminole Killer

Megalomania series

Believe it or Not
The Phantom
End of the World
China falls

This work is entirely fictional and any similarity to people or places is purely coincidental.

No part of this publication should be reproduced in any form, or by any means, without explicit permission from the author.

Copyright © 2020 Hugh Macnab

Lost Souls

Hugh Macnab

Copyright © 2023 Hugh Macnab

All rights reserved.

ISBN: 9798500430199

I'm on the Monday morning American Airlines flight from Naples to Washington D.C., with twenty minutes until we land. Two and a half hours in the air. Long enough for me to wonder what the hell I'm letting myself in for.

As a homicide detective, I reckon I've seen some pretty gruesome things and come across dangerous people, but when Lead Agent Fabia Mendez talked with me about this assignment to the Homeland Security Trafficking Division, she firmly emphasized that she only expects me to stay for six months. Or what she described as the maximum she would expect anyone to survive without burn-out.

This is what's at the root of my worry. How much worse can the work be?

I glance out the window as the pilot tells us we're passing over the Chesapeake Bay on the right and should be on the ground on schedule. As I arrive midday, the temperature is around average for October at fifty degrees, dropping to the low forties in the evening. When I left Naples a couple of hours ago, midday was forecast in the mid-eighties dropping to seventy-five at night. I'm in for a shock.

I've never been out of Florida before.

I grew up on the Seminole reservation, went to college in Florida, served as a patrol officer in Miami-Date County, moved to Highway Patrol, and then the Sheriff's office in Naples.

All vacations, such as they've been, were in Florida. The furthest I've been is down to Key West.

So, I guess I'm excited to be out of state and visiting the Capital. I know work will keep me busy, but I'll make sure I see some of the key sites. I want to visit the Whitehouse, Capitol Hill, the Lincoln Memorial, and most of all, the National Air and Space Museum. History is great, but space - so much more interesting. It's where our future lies.

* * *

On the ground, I disembark and wander vast corridors, following everyone else as they look for luggage recovery. Then after successfully picking up my large suitcase, I exit into the bright sunshine and cool air and follow the signs for Enterprise car rental. A car has been pre-arranged for me, as has accommodation. I'll be sharing an apartment with another six-month assignee who is starting at the same time. Hopefully, she'll be friendly.

Twenty minutes later, I pull out into the heavy traffic and follow signs for the Memorial Bridge. Ten minutes later, after crossing the Potomac, I get a first glimpse of the Lincoln Memorial as I loop around and head North, hugging the Potomac until turning inland and following the sat nav to Wisconsin Avenue. The apartment block is four stories tall, with underground parking.

My first problem is I don't have an entry card, so I park in a nearby public car park and walk to the apartment complex. There's a check-in area with a concierge, and he gives me a key to an apartment and a fob for parking. Just my luck, the apartment is on the top floor.

Twenty minutes later, I parked in the allocated spot in the underground parking area, traveled to the fourth floor in the elevator, and opened the apartment door to stand gawping.

Homeland must run with much higher budgets than the Sheriff's office for sure.

The place is brand new and very stylish. Wooden parquet flooring in the lounge area, but tiles in the kitchen, and carpets leading into what I assume to be two bedrooms.

I've made it no further than the middle of the lounge when a man opens one of the bedroom doors and gives me an odd look. He looks around my age, maybe three inches taller, with dark hair military-cropped.

'Are you Sam Greyfox?'

'Sammy, but yes, I am.'

'Ah. Seems like a cock-up to me. You're supposed to be a

man.'

'Sorry to disappoint, but as you can probably tell, I'm not.'

'Well, I'm expecting a man, so you'd better get it sorted out.'

And with that, he disappears into the bedroom and closes the door.

I spend the next few minutes considering my options. I can call Human Resources and see what's going on. I can ask for this guy to be relocated. Or I can move in.

Simple choice, really. Other than the fact he's an ass-hole, I don't have a problem sharing with a man unless there's a shared washroom.

However, I'm good when I check out the second bedroom and see full ensuite facilities.

The bedroom has a king-size bed with a massive padded headboard, two bedside cabinets, a walk-in closet the size of the apartment I left behind in Naples, and a great washroom with a walk-in shower.

I'm more than good. I'm ecstatic.

As virtually all my worldly possessions are in one suitcase, it only takes ten minutes to unpack, and I'm ready to find the coffee maker.

Back in the lounge, ass-hole still hasn't appeared, so I rake around in the kitchen to see what I can find. Not much. So, now I have a problem. If I stock up, is it for me or both of us? We need a kitty or else separate cupboards. And if we have to go down that route, I'll buy a heavy-duty padlock for mine.

I'm not ready to tackle this whole issue yet, so I decided to go find a coffee shop.

It takes ten minutes to find a Lavazza Creperie, but by the time I do, I'm cold. It seems I'll need some warmer clothes. I'm happy to sit in.

That's where I am when my cell buzzes, and I answer to find it's Fabia Mendez asking if I'm settling in okay.

I tell her everything's fine and ask when she expects me to

appear at the office. Apparently, I'm on a one-day course the following day. She gives me an address and says she looks forward to meeting up again personally on Wednesday. I ask her about the course, but she says I'll learn everything I need to know when I get there. Just take some keep-fit gear with me.

I've no idea why I need to take keep-fit gear with me, but I have a more immediate issue to worry about. I need some warm clothing.

Three hours later, heavily laden, I arrive back at the apartment to find Mr. Crop-top has left the remains of a Chinese takeaway littered over the kitchen worktop and thrown the dirty dishes in the sink.

He's stretched out in sweatpants and a T-shirt on the three-seater sofa, watching the Redskins play the Giants.

Not known for diplomacy, I put down the food shopping in the kitchen, then take the new clothes I've purchased into the bedroom and hang everything away. After that, I'm ready.

'You planning on tidying this away?'

All I get is a shout about some stupid linebacker's move. So, I try again. This time I get a grunt.

I choose a cupboard and load up my vital shopping - popcorn, Craft Mac & Cheese, Doritos, and Bagels Then pop the top off a Corona before putting the rest of the six-pack in the fridge along with the cream cheese, a slab of Cheddar and a small carton of milk.

As I'm doing this, I'm using the time to figure out the best approach with this guy. If we're to live together for six months, he needs some serious training, and I'm not sure that's something I can be bothered doing. But, needs must, I suppose.

I wander into the lounge area and see the Redskins are three points down in the third. Crop-top reluctantly moves across the sofa, and I sit. I try the smooth approach.

'Who do you think's going to win?'

'Money's on the Giants. Their QB's too good for the Skins.'
'You don't sound like a New Yorker?'
'I'm not. You asked who I thought would win, not where I'm from.'
'Okay. Where are you from then?'
'San Fransisco.'
'And you're starting a six-month assignment with homeland?'
'Sure. Just like you. Have you found somewhere to stay yet?'
'Yes. It's nice. You would like it.'
'Good.'
Now there's a shout as the Skins QB throws a thirty-yard pass into the zone for a score, and the Giants fall behind.
'Are you on a one-day course tomorrow by any chance?'
'Nope. I report into HQ.'
'What's your name?'
For the first time, he actually looks at me to reply. I don't know if I'm supposed to feel privileged or what.
'Teddy Macintyre. Folks call me Mac.'
I stick out my hand.
'Pleased to meet you, Mac.'
There's just a fractional hesitation, and then he shakes.
'So, you're not moving elsewhere, are you?'
'No. I like it here.'
'I hope you're not going to be difficult?'
I almost laugh, but I don't.
'I doubt it. I'm pretty easygoing,' I tell him, lifting the tv controller and starting to channel flick.
'Hey, what are you doing? I'm watching the game.'
'Oh, sorry. I thought we could share a Romcom film. Or maybe something on Netflix?'
'Shit! You're joking, right?'
By now, he's swung his legs off the sofa and is paying me real attention for the first time.
'Hey, unless we get some rules in place. You're in for a tough ride, Mac,' I tell him, waving the controller just out of

his reach.

Twenty minutes later, we've reached some agreements. He's put his dishes in the dishwasher and trash in the bin. We've agreed to share the costs of food and to shop alternately. Laundry, we each take care of ourselves. I'm not having him touching my undies, and I certainly don't want to be anywhere near his.

I give him the controller back when I'm convinced we're good. He gets to watch sports, and it turns out we both like MASH.

After that, we seem good.

At nine am, I turn up at the address I've been given, complete with my running gear. The door's already open, so I enter. The place turns out to be a small private gym. When I say small, I mean tiny. I doubt more than half a dozen people can fit in the place.

There's only one person there, and he turns toward me as I enter.

'Detective Greyfox, I assume?'

I nod.

'Hi. I'm Tarrant. I'm your instructor for the day.'

'What kind of instructor?'

'The kind who might just help you save your life.'

'So, a top-notch chef who will save me from a diet of popcorn and Mac & Cheese?'

He smiles.

'Why would I want to save you from the good stuff? I'm talking about more short-term life-threatening situations you may encounter without your firearm to rescue you.'

'You know about me not being allowed to carry for six months?'

'Ms. Mendez told me. What she didn't tell me is why? Care to enlighten me?'

'If we're going to talk, do you have any coffee around here?'

Ten minutes later, we're sitting on a workout bench, two

black coffees, and I'm telling him why the Sheriff has revoked my license-to-carry.

'So,' he asks. 'You don't shoot to kill? Is that the problem?'

'Look, I'm a perfect shooter. I don't take shots I'm not sure I can make.'

'Until you're wrong.'

'I've never been wrong.'

'Yet.'

'Sounds like you agree with the ban?'

'First, let me ask why you don't do what you've been trained to do.

'I don't need to.'

'You know better than your instructors, many of whom have been on the streets for much longer than you?'

'It's not that I know better. It's that I'm confident in my skills.'

'What's your percentage?'

'In competition or on the range?'

'Both.'

'I won the handgun shootout against all-comers with a one-hundred percent score.'

'Impressive. What about on the range?'

'Consistently high nineties.'

'What, ninety-five, six. Something like that?'

'Every time.'

'So you miss your target, say four times in a hundred? And your targets stationary at a fixed distance?'

'Usually.'

With that, he pushes me off the bench, and I land hard on my rump.

'What did you do that for?'

'Do you think the bad guys you hunt play by the rules? That they stand still and wait for you to take your shot?'

For once, I don't have a quick reply. I just sit there. I guess I get the point better than when the Sheriff told me it was for my own good.

'Detective Greyfox....'

'Sammy, please.'

'Okay, Sammy. How would you think I would feel if you were my partner and I knew that when we were in a life-threatening position, you would pull off some fancy shooting? Especially if the bad guy is aiming at me? Do you see? It's not just about your confidence in yourself. It's about other people depending on you as well. And I tell you, ninety-six percent doesn't sound too good right then.'

I stand up and rub my butt as I take in what he's telling me before giving it another shot.

'My Papa once told me that it takes years to create a human being but seconds to kill one.'

'And if I were your partner, I would be worried who that one would be.'

I've been beaten up enough, so I changed the subject. So, is that why I'm here today? For you to explain why I need to shoot to kill like a good soldier?'

'No. But you need to think about everything I've just told you. The phrase you just used about being a good soldier tells me you're still way off understanding what your Sheriff expects. Not just from you but everyone who carries a gun. If you can't get your head around that, I would get out before you get someone killed.'

I stare at him, stuck for words for the second time.

'So, today. We will work on keeping you alive in threatening situations where you do not have a gun to protect yourself or others.'

'Self-defense? I covered a lot of that at the Academy.'

'Not defense like this, you didn't. If the bad guys don't play by your rule book, you must learn to play by theirs. Some people call this dirty fighting. I call it learning essential survival skills for unarmed combat.'

The remainder of the day flies by. I spend much of it back on my butt or flailing around helplessly in his grip. Sometimes, he attacks head-on, sometimes from behind. Sometimes with a knife or a gun, other times bare-handed. He explains body mechanics each time, and I learn how to use the knowledge to gain an advantage, even against a much stronger adversary.

He explains where we're most vulnerable. I assume I know all of this. I'm wrong. Our most vulnerable points will depend on the situation. For instance, if the attacker wears a crash helmet with a visor, his eyes are unavailable. If he's behind me, the back of his neck is unavailable. So, I need to know which points to attack and adapt to the dynamics of a fight. They will constantly change.

Tarrant runs through attacking eyes, throat, neck, cojones, knees, arms, and breasts if the attacker is a woman. My weapons are disguise, pace, nails, fingers, elbows, hips, and knees.

I learned how to take a gun away from someone. I've learned this at the Academy, but Tarrant makes it seem more straightforward. Dealing with a knife attack is much more complicated. The attacker can hold the knife or come at you in so many ways. Then, there's how to survive being strangled from behind or being squeezed in a bear hug. How I can broaden my stance to make it harder for the attacker to get me down on the ground? Or how lowering my weight makes it more awkward for him, especially if the attacker is tall. I also learned how to punch without any tells. No body wind-up or elbows out to the side - both easy to see coming. Just a sharp, direct jab. With no warning, it can gain a vital few seconds to allow more severe moves to follow.

By the time we finish, I'm exhausted but feel much more confident. I can't remember ever having learned so much in such a short space of time before.

As we're relaxing, I ask where he learned all this from, but he's evasive. I like that. No showing off.

The last thing he says is that he hopes for everything I've picked up; I give most thought to shoot-to-kill when my license-to-carry is returned.

Back at the apartment, Mac and I order Pizzas, then I go shower and change into loose clothes just as they arrive. I hadn't realized it then, but I worked straight through lunch. I wonder if that's an omen of what's to come.

Homeland Security HQ is off Nebraska Avenue, fifteen minutes from the apartment. It consists of a dozen buildings, some of which are interconnected. I drive around looking for a parking space, but it's not easy. I end up parked beside two huge aerial masts adorned with various dishes and antennae. When I find my way to Lead Agent Mendez's office, it's a quarter after eight, and I'm late for my first day.

I introduce myself at reception and wait until a woman arrives and introduces herself as Anna, Mendez's administrator. She's friendly and welcoming.

Once I've been issued a visitor's badge, and we're making our way to a conference room where she says her boss and a few others are waiting for me, she tells me she's been with her boss for five years and loves working for her, and the job itself.

When we arrive, she opens the door and ushers me in.

Discussions in the room stop, and I get the horrible feeling everyone was talking about me.

My new boss rises and welcomes me, shaking my hand. She invites me to sit next to her as she introduces everyone around the conference room table. It seems these are members of an organization she refers to as Operation T.E.N., which she explains is a new anti-trafficking coalition comprised of U.S. Immigration and Customs Enforcement (ICE), the FBI, Homeland Security and other Federal, State, and local law enforcement agencies across the country. Apparently, T.E.N. means Trafficking Ends Now.

The next hour or so goes by in a blur for me. They're talking about improving education in schools, colleges, and the public in general, encouraging cooperation between agencies, and empowering victims of human trafficking to become thriving survivors. It's all interesting, but it's unclear where I fit in.

When the meeting finishes, most folks leave, but two don't. I remember who one is - Hiram Garfunkel, the head of Cyber-technology, but I've forgotten the other. He turns out to be

Agent Pat Cataldo from the FBI. My boss explains that they've stayed because I will likely turn to them for help when I start my new assignment, and she wants to make sure I know who they are. Each of them hand me a card, wish me luck, and tell me to call anytime.

I nod but still have no real idea of what I'll be doing or why I may need help from the CIA Cyber-technology group, or the FBI for that matter.

When the others have left, my boss suggests we get some coffee and move to her office. I'm more than happy to oblige. Coffee does that to me.

The office is on the top floor and in a corner, so it's light and airy. So much better than my dark cubicle back in Naples.

We sit side by side on a sofa with our coffees as she explains my role.

She starts by making life a lot easier for me. When we're in Homeland and surrounded by our own team, I should call her Fabia, as everyone else does. Only when we're in a T.E.N. meeting or when some non-Homeland personnel is present should I refer to her as Lead Agent Mendez.

She asks me to try it out.

'Sure, Fabia.'

It feels weird, but I know I'll get used to it.

'So, your role is much more practical than the TEN task force. I want you in recovery.'

'Recovery?'

'Yes. Some of our team are on Discovery, searching for leads that may reveal a trafficking operation. Like yourself, the remainder will follow up on these leads and attempt to recover trafficked children.'

'Here in Washington?'

'Anywhere in the Country, Sammy. One week you may be in Cincinnati, another Poplar Bluff. You go where the leads take you and bring these children back safely. You will use whatever local resources you need, and that's where Pat Cataldo, Hiram Garfunkel, and myself come in. If you want local Homeland or FBI help, we will get it for you. If you need local law enforcement's help, you can work that yourself or use me.'

'And Hiram Garfunkel?'

'He is most likely your best resource. He and his CIA group are techno-wizards. If you need something technical, he's your go-to. Internet, computers, data research, dark web, comms… the list goes on. He has a large team, but I suggest you initially go through him personally. Most of us mere mortals would collapse under the kind of daily pressure he's under, but he thrives on it. So if you need to call, do it. I don't think the man sleeps. Questions?'

'Practical things mostly.'

'Such as?'

'This is my first experience of cold weather…'

'And you've had to buy some warm clothes. You want to know about the cash disturbance allowance?'

'Yes.'

'That's all cleared and ready for you. Speak to Anna. In fact, if you need *anything*, speak to Anna. She's another go-to person for you. You're likely to be traveling a lot. You'll need rental cars, hotels, flights and such. She'll make all of that happen for you. The other thing is that you will also receive a per-diem allowance on top of your Naples salary to cover additional expenses. And you will be required to submit receipts with your expense claims. Is that all clear?'

'You seem to have thought of everything.'

'Good. Now, your first assignment.'

She crosses to her desk and returns, carrying a single page. Handing it to me, I see it has a man's name and contact details on it. That's it.

'This is your starting point. It may be something; it may not. It's your job to find out. This man disembarked from a Dutch cargo vessel at the Port of Toronto. He immediately reported an incident he saw onboard to the local police. He says. He thinks some children were offloaded somewhere on the North shore of Lake Ontario.'

'Canada?'

'Yes, but I believe if what he says is true, the children are likely to be intended for here somewhere. They would have taken them off much earlier if their destination was Canada. They had to sail down the St. Lawrence River, past Quebec and Montreal, to reach Lake Ontario. It doesn't make sense.'

'You want me to talk with him and follow up?'

'Yes. You okay with that?'

'Sure. Why not?'

'Okay. Let's get you settled in here first. You need a base to work from.'

With that, she passes me over to her assistant, who shows me to an empty office four doors along. It's not a corner, but it does have windows along one entire wall. I could get used to this.

Anna gets me set up with the computer, arranges passwords, and walks me through the systems I will have access to. She's incredibly patient as I ask one dumb question after another. She then repeats the process with the telephone system before handing me a typed card with a dozen key contact numbers I should program into my cell.

When we're finished, and she asks if I need anything else, I ask where I can get coffee and lunch. This leads to a quick tour of several buildings before returning to my office. The last thing she does is hand me a Homeland Agents ID and a car park sticker for my car. I'm no longer a Sheriff's Detective but a Homeland Security Agent. Not sure how I feel about that.

I have a low moment when Anna's gone, and I'm sitting at an empty desk in an empty office. I wonder how I could have left everything so familiar to me to sit here in this empty place.

Only one thing to do. I lift the phone and place my first call.

The man who answers has a European accent. I'm not an expert, but I don't think he's Dutch.

He confirms he is Emil Basara and that he's Polish.

I ask him to walk me through what he told the police in

New Jersey.

'I have traveled the route from Amsterdam many times. The journey is over three-thousand nautical miles, so it usually takes ten, maybe twelve days. On this last trip, one night, I was unwell and went on deck in the middle of the night to get some fresh air.'

'And that's when you saw something?'

'Yes. A fishing vessel was alongside, and our Captain was arguing with someone onboard. They were shouting at each other, but I couldn't understand what was said. There was a strong wind.'

'What happened next?'

'They seemed to resolve whatever problem they had, and our Captain signaled a couple of our crew to bring these children out from one of the holds. I wasn't close enough to be sure, but I think they were all young girls. Couldn't been more than ten or twelve years old.'

'What happened to them?'

'The crew lowered them down into the fishing boat.'

'And the boat took them away?'

'Yes.'

'What did you do?'

'Nothing. I'm not stupid. If I'd said anything, I would have joined the fish. I know trouble when I see it.'

'Is there anything else you can tell me that might be useful?'

'We were due to dock in Port Toronto the following day. So we were probably already in Lake Ontario.'

'Can you tell me anything about the fishing boat?'

'It was dark. The top of the hull and the cabin were white, and I could only make out the first few letters of the registration.'

'No registration numbers, or maybe a name?'

'No. It was too dark. Just ON 6.'

What about your cargo vessel? What's it called?'

'She is called the Baarn, after an ancient cruiser belonging to the Royal Netherlands Steamship company.'

'Is there anything else you can tell me, Emil?'

'No. I wish you luck in finding these girls. This is a terrible thing.'

After, I thank him for his time and for reporting the incident. I sit back to think about what he has told me. I know the ship he was on - the Baarn. And that the fishing boat has white on the top of the cabin and hull and a registration that begins with ON6. And that the girls were released somewhere in Lake Ontario. Not much to go on.

I take a quick look at Google Maps and see that the lake is a couple of hundred miles long, with far too many small ports along the route to check out everyone. I need a way to reduce the variables.

There's a vague stirring of a distant memory from a class at the Academy. We were covering smuggling routes and sea traffic coming into Florida from the Caribbean and South America. The instructor used a system that monitors transponders fitted to all commercial shipping over a specific tonnage, like the Automated Identification System - AIS for aircraft.

I try downloading several different AIS Apps, but the system restrictions on the Homeland servers prevent me, so it seems like my first challenge for Hiram Garfunkel and his cyber team.

Having made my decision, I decide that as it's my first contact, I should do it in person rather than call. He's at the CIA complex at Langley. It shouldn't take more than forty minutes.

The George Bush CIA Headquarters building is like a pile of kid's rectangular play bricks carefully laid beside other, between six and eight stories tall.

The most impressive thing is the Central Intelligence Agency seal on the floor in the entrance area. It's enormous and proudly displayed.

I confess to being a little starry-eyed at the whole

experience, but who wouldn't be visiting this for the first time?

I show my new Homeland badge at reception and ask to see Hiram Garfunkel.

'Director Garfunkel?'

'Eh, yes. I guess so.'

After waiting a few moments, the receptionist tells me to go through security and take the elevator to the sixth floor, where someone will meet me.

I thank him and follow the instructions, arriving at the sixth a few minutes later to find a guy waiting for me. I would guess he's in his forties, dressed in jeans and a casual sweater with a rainbow on the front.

'Agent Greyfox? Gene Hackman.'

I give him one of my suspicious looks, and he laughs.

'Most people fall for that. My real name's George, but Gene gets more kicks.'

We shake hands as he explains that his boss is tied up in an all-day meeting, but he will do what he can to help me.

We collect a coffee as we head back to his office. An office that turns out to be more like a Geek's playroom. I don't know what everything is, but it's an electronic nirvana, that's for sure.

George invites me to sit and asks how he can help.

I explain what I've got and the idea in my head.

He plays it back to me.

'So, you reckon the cargo ship had to stop to offload the kids and are wondering if I can find a historical log of your ships' movements in the AIS system to find out where that happened?'

'You got it.'

With that, he confirms the name of the cargo ship is Baarn, then turns to one of his screens and starts typing a hundred times faster than I can before giving me an ah-ha.

An image appears to my right on a larger screen. It's obvious straight away that I'm looking at Lake Ontario. I can see the St. Lawrence River at the top and Niagara Falls at the bottom.

As I watch the screen, a dot appears at the top end. It's stationary for thirty seconds, then moves a little. Same again and again. George explains that the freighter's transponder only transmits periodically, so I only see a single dot on the screen each time it does.

'But if we only see it occasionally, how will we know if the ship stops?'

'Patience. Let me hurry up what you're looking at first. We need to let it run down the lake.'

Five minutes later, the dot is offshore at Port Toronto.

'Now,' explains George. 'Let me replay the dots for you but at a quicker speed.'

I watch as the dot moves every second slowly down the lake, from top to bottom, but I don't see anything.

'Let me do something else to make it easier for you,' he says.

He turns back to his keyboard.

Two minutes later, he asks what I see now.

The dots are the same as before, but suddenly, one is larger than the other.

'There,' I almost shout. 'What did you do?'

'I changed what you are looking at to display the time between dots instead of just the location.'

'So, the larger dot is where the ship slowed down?'

'Yes.'

'George, you're amazing.'

'I try to please. Is there anything else I can do for you?'

'You can't detect the fishing boat, can you?'

'No, I'm sorry. They're not required to have transponders, and even if they were, they would have switched it off for a covert operation like this. Do you have any details I can work with?'

I tell him about the white top on the hull and cabin, then the two letters O and N at the start of the registration ID.

'Well, the color doesn't help, but your two letters tell you the fishing vessel is registered in Ontario. The first letters always ID the province. So, I guess that's something.'

I guess my disappointment is showing, but he reminds me that I'm now one step closer than I was when I arrived. The thought cheers me up a little.

'I don't suppose there are only a few fishing boats in Ontario?'

'I'm afraid there will likely be thousands. If you're registered in Ontario, you can fish four of the five Great Lakes. However, the boat you're looking for is unlikely to fish anywhere other than Lake Ontario. So that should whittle it down a lot. It's the smallest of the lakes.'

'Thousands?'

'Wait a minute, and I'll print you a list of all fishing vessels registered in Ontario with a registration number that starts with a six.'

'Two minutes later, he hands me a printout from the printer with three pages, approximately fifty numbers per page. The first column gives me the Registration number, the second the name and address of the registered owner.'

Feeling overwhelmed, I leave my car in the Langley car park and stretch my legs. I head up Pennsylvania Avenue, determined to get my first sight of the Whitehouse. It will give me time to think.

I stop off halfway, pick up lunch at Pret-A-Manger and take it with me to find a bench in the sun where I can admire the East Wing. It's still only fifty degrees or thereabouts, but I'm wrapped up and feel fine.

I've seen the Whitehouse many times on tv, but the real thing is impressive. I'm tempted to walk a little further to see it from the front, but that can wait for another day. I need to get back to Homeland and make my first travel arrangements.

I'm going to Canada.

Even with an early morning flight out of Reagan, with a stopover in Newark, it's already lunchtime when I land in Toronto.

It's a thirty-minute drive from Pearson International to the Marriott, but I check in before eating.

The Marriott is easily recognizable, especially when you see the six-story bright-red sign suspended from the front of the building.

My room is ready, so I drop off my new travel bag and head out to find somewhere to eat. There's a massive mall immediately behind the hotel, so finding lunch is easy.

Afterward, I set out on foot for the Toronto Police HQ. Fifteen minutes away. Even though it's such a short journey, I find the number of shops daunting. I guess I'm not a city girl. I wonder if I'll feel the same about Washington when I get more time to look around.

At the front desk, I present my badge and ask to speak to the Chief.

I won't say the sergeant on duty is rude, but he isn't overflowingly keen to help. I wait twenty minutes before asking for a second time, only to be told to sit back down.

It's one of these situations where my back is up, but I'm helpless, which I hate.

I bite my tongue and wait a further ten minutes before approaching the sergeant for the third time.

'Just appreciate you telling your chief that an Agent from U.S Homeland Security is operating on your turf, and if he has time to meet with me, he can find me at the Marriott.'

The Sergeant gives me a cold stare, but I don't wait for him to speak, turn and walk away.

Outside in the cold sun, I feel much better and decide to use the remainder of the day to go down and look around the Port area. Get a feel for the place.

After exploring the area for a couple of hours, I'm surprised. As this is a major cargo destination, I expect a heavy-duty loading and unloading area, but there's not much to see. Plenty of small marinas with yachts and motorboats, a Navy Frigate, and a dozen commercial vessels, but no sign of container vessels or a container yard piled high.

Just not what I'm expecting.

Having satisfied my curiosity, I head back to the hotel and find a message from a Captain Jon Adamson, Superintendent of Organized Crime Enforcement, leaving a number and asking me to call back.

Up in my room, I call.

'Adamson.'

'Captain, this is Agent Greyfox responding to your message.'

'Yes. An impatient Agent who didn't have the courtesy to wait until she could be seen?'

'That would be me, Sir.'

'Yes. If you're looking for cooperation, you're going about it all the wrong way, Agent.'

'I'm not aware I was asking for cooperation. I was paying a courtesy call to let you know I was in the area and following up on a case I'm working on.'

'You do know you have no authority here?'

'Yes, Sir. But there's nothing to say I can't ask questions.'

'What are you working on?'

'Possible trafficking of children.'

'I thought that was an FBI thing?'

'We're collaborating on this one.'

'Do you need anything from me?'

'No, Sir. Just that you are aware I'm here.'

'You should speak to one of my sergeants who heads up trafficking here. Sergeant Alex Higgins. I'll text you contact details.'

'Thank you, Sir. That could well be useful.'

With that, the line goes dead, and I'm left with my second sour taste of the Toronto police.

At least he follows through and delivers details for Higgins.

No point in hanging about, so I place the call.

'Alex Higgins. Serious Crimes.'

It takes me a few seconds to overcome my surprise. I guess I should be familiar with people thinking I'm a man with a name like Sammy, but I've fallen into the same trap. Alex is a woman.

'Hi, Sammy Greyfox here.'

'Yes?'

'Sorry, Agent Sammy Greyfox with U.S. Homeland Security. Your Captain suggested I call you?'

'Captain Adamson?'

'Yes.'

'That explains why I don't know anything about it.'

'To be fair, Sergeant. I'm just off the phone, so he hasn't had time.'

'Yeah, maybe. Anyway, what can I do for you, Agent?'

'Can we start with Sammy and Alex?'

'Sure, why not.'

I start from the beginning and tell her about the possible trafficking, tracking the cargo boat, and locating the most likely place for the children to be disembarked.

She asks me what my plans are, and I tell her I will visit the fishing villages on the North Shore and see if I can locate the boat used.

To my surprise, she asks if I would like some company.

We agree she'll pick me up out front at eight the following morning.

My plans now are to head to the gym and see if they have a running machine I can use, then get a bite to eat and a good night's sleep.

As promised, Alex picks me up at eight, and we leave the city heading East along the shore. As she drives, she tells me she has been researching where the most likely place for a fishing boat to land would be. Most of the small ports on the north shore are private marinas. If you want to rent a boat to go fishing, there's plenty of choice. But, if it's a bona-fida fishing boat we're looking for, she reckons there are only two ports it could be from. Gosport is the furthest east and is sheltered from the lake by Presqu'ile Bay. But we will reach the other choice first. Cobourg.

Alex doubts they would use Cobourg as there is a Coast Guard station there. But regardless, we decide to take a quick look at Cobourg, then focus our primary attention on Gosport.

It takes a couple of hours to get out there, and by that time, my new buddy is as ready for a coffee as I am. She heads down to the waterfront, where she parks at the rear of the Whistling Duck.

We order to go and wander for the next thirty minutes until we're both convinced that this is strictly tourist and playboy territory.

Gosport is about twenty minutes further East, and while we travel, Alex tells me that her father and brother have fished the lake for years, often bringing home Chinook, Steelhead Trout, or Atlantic Salmon.

I ask her what a Chinook is, and she tells me it's a large Salmon. That's news to me. I thought it was a helicopter.

When we arrive in Gosport, it all looks the same as Cobourg to me - mainly fancy yachts and powerboats. As I'm checking them out, Alex stops and talks to an old-timer mending some nets, and he tells her where we can still find a few fishing boats a mile further East.

When she returns, she's excited.

'Seems like we might have found your fishing boat. When I described the white cabin and top trim on the hull, he said the boat likely belongs to Charlie Curtis - been around here for years. He describes him as a bit of a rogue. Why don't you drive, and I'll see if he has a sheet.'

Five minutes later, I've parked, and we're examining Curtis's sheet. Nothing major, but he's a repeat offender many times over. Never been inside.

We get out of the car and walk towards the boat. The old-timer was right. This looks like the one we're looking for. The registration fits, and my three-page list confirms Charles Curtis as the owner.

Alex shouts out his name at the quay's edge but gets no reply.

She shouts that she's the police and intends to board the vessel.

Still no reply, so we jump aboard.

The boat has seen better days for sure. The deck is stained and heavily worn. Such nets that are visible are full of tears and large holes. The cabin paint has mostly peeled away, leaving the soft, rotted wood underneath exposed to the weather.

Alex steps down to the cabin and shouts once more, and I guess she's concerned for the owner's well-being because she opens the door and enters. I follow and start looking around.

It's a small place, so it doesn't take long, but the one thing I do find is a cell phone.

I switch it on, and it doesn't need a password. I quickly look through the call-log history back to the night the children were dropped off and find several calls to the same number in the middle of that night. I quickly note the number before we replace the cell and leave, closing the door behind us.

Back in the car, Alex calls the number in and is given the registered owner's name. When she hears it, she turns to me and smiles.

'Shamus O'Rourke.'

'You know him?'

'He's second in command of one of our local Organized Crime Gangs. So, yes. I know him well.'

'Do you know where we can find him?'

'Already heading there,' she replies, starting the engine.

'You do realize we need a plan?'

'Working on it.'

As she drives, she calls the information in and asks that an immediate phone tap be placed on the number we have. Then, she explains how the Serious Crimes Squad has a special provision agreed with a local judge. This allows them to tap a phone for twenty-four hours without seeking approval if there are exigent circumstances. In other words, they're free to use their judgment in fluid situations like we are now.

The tap is already in place in the two hours it takes to get back to the city. She drives straight to the home of Shamus O'Rourke and pulls up outside large double wrought-iron black gates. Without saying anything, she waits and holds her badge up to the windshield.

Twenty seconds later, the gates slowly swing open, and we drive up a sweeping drive toward a medieval house with towers and tall thin windows. I'm half expecting to cross a moat.

By the time we come to a halt, two men are already waiting at the front door for us. Alex whispers for me to follow her lead as we walk toward them.

'Afternoon, lads.'

'Ms. Higgins. Social or business?'

'Not sure. I'll let your boss decide.'

'Fair enough. You know the routine.'

I watch as she hands over her weapon before one of the two men asks me for mine. I open my coat and show I'm not carrying. There's something strange going on. They take me at my word. No searches for either of us, and we're shown through an entrance hallway and into a lounge tastefully decorated in pale warm colors.

There's an open log fire burning in a massive fireplace and a burly, bald man with a red beard warming his posterior, with a glass in his hand.

'Alex. What a pleasant surprise. You didn't tell me you were coming?'

'No, Shamus. I need to ask you about something, but can I introduce my colleague before I do? Agent Greyfox with U.S. Homeland Security.'

I can't quite figure out his response. He's curious but maybe also just a little worried. Whatever I think I see, it quickly disappears as he reaches out to offer a handshake.

'Please be seated. Can I offer you something to drink?'

After we decline, he focuses on Alex.

'So, what do you want to ask me about?'

'Your relationship with Charlie Curtis.'

This time, he's too slow to hide his reaction, and even though he asks who Curtis is, it's obvious he knows. Alex sees it as well and repeats her question.

'Specifically, I would like to know what the two of you were up to in the middle of the night a week past Tuesday?'

There's definite tension in the air now, and he's trying hard to pretend otherwise.

'As I don't know the man, I can't speak for him. But if you are asking about the middle of the night, then I would be asleep in bed. And if you are sure of which night it was, I can check my diary and see who might be able to corroborate that fact.'

After that, we to-and-fro a little, but it's job done. He's riled, so all we need to do is clear out and hope he makes the call we think he will.

Back in the car, I ask Alex about Shamus O'Rourke and why he seems so familiar with her.

'He's my father-in-law.'

'What?'

'Yeah. That's more or less what I said when my then-boyfriend told me who his old man was.'

'You're married into an OCG?'

'No, of course not. My husband's an attorney and works for the DA.'

'Does he know what his father does?'

'No. He's never been involved in the family business, and that's one of the things I love about him. Shamus, his three brothers, and virtually all of their combined families comprise the core of the OCG. My husband is the only one who made it out.'

***

By now, we're driving back to the Marriott when Alex's cell rings, and she answers with it on speaker.

'Okay, Alex. He made a call exactly as you said he would. It's an international call to a number in New York. I'll text you the details.'

As they come through, I copy them into my cell.

'It looks like it's back to you, Sammy. I don't think we can get anything else here.'

'Thanks, Alex. I couldn't have achieved this without your help.'

As she drops me off, I agree to keep her in touch with the investigation. After all, there may be more children coming through the same route.

I get an early morning flight back to Washington and arrive at my apartment by eleven. After leaving so early, I head for a shower and change into fresh clothes.

Just time for coffee and a couple of toasted bagels with cream cheese, then into Homeland.

When I arrive, there's already a message from George in cybertech. He seems to have become my go-to guy in their operation. Given how impressed I already am with his work a couple of days ago, I've no problem with that.

The message is a name and an address to go with the New York number I texted him.

Before I do anything else, I need to talk this through with someone, but that's something I don't yet have here. When all else fails, I call my real boss. Dan Weissman back in Naples.

Luckily, I catch him in a quiet moment, and he has time to listen.

I explain what I'm doing and how far I've managed to get, but I'm unsure what to do next. One thing I love about Dan. He's never short of ideas; I learn from him whenever we talk.

'So you have a name. Have you pulled his sheet?'

That simple question sets me back. It's so obvious.

'Not yet.'

'Once you have that, I'm fairly confident he will have a sheet. Check who the arresting officers were in each of the most recent incidents. Also, which precinct they're working out of. When you have that, call me back, and I'll see if I can get you a contact. Remember, I worked up there most of my career in several precincts and Central Plaza. Does that sound like a plan?'

'It sure does, thanks, Dan. I'll be in touch.'

Pulling the sheet for the name I've been given is straightforward, and there are no real surprises. It's similar to the fishing boat skipper. Many minor offenses and one charge of GBH that didn't stick. So, he's still out and about.

I text Dan everything I've got and head to get some lunch.

I haven't even bitten into my Tuna-on-Rye, and my cell buzzes. It's Dan.

'I've spoken to the precinct Captain where your guy, McGuire, is known, and he'll have one of his detectives call you. See where that takes you.'

'Thanks, Dan. I'm due you one.'

'Good luck.'

I'm two bites in when my cell buzzes again, and I have to swallow quickly before answering.

'Sammy Greyfox?' asks the unfamiliar voice.

'That's me.'

'Detective Roy Mallone from the One-Hundred-Seventh here. I hear you're interested in Jonas McGuire?'

'I am. Do you think you might be able to find him?'

'When by?'

I check the time and see that it would be pretty late at night before I could get there, so ask if he's around over the next couple of days.

'Can you tell me what you're after him for?'

'Trafficking children.'

'Shit. For real?'

'Yip.'

'In that case, I can be working whenever you want me to be.'

'I probably need to do some more work at this end first. Can you find him and sit on him for a day or so? Maybe I can get up there tomorrow afternoon.'

'I'll track him down and keep him in view for you. Just let me know when you want him.'

'Thanks, Detective. Speak tomorrow.'

I think that wandering in and accusing this guy of trafficking without any evidence isn't going to work. I need something more tangible and more help from my go-to guy.

This time I call ahead and ensure he's there before telling him I'm heading to see him.

It seems George is available twenty-four-seven for me. This T.E.N. thing seems to work.

'So?' George says. Your cargo ship drops the kids off. A fishing boat takes them ashore. Someone there, possibly an OCG member, takes them and passes them to this guy from New York who somehow manages to get them across the border. Is that about it?'

'Yes.'

'So, it's obvious what they do.'

'It is?'

'Sure. They must have come through Niagara Falls. That's the only place that makes sense.'

'Can't the fishing boat just drop them on the U.S. side of the Lake?'

'Too risky. The lake is well-policed, especially at night. Satellite eyes in the sky monitor all crossings twenty-four-seven. Then there's the Coast Guard power-boats, both Canadian and U.S., not to mention the U.S. border protection force on the shore, who use drones with thermal imaging. No, they wouldn't ship these kids all the way from Europe and

take a risk like that bringing them into the country.'
'So, how do they do it then?'
'Your talking kids. What? A dozen or so?'
'Yes. I'm not sure of the exact number but around a dozen.'
'So, they split them up into ones and twos, then transport them in individual vehicles, or use a school bus. Again, using individual vehicles is far too risky and involves too many people. I fancy they used the bus trick.'
'You've seen this before?'
'Yes. But, they usually get caught because of documentation problems.'
'So, can you check if they were caught that day or in the days since? Maybe I'm trying to find children who have already been found?'

Again he lets his fingers do the talking as he searches various data sources at super-fast speeds before declaring that no children have been taken into custody at Niagara Falls in the past couple of weeks.

Now, he's getting excited, and I ask him why.

'If they got through both Canadian and U.S. Immigration and Customs checks, either they had excellent documentation in advance, or someone has hacked the immigration systems of both countries. For me, that would be exciting. Can you leave this with me for a bit? I need to look into it and talk with Herman.'

No problem. You have my cell?'

I feel like I'm talking into a vacuum. He's already deep in thought.

Four am, Sunday morning. I'm sound asleep when my cell buzzes. I answer half-awake to find an excited cyber-tech on the other end. He's speaking gibberish at an incredibly fast rate, and I don't understand a word. I ask where he is and tell him I'll be there in thirty.

Pulling on my jeans, I figure out that the guy probably hasn't left his work area since the previous afternoon. Once I realize that, I don't feel so angry at being awakened in the middle of the night. I hope he has coffee available at Langley.

When I arrive, George and his boss - Herman Garfunkel, are there, poring over their screens. Before interrupting, I head for the Cona jug and check it's hot. It is. I fill a mug with black coffee and pull a chair to sit with them.

George notices me first and starts straight into explaining what all the fuss is about.

'You've given us a lead on a hacker we've been trying to track for years. He's the best we've ever come across. We call him the Phantom because he drifts in and out of highly secure systems and databases without leaving any trace.'

'How do you know about him if he leaves no trace?'

'Logic. There are too many times when something inexplicable has happened, and the only solution we have been able to come up with is someone with phenomenal hacking skills.'

'So, you don't *actually* know he exists. It's a theory?'

'Yes, but we're convinced he exists. And he has been responsible for getting your kids through Immigration at Niagara Falls. It has his signature all over it.'

'You mean it doesn't have any signature, right?'

'Technically, yes. That is his signature. The ability to access and alter data inside the highest secure firewalls without leaving a trace.'

'Okay. Tell me what he's done in this case.'

It's the Director who answers.

'For your trafficked children to enter the country, several things must be prepared in advance. First, they need documentation. I suspect that was already taken care of before they left Europe. But getting that false documentation into the immigration system should be impossible. However, assume for a moment that someone managed to do that in order for the children to appear to return to the U.S.; they would have to have left in the first place.'

'So someone had to create a false exit through Niagara Falls?'

'Correct. Again, that information is held in a different database from the passport and visa information, so not easy to do. But once they are in the system as having left, say on a school bus and probably on a day trip to see the Falls from the Canadian side, Immigration Officers would be less suspicious on their return journey.'

'Okay. I get why you're both excited about finding something the Phantom may have done, but how about what I need? Information to help me track the children?'

At that point, George picks up the story.

'Sorry, Sammy. This is the biggest break we've had on this guy for some time. Let me tell you what you need to know. We examined all school buses entering and leaving a couple of days after your cargo ship delivered the kids. There were eighteen buses, but we quickly ruled most out based on the number of kids aboard. That took us down to three. Then, if you want to sneak through Immigration with minimal attention being paid, when would you choose?'

'Middle of the night?'

'No. You're much too visible. You would pick rush hour when all immigration officers are stressed out. That's how we initially singled out a particular school bus. There were twelve kids and three adults. When we looked into the adults, two were clean, but the third guy had a sheet a mile long.'

'Don't tell me. Jonas McGuire?'

'Right in one. Of course! You already know him? He's the name I gave you yesterday.'

'Yes. And I'll know him much better real soon. He's a person of interest at the moment, and you've just made him more interesting still.'

'What about the other two adults?'

'They're teachers at a school in Queens.'

'No records?'

'Totally clean.'

'Can you send me all the details?'

'Already done.'

'Can you give me the passport photos used for the twelve

girls and the three men?'
'Sure. I'll send those as well.'
'Anything else for me?'
'Nothing right now, but I'll let you know if anything turns up.'
'Thanks, both of you. Good work.'

Six-thirty on a Sunday morning isn't a time to make for the office, so I head back to the apartment and make a fresh coffee while I wonder if my roomie is there. I haven't seen him since moving in, so I don't know.

While drinking my coffee, I review the information George has sent me. The guy is thorough. It's a good ten-minute read through details I hadn't even thought to ask about.

I'm doing fine until I get to the photos of the girls.

They're so damn young. I doubt the upper age is as high as twelve. But I have to run with something.

When I'm finished, I change into my running gear and start for Rock Creek Park, named after the creek that runs through it from the lakes to the north of the city down to where it joins the Potomac opposite Roosevelt Island.

The main feature in the park is the Smithsonian National Zoo, which I'll try to visit sometime, but not today. I would love to see the Panda enclosure. They must be one of my favorite animals.

As I run, there's no chance my mind is going into my preferred quiet zone. I've too much new information floating around to be able to push it aside.

Instead, I set a regular pace and summarize what I learned earlier.

First, I've confirmed the number of children involved as twelve. The crewman who started this whole thing off could only estimate the number he saw on the deck in the dark. But now, I'm definitely looking for twelve children.

Next, assuming the fake passports are at least based on some truth which is how the best fakes work, the children range in age from eight to twelve, and they're all girls. That information makes me uncomfortable, and I have to stop my mind from wondering what's happening to them right there and then.

I have all the IDs, but I doubt that will take me anywhere. Once in the U.S., these would more than likely be trashed. Wherever the end destinations for girls are, they won't need IDs. Of that, I'm sure.

Another thing I also know is that the guy I intend to visit in New York is definitely involved. McGuire. This should give me enough leverage to get him to talk.

Then there are the two school teachers. How did he manage to suck them into this? And why would teachers help to trafficking young children in the first place? It's also interesting that they both teach at the same school in Queens. Maybe a coincidence, perhaps something else.

Did they provide the bus?

If they've no records, maybe they'll break the easiest. I need to get their names to Detective Mallone ASAP.

As for this Phantom that George and Herman are so excited about, I don't see him directly involved in anything I'm working on. He's more a back-room type of guy, although he'll be expensive if he's as good as they think. Nor will he work for just anyone. He'll be very particular. So whoever is behind the trafficking operation is wealthy, powerful, or both.

It strikes me as odd that this is the first time I've thought about who might be behind the operation. I've been so focussed on tracking the children. I wonder if Fabia has any ideas about who this may be.

Back in the apartment, I shower and change. Make some poached eggs with bagels, and consider my next steps as I eat. As soon as I'm finished, I'm on my cell.

'Detective Mallone?'

'Yes.'

'Sammy Greyfox here.'

'Oh, yeah. Sure. I was expecting you to call.'

'I'm flying up this afternoon. Will you be able to meet me?'

'Try and stop me.'
'Thanks, Detective.'
'Can we drop the Detective, Agent thing? I'm Roy.'
'Sure, Roy. I'm Sammy.'
'Anything else you want me to do before you get here?'
'I have two more names for you. No priors. Both teachers at St. Charlotte's in Queens. They were on a school bus with McGuire, bringing twelve underage girls down from Niagara Falls. Maybe we talk with them before McGuire or the other way round. Why don't you look at them and see what you think best? I'll text you my flight details.'
'Fly into La Guardia and exit directly. I'll be upfront in a murky-fawn unmarked with a blue light flashing on the top.'
'Thanks, Roy. See you later.'
My next call is to Anna, who listens to what I need and asks me to give her twenty minutes.
As I wait, I knock on my roomie's door, but there's no reply. I guess he's on some remote mission like myself. Who knows where?

I spend the next ten minutes packing for another short trip. I wonder if this is how the job will be and whether I'll ever get time to enjoy the relative luxury this apartment offers.
I'm just closing my case when Anna calls back to give me flight information and tell me I have a reservation for two nights at the Queens Hotel. Seems appropriate. It's only then that I realize I've just taken Anna and Mallone away from their weekends.

The United Airlines flight to La Guardia is only ninety minutes, so I'm leaving Terminal B by five in the evening. The sky is dark, and the rain is incessant. It's also cold.
I pull up my collar and see my ride pulled onto the curb, fifty yards off to my right. Sure enough, there's a blue light flashing on top.
I run the short distance, pull open the passenger door and dive in to find myself in a cloud of smoke.

'Roy?'

'That's me. Sorry about the smoke; I didn't want to wind down the windows and let the rain in,' he explains, doing just that. I copy him and, after a few moments, risk breathing again.

'Welcome to the big smoke,' he says, laughing.

'And I always thought smog referred to traffic fumes,' I reply, as he pulls the car out and heads for the airport exit ramp.

The rain on the roof is deafening, and the wipers struggle to clear the screen. This must be common here, as it doesn't seem to phase Roy. It certainly doesn't slow him down.

Roy Mallone would be a great undercover cop. There's no way you would make him. He's unshaven, with a mop of unruly hair. Battered features with a broken nose he's never bothered to have straightened. I wouldn't say fat, but that's only because I'm being kind. Let's say there's not much space between his belly and the steering wheel.

'Let me guess, ' he says. 'You reckon I would be a good undercover cop?'

I don't say anything, which I guess answers his question.

'Don't worry. It's all part of my charm. Scumbags relate. Besides, my diet's unhealthy, and my exercise routines are worse. Not like you,' he says, looking my way.

'Whatever works for you, Roy. I'm not a judge. What did you find out about my two teachers?'

'They've quit and are gone.'

'Gone?'

'Vamoosed. Upped and gone. No one knows why they quit or where they've gone.'

'APB's out?'

'Sure, but if these guys want to disappear, I wouldn't hold your breath until we find them.'

'So we're down to McGuire? Are you sitting on him?'

'I've had a patrol watch him since you first called. He's been out for breakfast this morning but went straight back home. Do you want to come into the Precinct, and I'll have him brought in?'

'No. Can we go to his place?'

'Sure can. You'll love it. Real classy.'

'Does he live on his own?'

'No wife or kids, a bit of a loner. Got a dog you need to watch out for - mangy big thing. An Irish Wolfhound, I think. Stinks to high heaven.'

With that, I settle back, thinking about how best to tackle McGuire.

It's a fifteen-minute drive to Queens from La Guardia, past The Arthur Ashe Tennis Stadium and Flushing Meadow. When we arrive, I can see McGuire's home is opposite a derelict burned-out shopping center and backs onto a major rail siding with a dozen or more tracks, most of which seem to enter an extended work shed that looks large enough for at least ten carriages.

There's rubble from a demolished outhouse and an old rusty wheel-less Chrysler Cordoba from the seventies mounted on piles of bricks in the front yard. The entranceway has black trash bags piled high on either side, and Roy and I have to be careful where we stand as evidence of the Wolf Hound is all around.

Roy knocks on the door and waits before knocking a second time. Eventually, we hear floorboards creak inside, and the man I immediately recognize from his passport photograph opens the door while tightly gripping his pet's collar.

Roy shows his badge and asks if we can come in to talk, which McGuire surprisingly agrees to by just turning away with the dog and leaving the entranceway empty for us to follow.

As I've been warned, the house is in much the same state as the yard, but without dog excrement everywhere, which pleases me, although the smell is awful, and there are long, wiry dog hairs covering the sofa. McGuire indicates that we should sit while he takes the dog and closes it in the kitchen, where it whines and scratches annoyingly at the kitchen door.

We choose to stand.

Returning and sitting, he asks what he can do for New York's finest.

I don't want to tell him I'm from Homeland Security, so let Roy start the conversation. He goes straight on the attack.

'So how are you enjoying ripping off the elderly, then McGuire?'

McGuire doesn't answer. Instead, he sits back in his chair and shakes a cigarette loose from a pack. 'Like one Detective?' he asks, offering the packet.

With his offer declined, he offers the pack to me, then places it back on the small table beside his chair before lighting up and drawing deeply. 'Don't know what you're talking about.'

'Well, I just want you to know we're watching you and will catch you out soon enough.'

'Thanks for the warning, I'm sure. Very kind of you,' McGuire says, grinning through badly stained teeth. 'So you didn't drop by just to warn me. What do you want?'

I remove a photocopy of the passport photograph from my pocket, unfold it and hand it to McGuire. 'I'd like to talk to you about this.'

'Sorry, Sugar. Didn't see you there. Are you the Detective's sweet little *partner*?'

The way he emphasizes partner gets under my skin, but I know that's what he's trying to do, so I ignore it.

McGuire looks at the picture and says he doesn't know where it came from. That someone must have made it up like people can do with computers these days, but I shrug that away and warn him that using a falsified passport is a Federal offense and conviction can lead to up to ten years inside.

At this, I show him my Homeland Security credentials and tell him that trafficking minors is also a Federal offense, which, when added to the use of a false passport, could see him inside for most of the remainder of his life.

'What? I don't know what you're talking about,' said McGuire, blustering, not sure how seriously to take me, but now clearly worried.

***

'Let me tell you a story, Mr. McGuire. Then you can decide if you want to help us or not. Once upon a time, a container ship stopped off in Lake Ontario, near a small fishing village in Canada called Gosport. The ship offloaded twelve underage girls to a small fishing boat which took them ashore and delivered them to a man named Shamus O'Rourke, who, as you should know, is involved in various criminal enterprises we're already watching.

You, Mr. McGuire, with two teachers from St. Charlotte's school, transported these children in a school bus through U.S. customs at Niagara Falls and brought them down to Queens.'

'Still don't know what you're talking about.'

'Here's the thing, Mr. McGuire. My job isn't to bring you to justice, much as I would love it to be. My job is to track down and recover these underage girls as quickly as possible. So, any help you can offer would be most welcome, and I'm sure the detective here would have a kind word or two to say at your trial.'

McGuire is now so focused that he hasn't even noticed his cigarette has burned right down to his finger and suddenly yelps as he drops it on the floor. Stooping, he picks up the end and stubs it into an overflowing ashtray at his side.

'So, imagine for a moment that I might know something about this. I would need some guarantee from you, wouldn't I.'

'I can give you that, Mr. McGuire. But if you refuse to cooperate, I will bring the full force of not just Homeland Security to bear but also the FBI. As you know, trafficking is within their remit, and they don't like child traffickers, Mr. McGuire. And once you're banged up for the rest of your life, I can ensure that the general prison population knows exactly why you're there. I doubt your sentence will be very long after that.'

'You can't do that. That's not fair?'

'Neither's kidnapping young children from their families, transporting them thousands of miles from their homes, and selling them to perverts like you, to do who knows what with. The choice is yours, Mr. McGuire. And it would be best if you made it now. When I walk out that door, I'm gone and taking any offer with me.'

I give him ten seconds, then turn for the door.

'I...I don't know much.'

I turn back to face him, giving him my most incredulous stare.

'I mean, I was to pick them up and bring them back. I don't know what happened to them after that. I don't know what else you want from me?'

'We want to know everything from when you were first contacted to when you dropped off the girls. But we don't want it here. We'll do it downtown. Get your coat. It's wet outside.'

After a lengthy interview session at the Precinct, I leave Roy McGuire to complete the paperwork and grab a cab for the Queens Hotel. There's nothing else I can do here, but it's too late to get a flight back to Washington, so I'll change my ticket in the morning and go back then. Besides, a few hours of peace will allow me to catch up again.

I check in and immediately place an order for room service while I freshen up. The menu isn't five-star, but neither is roast beef on Rye, a packet of Ruffles chips, and a couple of cold Corona. That's a significant plus for my diet. I can find something wherever I am, no problem.

Half an hour later, as I'm working through this culinary treat, I'm thinking about the details that spilled out of McGuire. When we got him to the Precinct, he was wetting himself and couldn't wait to talk.

He implicated Shamus O'Rourke, and I intend to pass that information back to Alex Higgins in Toronto. I'm sure she'll be more than happy to follow up on her end. I wonder how her husband will take to her locking his father away?

McGuire also confirmed the names of the two teachers that helped him and told us that one of them arranged the bus as I

Lost souls

suspected, and the other that the schoolyard be left unlocked late at night to allow the bus entry and other vehicles to be parked off-street waiting to collect the girls. He said that the bus arrived more or less dead on midnight.

O' Rourke said there were eight vehicles, so some girls didn't travel onwards alone wherever they were going. When I asked if he paid attention to the plates, he said one with local plates had taken two girls. But he didn't notice the others.

So, two girls in New Jersey and ten spread elsewhere across the country.

By now, I realize why Fabia made such a big deal about me knowing the CIA Cyber-tech Division because that's where I need to go next. I hope I'm still on George's good side.

I'm at United's ticket desk by seven, and as luck would have it, I can change my return flight for the eight-fifteen back to D.C.

On the way to the gate, I stop at *Au Bon Pain*, order a two-egg & Cheddar on Ciabatta with an espresso and have time to finish this before being last onboard the flight.

When I land back at Reagan, I pick up my car and make straight for Langley, calling George to let him know I'm coming.

He seems happy to hear my voice.

Thirty minutes later, I lay out my new information for him and ask him what he thinks.

'What's the school?'

'St. Charlotte's, in Queens.'

I watch as he turns away and begins doing what I'm rapidly becoming familiar with. I don't even have time to ask him what he's doing before he tells me to look at the larger screen again.

'What am I looking at?'

'Most schools are very security conscious these days, so the top two pictures are from their front yard security cams. The other two are traffic cams from the two ends of the street the school is on.'

'Is this live footage?'

'At the moment, yes. But give me time....'

'Damn. The school cameras were down for an hour before and after midnight on the night we're interested in.'

'Probably one of the teachers arranged that.'

'Sure. But they couldn't do anything about the traffic cams. Look.'

As I watch the two remaining videos, I see vehicles appear one after another, turning north or south at the junctions.

'Can you slow these up and get the plates?'

'I can do better than that. Watch.'

He rewinds to the first vehicle and blows up the plate so we can make it out. In this case, it's from Georgia. But before I can comment, he blows it up even further until we get a picture of the driver.

'It's grainy, but we might get a hit with our recognition systems. Certainly worth a try.'

He prints a copy and then does the same with all eight vehicles and drivers.

When he's finished, we lay out what we have in front of us.

We have Georgia, Colorado, California, Washington, Florida, Illinois, and two from New Jersey to account for all eight vehicles.

We also have pictures of four of the drivers. The other vehicles have tinted glass, so there's no chance there.

'What do you want to do from here, Sammy?'

Can you find the registered owners of each vehicle?

'Give me a minute.'

While he's doing this, I pick up some coffee, and he's finished by the time I return.

'Got four names for you from the facial recognition system, and I'm just pulling their details now. Can you get them from the printer? I'm still waiting for the vehicle registration owner's information.

I give him his coffee, lay mine down, cross to the printer,

and wait while it spews records for the four drivers we've ID'd. When I have them, I sit back with George, and we look through them together.

'No hits for criminal activity in the system. They look clean.'

'Yeah. That's a surprise.'

'A fairly international bunch. South African, Canadian, Chinese, and one from the Empire of the South. Atlanta.'

'But their current locations give us four cities to focus on, and that's a start.'

Name: Arnou Chikumbutso
  Nickname: Chiko
  Born: South Africa
  DoB: 6/19/69
  US Citizen from 11/1/90
  Location: Chicago
  Family: Married with two sons.

Name: Francis Lemoine
  Nickname: The monk
  Born: Quebec
  DoB: 2/9/66
  US Citizen from 11/1/90
  Location: Seattle
  Family: None

Name: Wilson Clampett
  Nickname: Jed
  Born: Atlanta, Georgia
  DoB: 3/22/75
  Location: Atlanta
  Family: Wife deceased, one daughter.

Name: Zhan Wu
  Nickname: None
  Born: Shanghai, China
  US Citizen from 11/1/90

DoB: 5/15/79
Location: San Francisco
Family: None

'Hang on, Sammy, here's the vehicle registration info.'
We both look on-screen and recognize the four names we already have, with four more to add to our list.

Name: Pike Clayton
   Location: Denver, Colorado

Name: Tony Carletto
   Location: Pompano Beach, Florida

Name: Svetlana Kazakova
   Location: Brighton Beach, New Jersey

Name: John Smith
   Location: Avis New Jersey rental. Drop-off also New Jersey - overdue.

'Can you pull the sheets for the first three? The fourth seems like a waste of time. I'm pretty sure it's a false name.'
'I can for the first two, but you should talk with Lead Agent Mendez about the third one.'
'Why's that?'
'I recognize the name from a case she was working on recently. She can fill you in on the details. Let me get the other two up for you.'

Name: Pike Clayton
   Born: Colorado Springs, Colorado
   DoB: 8/9/85
   Location: Denver, Colorado
   Family: None

Name: Tony Carletto

Born: Miami, Florida
DoB: 2/2/82
Location: Pompano Beach, Florida
Family: Married, two boys

'Let me pull up their driving license pictures for you. Give me a moment.'

As George is doing his thing again, I wonder why he avoided telling me about the woman in New Jersey - Svetlana Kazakova. I'm still wondering when he hands me a page with copies of four driver's license photographs. So, now I know what the eight people look like - the people who have taken the girls.

'What do you want to do now, Sammy?'

'I'm not sure, George. I need time to mull all of this over. I probably want to put the pictures of the twelve girls out over the wire to all the States on our list, but I need to think about the best approach with the drivers we've identified. Knowing their addresses doesn't necessarily tell me where they've taken the girls, and I don't want to let them know we know who they are.'

'I agree, Sammy. I'll put an APB out on the girls for you with your contact details. I'll make it Country wide and for all agencies.'

'Thanks, George. You've been a tremendous help again. I appreciate it.'

After we say our farewells, I make my way back to Homeland HQ, my mind spinning with details but still curious about the name George suggested I talk with Fabia about. I reckon I'll start there. First, I need some food.

Suitably fuelled with a burger and fries from McDonald's, I find Fabia in her office back at HQ.

She looks up and smiles as I tap at the door and enter.

'Sammy. Anna tells me you've been keeping busy. Sorry, I

haven't been around much. Why don't you bring me up to date on your investigation? It sounds like you're making progress.'

I sit and spend the next half hour talking through the past few days' events until I get to the question I really want to ask.

'So, it turns out that when the girls were divided up in the Schoolyard, one of the seven vehicles taking them away was registered to a Svetlana Kazakova. I believe you know this person?'

I see a look cross Fabia's face. Certainly recognition, but mixed with something else. Sadness perhaps?

'Yes, I recognize the name. She was one of two daughters of Grigor Kazakova, the leader of one of the most dangerous organized crime groups in the Country. Your sergeant helped us take him and his daughters down recently. Well, to be more precise, we were closing in on them, and we believe Grigor killed not only himself but everyone in his mansion up in the Hampshires rather than face imprisonment. Eighteen people in all.'

'Including Svetlana?'

'Yes. And also including two under-age girls we have been unable to identify.'

'You think these might be two of the girls I'm looking for?'

'Let me pull up the file for you.'

When she's found what she's looking for, she turns the screen toward me. It shows two pictures of the girls in the morgue.

I quickly pull the copy of the twelve girl's pictures that George has put onto one page for me and compare. Sure enough, there's a match.

I sit back. The loss hitting me heavily.

'Sammy, this is not on you. None of this case is on you. These girls were dead before you even started this case. And you need to accept there may be more of this ahead of you. We rarely recover these children, and when we do, they are often so damaged their future lives will be difficult at best.'

I'm lost for words, so remain quiet. I didn't see this coming, and as I leave, Fabia's warning is ringing in my ears, and that's not helping.

I'm just about aware enough of my surroundings to fetch a coffee and find my way to my office, where I stand and stare out the window.

When I hear a noise behind me, I turn and find Fabia standing in the doorway.

'I'm fine. Honest, I am,' I bluster.

'Remember I explained why these assignments are a maximum of six months, Sammy?'

'Sure. I remember.'

'This is why. It's not the workload, although you'll put in the hours. It's this - what you're feeling right now. The senselessness of it all, and the sadness and pain.'

'How do you do it, Fabia? Day in and day out. You're not on assignment.'

'I focus on the ones we *can* save, Sammy. It's the only thing that can get us through.'

'I don't know how to do that. What if all the others are dead?'

'Sammy. When you started this case, you only had a crew member reporting what he thought he saw. Since then, you've moved mountains to find it was true. That there were twelve girls. Now you know the fate of two but not the other ten. That's where you focus. The other ten. Do your job!'

With that, she turns and leaves me alone once more, and just as happened when I left her office before, her final words are ringing in my ears. I need to get on with my job.

I shrug off how I feel and draw on the whiteboard. I start with a circle marked St. Charlotte's in the center, then draw eight circles around it and fill in the details I know for each. Seattle, Chicago, New Jersey, Colorado, Miami, Atlanta, California, and a rental car with New Jersey plates.

I add the four names from the facial recognition system to

Seattle, Chicago, Atlanta, and California.

Next are the four names from the vehicle registration data. After the conversation with Fabia, I can dismiss Svetlana Kazakova. For now, I also ignore the car-rental driver, John Smith, leaving me with two more names.

I start checking them for previous convictions. Pike Clayton and Tony Carletto.

Clayton is clean as a whistle. But there's a lot of detail on Carletto. No convictions, but a lot of charges, most of which relate to organized crime activity in Miami. He probably has an expensive hotshot attorney. None of the charges relate to trafficking.

Whichever I start with, I'll get nowhere going in all guns blazing. I need more information before I can get anywhere. Besides, if I go direct now, they'll know I'm onto them, and the chances of me finding any of the remaining girls alive will drop to zero.

I need to start somewhere, so it might as well be on my home turf. And thanks to my recent experiences in Miami, I have an in with a Captain in Miami-Dade.

Twenty minutes later, I end the call and ask Anna to arrange a morning flight to Miami. I'm heading back to the sun.

I'm on the ten-thirty United flight arriving in Miami International just after lunch. I had to choose my clothing carefully, and I'm glad I did. When I exit arrivals, a wave of heat and humidity blasts my face. It's blues skies above and in the low eighties.

I've only been gone a week, but it seems like forever.

A sergeant is leaning against a patrol SUV out front. As I walk towards him, he asks if I'm Detective Greyfox.

I tell him I am.

He tells me to climb aboard.

I get the third degree from him on the way to HQ. It seems

that my previous involvement down here hasn't gone unnoticed, and he wants to know all about the case I was working on then.

I fill him in on some details, skipping over how hazardous the operation was, and he seems impressed.

When we pull up outside the front of HQ, I thank him for the ride, and he thanks me for taking down some bad people in his area. I think he likes me.

The South Beach Precinct is like no other. It's a brilliant white Art Deco six-story building with a broad, curved entranceway from the twenties. It's been featured in many Art Deco magazines over the years, but the pictures I've seen don't do it justice.

I show my Detective's credentials at the front desk and ask to speak to the Captain. I'm told he's expecting me, and after I sign in, I can go right up to the sixth floor.

It's funny coming back to this place. I know it's only a few weeks since I was last here, but so much seems to have happened since then. It seems forever ago.

I'm shown straight into the Captain's office, and he rises to greet me with a handshake and a smile.

'Didn't expect to see you again so soon, Detective. Still, if you keep solving major crimes for us, you're welcome anytime.'

'Good to see you again, Sir. Thanks for offering to help.'

I sense someone behind me, and as I turn, the Captain introduces the new arrival as Lieutenant Jim Walker from the Trafficking division.

We shake hands, and the Lieutenant asks if I've had lunch.

With that thought in mind, I thank the Captain once again and follow the Lieutenant's lead.

By the time we have our food, the cafeteria is relatively quiet, and we find a table by the floor-to-ceiling window that runs the entire room length.

As we start to eat, at his insistence, we've already dropped titles, and I'm feeling relaxed in his company.

'So, you're interested in Tony Carletto?'

'I am. You know him?'

'Sure do. He's second in command of the main OCG down here.'

'Whose the main player?'

'A guy called Vladi Popov.'

'Russian?'

'Yes. But a clever one. He stays in the background and pulls the strings. Never gets directly involved.'

'Same as Carletto. Seems no one has been able to nail him either.'

'True. We've been close several times but made some procedural errors, and his attorneys played us.'

'Are you aware if they are involved in trafficking?'

'That's a new one on me. I know these guys from my previous role in Serious Crimes, but I haven't encountered them for trafficking. Having said that, there's trafficking going on every day down here. In the past twelve months alone, we've already broken up twenty trafficking operations. In some of these, they brand their women like cattle, and the pimps beat them if they don't deliver their daily cash quotas. So, we're dealing with this stuff every day.'

'What about underage girls?'

'Much less common, I'm glad to say. Most of the women are late teens and early twenties and come from as far away as Serbia or Alaska, would you believe?'

'Have you circulated the photos of the girls I sent out?'

'Yes, but no one has seen any of them down here. But you have some evidence we can use to nail Carletto, right?'

'Possibly, although a decent attorney can probably get him out of it.'

'But the Captain says you have a plan?'

'I do. Do you have a good car mechanic?'

Late afternoon and we're all set. The Lieutenant and I are

parked up in an unmarked where we have a clear view of Carletto's residence in Pompano Beach. We've timed the operation to catch Carletto at home while his wife is still at work and the kids are in after-school activities.

We watch a patrol car pull up outside Carletto's house, and an officer walks up the drive and knocks on the front door.

When Carletto answers, their conversation upsets him before the officer returns to his vehicle and pulls away.

Five minutes later, Carletto hurries out of his house and jumps in his car. We watch as he gets increasingly upset, thumping the steering wheel in frustration before climbing out and making a call on his cell.

It only takes two minutes for an Uber to pull up and for him to climb in the back, then disappear south to the city.

At that point, another unmarked pulls up beside Carletto's vehicle, and a plain-clothes detective gets out, spends thirty seconds fiddling with the driver's door, then opens it and gets inside.

He's in there for five minutes before climbing out and re-locking the car. He gives us a thumbs up and drives towards us.

After pulling alongside, he tells us what he's discovered in the vehicle's sat nav history.

Yes. The vehicle had been in New Jersey on the night in question, and more importantly, it stopped four times on the long drive south, with the last stop being only thirty minutes to the north.

Our plan had been simple. A mechanic disabled Carletto's car. The Traffic officer told Carletto his wife's car had been towed, and the recovery cost was rising by the hour. This got him out of the house so the mechanic could access his sat nav. It all worked perfectly.

Looking through the information with the Lieutenant, we reckon the drive down from New Jersey would be around eighteen hours with maybe a few stops, so the first three stops on the sat nav would probably be for food, drink, or the washrooms. But with the fourth, why would he stop less than thirty minutes from home? Surely he would keep going.

This is where we figure he dropped the girl or girls.

Thirty minutes later, I'm standing behind a patrol car listening as the Lieutenant gives instructions to the local officers from the Marin County Sheriff's office.

The house we're looking at is a sprawling affair on Jupiter Island, on the other side of the Inter-Coastal waterway from the mainland. The owner is a retired financier from New York. He moved here the previous year, but other than that, we don't know much about him. No sheet, that's for sure.

As the local officers spread around each side of the property, the Lieutenant hands me a Kevlar vest and tells me we're getting to the fun part - the front door.

Stepping ahead of me, he knocks firmly, and we wait. I can hear the sound echoing through the hollow interior of this place.

He's about to knock for a second time when the door swings open, and a thin, wiry man wearing lycra shorts and a sweat-soaked T-shirt opens it.

As soon as he sees the Lieutenant's badge, he tries to slam the door shut, but he's way too slow, and the Lieutenant gets his foot in first, then pushes the door so quickly that it catches the guy off guard. He loses his balance and falls on his butt on the hard, expensive wooden flooring.

The Lieutenant flips the guy over and secures his hands behind his back with nylon ties.

'You can't treat me like this. You've no right to burst in here!'

I hold up the search warrant in his face and tell him we have every right; at this point, he starts demanding his attorney.

I assure him that he will see his attorney soon enough and leave one of the officers keeping an eye on him as I join the others who have already started the search for any evidence that the girl or girls may have been here.

There are eight of us searching, but it still takes twenty minutes to check every room and look for anywhere less obvious he could keep someone against their will.

I find a small basement with a boiler, but not much else. There's an attic in the house, but other than some storage boxes, there's nothing there either.

I open the sliding doors at the rear of the house and step outside. He has an infinity pool running the entire length of the house. It must be close to Olympic size. The water level is carefully designed to merge into the Atlantic in the background, although the calmness of the pool doesn't at all match the ocean's turbulence. There's a small changing room, an outdoor shower, a few loungers, and a set of patio furniture - a table, six chairs, and a massive umbrella.

I begin to feel foolish. Each time an officer reports back, it's the same - no sign of anyone in the house apart from the owner.

I chat with the Lieutenant outside, and we agree that there's nothing more we can get at the house, but it's worth taking him in for questioning about why Tony Carletto stopped by in the middle of the night. Even then, I doubt we'll get anything if he refuses to talk until his attorney arrives. This feels like a dead end.

We're heading inside when I ask for a few more minutes. I go over to the far side of the pool and peer over the edge. Just as I thought, there's a steep fall to the rocks below. But I'm still hopeful and look carefully at each end of the pool, and sure enough, I find what I'm looking for. Trampled grass leads to a narrow trail down to what appears to be a small private beach. I kick myself. I should have known a place like this would have access to a beach.

I shout for the Lieutenant and start carefully picking my way down the rocky, uneven path and, as I had hoped, come to a door in the cliff-face, locked with a shiny new padlock. This place will be for the pump and filtering equipment for the pool, but it may also be for something else.

I climb back up to the Lieutenant waiting for me at the top and explain that we need to find a key, and it doesn't take long.

The next time we descend the path, we're joined by a female patrol officer. I unlock the padlock, remove it from the hasp and gently push the door open, allowing some light to penetrate the dark interior.

The Lieutenant and I take out our cell phones and switch on the torch apps, casting light deeper into this underground cave carved from solid rock. Inside, the atmosphere is icy-cold and damp, and water trails glisten on the rocky walls.

As I move further in, I find the remains of several candles and an empty water bottle beside a grubby sleeping bag. The place smells of excrement and fear.

I raise my cell, look into the furthest recess and find what I'm looking for.

Huddled in a corner is a young girl sitting with her knees up and arms wrapped protectively around them. I get the impression she's trying to make herself as small as possible. It looks like all she's wearing is a T-shirt that's too large for her, and she's cold and shivering.

As I walk slowly towards the tiny figure making hushing sounds, I can begin to see how badly she's been treated. One eye is swollen shut and badly discolored, and there are angry weals on both arms and legs. I can't imagine the emotional scars she must have, perhaps for the rest of her life.

I stand to the side and allow the female officer to approach the girl, whispering gentle encouragement and telling her she will be alright and that we're there to help her.

Even then, the girl pulls herself into an even tighter ball and starts whimpering, terrified.

I don't think I've ever been so angry. Unable to watch anymore, I turn and head back into the light, my temper barely in control.

I'm about to start back up the path when the Lieutenant catches me by the arm.

'You've done your bit, Detective. Leave everything else with me. Trust me; I'll take good care of Mr. Lycra. And after the Law is finished with him, he'll undergo the same fate all child molesters suffer in prison. They don't like Chomos. They're considered sick freaks. That'll be his real punishment.'

'Well, I can't have any sympathy for him. He deserves whatever he gets as far as I'm concerned.'

The Lieutenant's tone reminds me of my sergeant when he's giving me a command without actually saying so. But I know he's right. If I go back up there and tear the guy's throat out, I'll be the one to suffer.

But to think that someone has ripped this child from her family in some distant country, transported her across the Atlantic to end up in some sick wealthy pedophile's cave, locked away in the dark, to be abused in God knows what ways, just turns my stomach. I'm truly beginning to understand Fabia's six-month rotation plan. The worrying thing is I still have nine more girls to find.

I call Anna and ask if she can book me somewhere at the airport for the night and change my flight to the following morning. I can't face traveling tonight.

When I tell the Lieutenant my plan, he offers to drop me off at the hotel.

We talk on the way.

He's as horrified as me about how the girl has been treated but delighted to have taken Mr. Lycra off the grid.

He also tells me he has officers picking up Tony Carletto. He's hopeful that this time he can make the charges stick.

The girl we found is receiving specialist care and, when she's ready, will be transported up to Homeland in Washington, where recovery facilities and support are already in place.

Before I leave, he thanks me for my help as he hands me my traveling case from the trunk.

I'm too numb to say much, so I mutter something unintelligible and watch as he pulls away.

I check in and head for the bar. My room can wait.

The first flight Anna can get me on isn't until midday, which

I'm not at all upset about. I never travel without my running gear, so by seven, I'm already pounding the streets of Miami. By nine, I'm showered and enjoying a full-cooked breakfast; by eleven, I'm sitting at the gate waiting for my flight.

My cell buzzes, and I answer it to find myself speaking to Lieutenant Colonel Rochelle Sack, head of the Bureau of Investigative Services in St Louis. She tells me that a State trooper had pulled in behind a vehicle stopped on I70 between Pocohantus and Greenville. When he checked inside the car, he found a young girl curled up tight in a ball in the rear seat, paralyzed with fear and refusing to get out.

The girl is now in the Precinct and is being cared for by Children's Welfare Services. The LC thinks this might be one of the girls I'm looking for, and she wants to know what I want to be done with her.

I ask if the girl's ready to travel, but she thinks not. So I thank her for being in touch and tell her I'll get a flight out there as soon as possible.

As soon as I end the call, I go to the United ticket desk and ask to change my ticket, but the best I can get will be late afternoon with a stop-over in Orlando. The agent suggests I try Delta, and they offer a flight in one hour, with a short stop-over of forty minutes in Atlanta and a total flight time of four hours. I snap it up, grab a muffin and coffee, and eat it at the gate as I wait. I should be in St. Louis by five. I text that information to the LC, and she replies immediately, saying a patrol car will collect me and take me straight to Children's Welfare Services. She also attaches a picture of the girl.

I compare it to the one I'm carrying and feel confident that she's one of the girls on my sheet.

I text Anna, telling her my new plans just as they call the flight.

Here I go - girl number four.

Air traffic control holds us circling St. Louis for the best part of an hour, so it's just after six before I exit arrivals. Fortunately, my pick-up is still waiting for me.

Lost souls

It's a twenty-minute ride to Police Headquarters. The officer driving explains that children's welfare Services have a department co-located there, where the girl is waiting for me.

As we get close, he asks me if I follow baseball. I tell him I'm more of a football fan but wonder why he's asking.

It turns out that we're just passing Busch Gardens, home of the Cardinals.

He drops me right at the front door and tells me to ask for Pam Ellis.

I thank him for the ride and enter a bog-standard multi-story building, unlike Miami-Dade. No Art Deco. No art full stop.

I show my badge at the front desk, ask for Pam Ellis, and am told to sit.

Rather than sit, the flight was enough sitting for one day; I review whatever is on the walls and come across the familiar plaque which honors the dead in service. It tells me that one-hundred-seventy police officers have given their lives and that ninety have died from gunshot wounds. It also tells me that October is the most dangerous month. Not a cheering thought.

Pam Ellis is miniature in every way, apart from her personality. She's a strange mix of bubbly and calm; I can't quite figure out. She can't be any taller than five feet and skinny as a spring lamb. Her silver hair is tied neatly back in a tight bun, and from her face, I would guess she's around fifty. She's wearing rimless glasses that seem way too big for her face.

She holds out her hand and welcomes me to St. Louis.

As we walk to her office, she asks if I've been to the city before, and I tell her I haven't. She seems to be a big fan and has a part-time voluntary job working for the local tourist association.

When we get to her office, she sees me eyeing the Cona jug in the corner and offers me a coffee before we sit.

I hand her the sheet with the photographs of the girls on it and ask if she can ID the girl in her care.

As she studies it, I can see her reaction and already know her next question. Incredibly, I'm now so calm about the whole thing. It turns out I'm right.

'All these children are being trafficked?'

I nod in agreement.

'My God. How can people do this sort of thing?'

I recognize a rhetorical statement when I hear one, so I remain silent until she points to one of the pictures.

'This is her. I'm sure of it. Do you know her name?'

'No. I don't know their names or where they're from.'

'Well, I can help you a little with this girl. She's from Bosnia?'

'She told you this?'

'No. But I've had a few language experts listen to what little I've gotten her to say, and one of them is quite confident.'

'What has she told you so far?'

'Nothing. I don't even know her first name. The good news is that she's not nearly as agitated or panicky as she was when they first brought her in.'

'She's calmed down?'

'A little. But she's still frightened. Do you want to see her?'

'You say you have someone who can speak her language?'

'Only a little. But if you wait till tomorrow, I can probably find someone from the University that's a lot more fluent.'

'That sounds better. There's no point in me adding to the girl's discomfort if I'm unable to understand her. Can you arrange someone for tomorrow morning?'

'I'll make some calls and try to have someone here for nine. How's that?'

Before I leave, I call Anna to find I already have a booking at the Drury Hotel, just a few blocks away. The walk will do me good.

The hotel is an unimaginative twelve-story rectangular block close to Union Station. The room rate includes a complimentary hot breakfast and a daily newspaper. The breakfast interests me, the newspaper I can do without.

Given everything I've been through in the past few days, I ask reception where I can find the best Steak House in the city. The recommendation is for Al's restaurant down close to the mighty Mississippi. I need a treat.

The recommendation is first class. The steak is even better, and by nine-thirty, I'm strolling through the Gateway Arch National Park along the side of the river. It seems I'm on the wrong side as the other side has parks as far as I can see in both directions, whereas I'm out of Gateway Arch in ten minutes.

Anyway, I stand admiring the sheer power of the mighty river for a while, wondering if it's true that Chicago built a canal to connect with the Mississippi up north so they could use it to remove treated sewage from the city down to New Orleans and into the Gulf rather than into Lake Michigan where they get most of their drinking water from.

When I get back to my room, there's a message for Fabia asking me to call. I sit on the bed and place the call.

'Fabia?'

'Hi, Sammy. Thanks for calling back. I hear you've managed to recover one of the girls?'

'Yes, but she's in terrible shape. You wouldn't believe how she was being treated.'

'I suspect I would. I hope that hasn't put you off?'

'It probably did at the time, if I'm honest. But with time to think about it, it's all the more important that I carry on. There are still nine others to find. Although it looks like I have another one here in St. Louis.'

'Good news. It's the girls I want to talk with you about. We recently created a special facility here in Washington to house, treat and help trafficked children re-enter the World. Sometimes, that will mean tracing their origins and sending them home. In others, perhaps U.S. citizenship and long-term care or adoption.'

'That sounds fantastic.'

'It was a bear getting it funded, but we're good for five

years. So, I wanted to tell you that I've already arranged for the first girl you found to be brought up here from Miami. When you're ready, I'll do the same for the one you have discovered in St. Louis. Just let me know. Do you need anything else from me?'

'No. I'm good, Fabia. Thanks. I should be back tomorrow sometime.'

'See you then.'

I meet Pam Ellis as arranged in reception at nine in the morning. It takes me a few moments to recognize her. Her hair is combed-out and hanging loose to her shoulders, and she's no longer wearing glasses and, most confusing of all, has high heels on, which brings her a few inches closer to my height.

She obviously recognizes my confusion and explains that she was dressed casually the previous day because she was called in from home at short notice. She didn't even have time to put her contacts in.

I nod acceptance and ask if she has seen the girl yet.

She hasn't but assures me that she would have been okay overnight. She has two converted cells in the detention area for use in circumstances like this. They're comfortable and safe with twenty-four-hour video monitoring.

As we wait, we're joined by a young man, college-age. Pam introduces him as Abraham and tells me he speaks some Serbian.

We shake hands.

This guy seriously needs a diet, but who am I to tell him? He seems friendly enough, and I wonder what the young girl will make of him.

Ten minutes later, Pam brings her into a small conference room where the four of us can sit around a table.

Having seen the girl's state in the underground cave in Miami, I'm more prepared than I might have been, but I'm still shocked.

She doesn't look too undernourished, yet the skin on her

Lost souls

cheeks seems drawn and sunken, which exaggerates the fear in her eyes. She's still terrified.

I ask Abraham to introduce us by first names and to ask hers.

She's surprised when he speaks.

When he pauses, she remains silent.

He tries for her name again, but she doesn't respond.

He keeps trying in various fashions for around fifteen minutes but is not getting anywhere.

I sit back and talk to Pam in English. I tell her about the special arrangements made in Washington and that when we're finished here, that's where she will be going.

I barely finish when the girl throws her chair back, jumps up, and starts screaming.

The door opens, and an officer asks if everything is okay.

I wave him away as Pam tries to console the girl and bring her back to the table.

Clearly, she understood something I said. I don't know what.

I decide to try talking directly to her.

'I understand you're frightened, but you're safe now. We'll look after you, and you'll come to no more harm.'

I await a response, but it doesn't look like she understands.

'I want to move you to somewhere more comfortable than here. Somewhere extra safe. Do you understand?'

Nothing.

I ask Abraham to repeat everything I said, and he gets to the point where I was saying we want to move her when again she starts to scream and cry.

I hold up my hands and try to soothe her, and this seems to have some effect as at least she sits back down again.

I turn to Abraham and ask him to ask her why she doesn't want to move.

After this, she looks at me and says,' Safija.'

We all look at each other before Abraham tells us it's her name.

'You are Safija?

She nods.

Over the next hour, mainly with Abraham's help, we discover that she doesn't want to leave because she wasn't alone in the car when the State police found her. Her elder sister was also there.

We can't get much more from her, but it explains why she doesn't want to leave the area.

I show her the page with the twelve girls on it, and she points to one immediately.

'Tiana.'

'Her name is Tiana?'

She nods again.

Given this new information, I leave Pam and go find the duty desk sergeant of the day, who directs me to Lieutenant Colonel Rochelle Sack, who had called me originally.

When I explain what we've found out, I show them the picture Safija ID'd as her sister, and she immediately calls a sergeant in and explains what she wants to be done.

A search within an initial five-mile radius of where the vehicle broke down. Every farm, barn, and outhouse is to be searched.

When this is arranged, she tells me she'll contact me personally when the girl is found.

I thank her and return to the interview room downstairs. I find the girl has been returned to her room, and Abraham has left, but Pam is waiting for me.

We agree the only possible solution is for Safija to remain under her care until the sister is found and that they can be transferred together when they are reunited.

After this, nothing is keeping me in St. Louis, so I make for Louis Lambert Airport and another ticket change. This time, I'm definitely going back to Washington. I'm out of clean clothes.

* * *

It felt great to get back to the apartment at a reasonable hour last night. I managed to get some laundry done and chill in front of the box for a while. I didn't have to fight for the controller and again wondered where my roomie was. To my knowledge, he hasn't been back since I first met him.

Most of Friday morning, I spend writing reports. I have to cover my activities in Toronto, New Jersey, Miami, and St. Louis.

It's sure been a busy week. I'm looking forward to finishing up and taking the weekend off. It's time I have a chance to look around the Capital City.

I'm just getting ready for lunch when my cell buzzes. I'm never sure whether to use the Agent title or Detective, so I go the simple route.

'Sammy Greyfox'

'Agent, this is Deputy Chief Margaret Scott, Criminal Investigation Division in Atlanta.'

'Yes, Ma'am. How can I help you?'

'It may be the other way round, Agent. We may be able to help you.'

'You have my attention, Ma'am.'

'As you may or may not know, In Atlanta, we have developed a strong community-led policing philosophy which relies heavily on community involvement and collaborative problem-solving.'

'I've heard a little of the approach, Ma'am. I believe you are having some notable success?'

'Yes, Agent. We are very proud of some results, but although the overall level of crime has dropped for three consecutive years, we're still finding it difficult to deal with Organized Crime. However, in collaboration with the local community, we now have a joint focus on cracking that particular problem. I'm sure you know we have significant OCG activity down here, and we have just received information that underage girls are being rented out by the hour in some of the less salubrious areas of the City.'

'And you think this may involve some of the girls I'm looking for?'

'On the nail, Agent. Are you interested in being around when we bring this activity down?' We're trying to get more detailed information from an inmate we have in detention over the next twenty-four hours. After that, we'll be taking action, and you are welcome to join in if you have the time.'

'Most definitely, Ma'am. I can catch an early flight in the morning.'

'Excellent. I look forward to meeting you. Please let my office know your travel arrangements, and we will have you collected at the airport. No one enjoys driving downtown these days if they can avoid it.'

'Thank you again, Ma'am. I'll see you in the morning.'

So much for a quiet weekend, I need to talk to Anna.

Faced with the choice of an early flight at either six or eight, I opt for the latter, which with time-change, will still get me into Atlanta by ten, courtesy of Delta Airlines.

On the flight, the pilot informs us that Hartsfield-Jackson Airport is the busiest airport in the United States, with over a hundred-ten million passengers yearly. Twice as much as Orlando International, which I always assumed would be one of the busiest.

The landing is smooth, and I step out of the south domestic terminal by ten-forty-five with only my carry-on luggage.

As promised, a car is waiting for me, but it's not what I expected. I'm looking for a dark blue vehicle with Atlanta Police across the front doors and two go-fast red stripes. Instead, this car is white with a gold hockey-stick design and 'Atlanta Police' in large gold letters across both doors.

The officer driving me is a talkative man who keeps up a running commentary into the city on I85.

The car is an all-electric Tesla. One of the first in the force on a trial basis bought and paid for using confiscated drug funds. The vehicle has already undergone rigorous speed and performance tests and has come through with flying colors.

The only problem is the cost.

After learning about the vehicle, I mentally switch off and no longer pay much attention until I hear him mention the Mercedes Benz Stadium, the home ground of the Falcons. It's only a few years since I watched them play the Buccs at the Georgia dome when they ran up fifty-six points with the QB, Matt Ryan, leading a high-powered offensive assault - a game to remember.

The stadium is an unusual geometric design with adjoining triangular sections pointing both up and down, and of course, the Mercedes logo is prominently displayed.

A few minutes after we pass the stadium, we pull into the car park in front of a four-story red-brick building shared between the Atlanta Police Headquarters and the Fire Rescue Service.

I thank the officer for the ride and being a free tour guide, then enter the single-story reception area and show my credentials. This time, I'm Agent Greyfox.

I'm told that I'm expected and asked to sit while someone comes to collect me.

Rather than sit, I look for and find the same board I looked at in Miami. Those officers lost in the line of duty. In this case, there have been eighty-seven, with fifty-two by gunfire. Much less in total than in Miami, but a significantly higher percentage of gunfire deaths. Given that I've offered to help with taking down an OCG here in Atlanta, I'm suddenly only too aware of my carrying license being revoked. Given that I know the equivalent number of shooting deaths in Naples is two - I'm even more alarmed.

I can't get my head around why gun laws are still so unregulated in many of the States. Or maybe it's not the lack of regulation that's the problem. It's which guns are allowed. In many States, virtually anything can be legally purchased.

In the past three months, over hundred-twenty people have died in three mass shootings alone - two in Texas and one in Ohio. In a recent article, I read that US citizens own nearly four hundred million firearms, and around forty percent of households have at least one firearm. Run the math, and you see that this works out at one-hundred-twenty guns for every one hundred adults - all thanks to the Second Amendment, which enshrines people's right to bear arms.

As I ponder this, a thirty-something female officer taps me on the arm and asks if I'm Agent Greyfox.

After my acknowledgment, she has me issued a visitor's badge, then swipes us through security and into the headquarters building properly.

We take the lift to the third floor, where we exit and turn right towards a glass-fronted suite of offices with senior officers busy at work.

I'm shown to the one on the far right, where a woman rises from her chair and offers her hand.

As we shake, she thanks me for coming down and tells me she's a big fan of inter-organizational working. Hence her call to me in Homeland Security. I'm guessing now would be the wrong time to tell her I'm really a homicide detective, so keep that to myself.

I tell her that the trip will be worthwhile even if we only recover one of the girls I'm looking for.

'Well said, Agent. Why don't you sit, and I'll bring you up to speed. How about we get some coffee first?'

I expect a secretary to bring us coffee, but the Deputy Chief prefers to get her own. I tag along to be rewarded by none other than a Folgers strong brew.

She apologizes for the strength, but I tell her no apology is necessary. Strong is good.

Back in the office, she starts the update.

'First and foremost, we have to consider the danger the girls are in. With that in mind, the District Attorney has made a one-time offer to the individual we have in custody if he gives us help which leads to the rescue of all the girls involved.'

'Do you know how many?'

'No. Nor do we know where they are being held or even if they are being held in one place. And that's the problem. We can take down one or more gang members as they deliver the girls, but there's no guarantee they'll give up where the others are.'

'But if you don't take these initial ones down, you're condoning whatever will happen to these girls that night?'

'Precisely. And we can't do that. Which is why the offer expires at four o'clock this afternoon.'

'What do you know about your detainee?'

'He's low-level, used to run girls around. His name is Wilson Clampett, although his nickname is....'

'...Jed?'

'Either you're a fan of the Beverly Hillbillies, or you know this man?'

'Sorry, Ma'am. I've recently discovered some information about people involved in my trafficking operation, but I haven't had time to do anything with it. With help from the CIA cyber-tech group, I've identified some drivers responsible for transporting the girls I'm looking for from New Jersey across the country.'

'And one of them is Clampett?'

'Yes, Ma'am.'

'Then it looks like you've found at least one of the girls in Atlanta.'

'It looks that way.'

I take out my cell and show her the pictures of the drivers in New Jersey, and she immediately identifies Jed Clampett.

'Can you send this to me? I think this will prove useful in our negotiation'.

I forward it to her immediately.

'So, we are trying to achieve several things from Clampett, and the DA is drawing up a specific agreement that will include all of them. First, we want to know how many girls are involved, then where and how they are being detained - together or separately. After that, we want to know where they take the girls each night, how they supervise them, and as many names as possible of their paying customers. Until we turn off the demand for these girls, more will take their place.

We also need his help figuring out the best timing to ensure that we can free every girl, not to mention rounding up the entire gang.'

'Clampett gets immunity from prosecution?'

'No, Agent. That's definitely not on the table. But we will allow him to plead to a lesser charge. What he doesn't know is that the Judge will advocate the longest sentence available to him and disallow parole.'

I nod my appreciation and only hope he falls for it.

Twenty minutes later, I'm in a viewing room with a one-way window looking through to the room beyond, where I recognize Jed Clampett immediately. He has a suit beside him who is undoubtedly an attorney. They look the same the world over.

Opposite him are two detectives and someone who must be the DA. He has that look about him. Authoritative. Powerful. Smart.

The interview has just started when I arrive, and one of the detectives is speaking for the sake of the recording, stating the time and who is present in the room.

After that, the DA starts the conversation by saying that the detainee has had sufficient time to consider the deal on the table, and now was the time to accept it, or he would proceed with the charges.

As Clampett turns to his attorney, the DA produces a printed copy of the photograph I gave to the Deputy Chief - Clampett at the schoolyard in New Jersey.

As the photo is explained to Clampett, I can see him realizing he's in deeper trouble than he thought, and after a brief whispered conversation with his attorney, he turns back to the table and signs the document in front of him. After that, the DA adds his signature and leaves the room.

The detectives start working through the agreed questions until they have everything they need.

When they finish, one of them produces a copy of the page with the photographs of all twelve girls and asks him to ID who was in the car with him on the way down from New Jersey.

After studying the page, he singles one out with a finger tap.

To my surprise, the Deputy Chief appears after Clampett is taken away and offers to treat both detectives and myself to lunch. What can I say other than yes? It's already gone two, and breakfast seems a long time ago.

In the corner of the cafeteria, the Deputy Chief tells everyone the remainder of her afternoon is busy, so we need to talk through what needs to happen before the round-up operation later that night.

While we eat, one of the detectives gives us his take.

'It's potentially a more straightforward operation than we thought. Only five girls are involved, and during daylight hours, they're held in one location. At night, they're transported singly or in two's to various hotels well known for room-rental by the hour or hot-cotting.'

The Deputy Chief asks if the girls are supervised at that point.

'Yes, and no. When a girl is working, one OCG member stays nearby to collect the girl or girls after they've satisfied their clients. This isn't for the girl's protection. It's purely transport. All clients are told they will pay heavily for damage, particularly external and visible damage, or any internal injury which might result in the girl being unable to work.'

'How many tricks would a girl expect each night?'

'According to Clampett, they're busy from eleven to six in the morning. Not every night, though.'

'Seven Johns?'

'At five hundred an hour. That's thirty-five hundred per girl per night.'

We all take a moment to let this sink in before the detective continues.

'The girls never work before eleven at night and are held in a small ranch house on the city's outskirts where two men are with them throughout the day. Each evening, depending upon how many clients they sign up for that night, OCG members will turn up around eight o'clock to be ready to transport the girls to the hotels. Clampett has given us some names but says the gang is too big for him to know everyone, and although he would sometimes drive the girls, he wasn't involved in whatever they got up to - as if this might reduce his liability.'

'No chance of that,' says the Deputy Chief. 'So, we go in sometime around nine tonight to catch as many OCG members as possible and recover all the girls simultaneously. How does that sound?'

Everyone nods in agreement.

'I'll leave the three of you to make the arrangements. We leave here at eight-fifteen. Count me in.'

A convoy of four vehicles leaves the Atlanta headquarters at eight-fifteen as planned, heading southwest on Rte70 through Cedar Grove and into the Chattahoochee foothills.

When we reach Rivertown Road, we turn south and follow the exact directions given by Clampett. This area is densely wooded, and as we turn off again, the road becomes a rutted single-track, which slows our progress to a near walking pace.

The convoy halts at around a hundred yards from the target farmhouse, and everyone gathers around the Deputy Chief.

Having such a senior officer in the field is a new experience for me. Wherever I've worked before, a Sergeant would be the most senior in most cases. In a significant case, a Lieutenant or Captain might turn up to ensure everything is running smoothly, but they won't become involved. This Deputy Chief is leading the operation.

We're studying a detailed map of the area on the hood of the lead vehicle, with several of us using cells to provide light. The DC issues instructions for where she wants everyone to position themselves.

Two officers then give out Kevlar vests, one of which I'm glad to put on. Only then does the DC offer me a weapon, then give me a disbelieving stare when I refuse. She realizes now's not the time for an explanation, so she shrugs and tells me to stay close.

The officers are armed with a combination of .40 caliber Glock 22s and AR-15 light-weight semi-automatic rifles.

It's already dark and even darker under the canopy of trees, but I can still make out each group making their way to their designated locations in the gloom.

The DC and I creep closer to the farmhouse, and I'm surprised by what I see. This building has been recently completed, and piles of unused construction materials are still on one side.

The building itself is a simple Cinder-block structure with a red tin roof. Basic but functional. Given what it's being used for, it's more than adequate.

Felled trees lay across the field to the left, creating an open clearing, whereas the rear and other sides of the building are both tight to the dark tree line.

Out front, several rust buckets are parked randomly. I recognize an old Ford Explorer and a Jeep Wrangler from quite some years back.

One of the preparations we made earlier was to get copies of the building construction from the local Municipal planning authority. This shows two rooms inside, separated by one wall that runs the entire building. We assume the girls are held in the rear, and the OCG members are in the front.

The fact that someone behind this scheme has gone to the expense of building this place confirms how much this business is worth, and also, they're planning on being in it for the long haul. I imagine they probably bring in replacement girls regularly.

After checking the time on her watch, the DC is just about to give the go command when the front door of the building opens, and two men come out onto the front porch, light up and start talking in hushed tones.

The clearing at the front of the house is too wide to go while they're there, so we have no alternative other than to wait.

Settling back, we're surprised as lights suddenly appear behind us, coming along the rutted path.

The DC immediately signals to some officers that she wants them to move that way and cover our flank.

We hear the new arrival come to a halt, but with the engine still running. He'll have seen our vehicles by now and will probably be raising the alarm.

Sure enough, one of the men on the front porch takes a cell from his pocket and listens for a few minutes before hustling the two back indoors.

'We're blown,' says the DC. 'Any ideas, Agent Greyfox?'

'Do any of your officers smoke?'

Ten minutes later, I've worked my way around to the right-hand side of the building and am huddled with three officers, one of which can give me a lighter. I explain what I'm about to do, and they say they'll have my back.

I move towards the building until my back is firmly pressed against the wall, then slide towards the trash bins at the front corner.

Still unseen, I fish out some discarded copies of newspapers and take them with me as I hunker down beneath a window and listen to the conversation inside.

At first, it isn't easy to determine how many men are there, but eventually, I reckon four, and they're not happy. They're arguing loudly, one advocating they head for the woods and don't look back. Another that they should call for help, and yet another that they should wait and see what the cops intend to do. I can almost feel the testosterone flying around.

I signal back that I think there are four men, then ease forwards towards the front door, keeping as close to the wall as possible to avoid creaky planking on the front porch.

When I get there, I wedge the papers under the door and set them alight. Shielding the flame, I carefully blow the smoke through the gap under the door and press myself back against the wall hoping the others have covered me. I'm definitely missing my Glock.

It doesn't take long to get a reaction.
　'Christ! What are they doing?' One of them shouts.
　'They're burning us out!'
　'Don't be stupid,' shouts the first. 'They wouldn't do that.'
　'Maybe, maybe not, but that smoke's real, and I'm getting out of here.'
The front door opens, and two men rush out, off the porch, and make for the woods, without noticing a few scraps of smoldering paper blowing up in their tracks.

I stand, intending to leave the entry for the armed officers behind me, but as I do, a third man comes out no more than three feet from me.

He has a gun in his right hand, pointing toward the ground.

I clasp my two hands together with the forefingers pointed towards him, and the thumbs raised and shout in my most commanding tone.'

　'Armed officers! Drop your weapon!'

I can read the guy like an open book. His first thought is that he's nicked. Then, there's confusion as his brain figures out what I'm doing, and this gives me valuable time to practice one of the moves I learned in my one-day survival course.

As he raises his gun, I grab the barrel in my left hand and bend it away from me while ducking my body in the opposite direction in case he manages to get a shot away. Then I bring my right hand to bear on the gun and twist it further away until it springs out of his hand in one quick movement, and I end up pointing his gun at him.

　'Hands above your head!'

By the time I've done this, he's already surrounded by officers, one of which pushes him to the ground and cable-ties his hands behind his back.

But this only accounts for three, and I realize another must still be inside.

I give the gun to one of the officers and peer in through the open doorway. The room is empty, with the door to the room at the rear of the house standing wide open.

I have two officers enter and go to each side of the open doorway. When they're in position, I shout out aloud.

'Inside. I know you're there. We have the place surrounded, and this door is the only way out. Throw down your weapon and come out now!'

'Come and get me. But you won't like what you see.'

I move towards the door until I can see inside.

The man stands six feet in, with a young girl in one arm and a gun against her head. She looks no more than seven or eight years old, and my blood begins to boil just thinking about what this man is putting her through.

'Don't come any closer. I'll shoot her.'

'No, you won't, I tell him taking a step into the room.'

'I told you. Don't come closer!'

I take another step.

'You can't shoot her.'

'Why not. Of course, I can.'

I take another step and see him begin to panic. He doesn't know what to do. I'm only three paces away.

'If you shoot her, that's first-degree homicide. That means twenty-five years to life, with at least the twenty-five before any possibility of parole.'

'I don't care. I'm telling you I'll shoot her.'

I take another step as I speak.

'Do you know what a Chomo is?'

'What the fuck? Who cares? Stay where you are.'

'A Chomo is prison slang for a child molester, what inmates and prison officers call bottom feeders. I think they're ranked even below snitches.'

'So what?'

If you shoot that girl, I will personally make sure that whichever State penitentiary you are locked up in will recognize you as a Chomo. Not a murderer, a Chomo.'

I take one more step and reach out for his gun. I can see his indecision. He needs the carrot now, not the stick.

'I tell you what I'll do if you let her go. I'll talk with the DA about what you've been up to here and put in the best word for you that I can. You're not walking free, but at least you won't be a fuck-bunny to be passed around cell by cell in your new home.'

I place my hand on the gun and gently ease it away from the girl's head, then watch as all his bravado leaks away, and would you believe he starts to cry?

Within seconds, the two officers from outside have him safely tie-wrapped on the floor.

'Hey, Agent. That's the craziest thing I've ever seen,' says one officer.

'Not as crazy as the stunt with the make-believe gun on the porch. You must have balls the size of a wrecking ball,' says a second.

My attention isn't on what they're saying. It's on the small child the guy had been holding. She's standing alone, completely bewildered.

I bend down until I can look her in the eye and make reassuring sounds, but they don't seem to register. I reach out toward her, but she flinches, and I stop immediately.

I stand again and suddenly become aware of the other children in the room. There are four more, all young girls but older than the one in front of me. A couple of them are wearing make-up which I assume is to satisfy particular clients' needs. They all look thin, malnourished, and pale. How can anyone do this? It's inhumane.

I back towards the entrance to their room as the DC encourages two women from Child Welfare to enter and start dealing with the children.

Only now do I become aware of the smell? Urine and fasces. Looking around, there are no facilities, just a galvanized pail. And a tap with a short hose connected.

I can hear the sound of ambulances arriving in the background. This is going to be a pretty busy crime scene shortly.

I unfold the sheet I have in my pocket with the twelve

photographs and scan the room, settling on one of the older girls. I have my fifth girl.

As I turn away, the Deputy Chief offers her hand and congratulates me for doing what I had done.

I'm not good with praise, so I mutter something and try to escape. But she smiles and reminds me we're traveling together.

I'm back in the apartment in Washington by lunchtime Sunday, feeling drained. It's my time of the month, and I know I'll feel like shit for the next three days. There's never a *good* time for this, but this is a particularly bad time. I take a long shower to freshen up after the flight, put the running gear on, and head out.

My objective for today's run is to see more of the Capital. So, speed's not essential. One of the places I've always wanted to see is Arlington National Cemetery. Not maybe a glamorous location, but maybe it's more like a patriotic thing I feel I should do. It can't be more than an hour from the apartment, so I set off at a comfortable pace.

I'm only a couple of blocks in, and I pass a place called '*Smile Therapy Services*' which claims to transform individuals from the inside out. I wonder how they would get on with some of the young girls I've encountered in the past few days. Transform yourself - sounds so damn simple, it knocks me off my stride for the next ten minutes.

I cross Mass. Avenue and skirt the edge of Columbus Circle before picking up East Street and heading towards the Whitehouse. When I hit the South Lawn, I go round the ellipse where they usually have the National Christmas tree I've seen in pictures with the Whitehouse in the background. It won't be up for another four weeks or so. I should still have four and a half months to go by then, so I'll be able to see it for real this year.

I cross Constitution Avenue into the park and head for the Lincoln Memorial. This is an impressive place. The Lincoln

Memorial is at one end of the reflecting pool, and the Second World War Memorial is at the other.

I take a few minutes to take everything in and enjoy a real sense of history. I don't get this stuff in Naples, or anywhere in Florida, for that matter.

When I'm ready to continue, it's only a couple of minutes later that I'm on the Arlington Memorial Bridge crossing the Potomac, leading directly into Arlington Cemetery itself, but before I go there, I divert slightly north and make for a place I've already planned for a late lunch - the Quarterdeck. It's a popular place that George has told me about, and I have to wait ten minutes to get a table, but it's worth it. The pan-seared Salmon and chips are to die for. I stick with iced water to drink but allow myself to think ahead to later when I can help myself to a Corona back at the apartment. I may even have two.

Arlington is worth the visit, and I may come back another time. I've visited John Kennedy's grave and watched the changing of the guard at the tomb of the unknown warrior, two things I wanted to see, but I know it's an hour to get back, and the past week is catching up with me so I head back towards the Arlington Memorial bridge. As I make to leave, I pause to read an inscription that tells me, *'The price of freedom is buried here,'* and that says it all for me. Thousands and thousands of plain tombstones stretch over acres of the cemetery. How many people have given their lives for the freedoms we enjoy?

Happy with my tourism jog, I take the elevator up to the apartment only to find the door jam splintered and the door slightly ajar.

I step back and call nine-one-one, saying that an officer needs assistance, and give the address.

This is another time when I regret not having my carry license. To go in unarmed would be crazy, but Mac could be in trouble. My fear for Mac overcomes the fear for myself, and I crouch as low as possible and gently push the door open. If bullets come my way, at least the initial volley should pass overhead.

No shots, but I can hear voices inside, and they don't sound friendly.

I slowly ease into the apartment until I can glimpse what's happening. Mac is on the floor in front of the tv, and it looks like he's already taken a beating. One man is standing over him, pointing a gun, and another is closer to me, facing away from me and watching the action as I am. He also has a gun, but it's held casually in his hand.

Both guns have silencers fitted. This is no simple robbery.

I realize that If I'm spotted, I'm just as vulnerable as Mac, and I'm trying to figure out what to do about it when the one pointing the gun fires twice in quick succession.

I've no choice now. I have to act.

I spring forward and grab the gun hand of the one with his back to me, pull it upwards, and fire at the other man. The shot goes wild, but I still have the element of surprise.

As I'm about to take the gun, I glimpse movement to my left and am only dimly aware of a heavy punch coming toward me before I go down and out.

When I come to, the room is crazy with people. I have a neck brace on, and a paramedic is leaning over me, attending to the left side of my face, which hurts like hell. Looking over her shoulder, I see two other para's working on Mac. They already have him on a stretcher and a couple of drips in his arm. I take this as a good sign that he's still with us.

There are several police officers, FBI Agents, and Homeland Agents - too many to count, milling around.

The only one I recognize is Fabia.

When she sees I've come around, she comes over to see how I am.

I sit up and, with help, move to sit on a chair.

Mac's gone, but he's left a lot of his blood behind. I hope he's going to be okay.

Fabia's talking to me.

'Are you okay, Sammy?'

I shake my head and tell her I'm fine, although I now realize it's my jaw that hurts, not my head.

The para tells me she wants to take me to the hospital for a concussion check, but I say I'm really fine, other than I would appreciate a couple of painkillers.

Two Percocet later, and both the neck brace and para are gone. Leaving me with Fabia and a dozen others. I have to say, if Arnie Collins, our ME, were here, he'd be throwing a tizzy fit at how many people were trampling all over his crime scene. Not my problem.

I focus on Fabia.

'What was Mac working on?'

'Why do you ask?'

'Because these guys were professionals, and I'm not working on anything that would attract their attention. So it has to be Mac.'

'He's been working with me on a South American trafficking ring, bringing people in from Honduras, Guatemala, and Nicaragua through Mexico.'

'An Organized Crime Gang?'

'Most definitely, although we haven't figured out exactly who they are yet.'

'Well, they know who you are, so I would be careful if I were you.'

'I doubt your right, Sammy. There's no way they could have found out who was on the case or where Mac lived.'

'Regarding OCG's Fabia, I've learned nothing is ever impossible. They usually have long reaches and ways of getting to people.'

'You mean an inside source at Homeland?'

'Or the FBI, if you guys are sharing information.'

At this point, the Forensics team arrives and chases everyone out of the room. Fabia confirms that I can't stay there for a night or two, so she suggests I pack a small bag and stay at her place. With nowhere else to go, I'm happy to accept.

Fabia's car is parked outside the apartment with a Homeland Permit prominently displayed on the dash. It's a white C-class Mercedes cabriolet - very classy.

Inside, it's as luxurious a car as I've ever been in, and Fabia smiles as she tells me what it's capable of doing. Most of it goes over my head, but it sounds like it can more or less drive itself.

It takes thirty minutes to get down to her place in Forest Hills. It's over the Anacostia and south on I295.

When she pulls the car into her driveway, an automated garage door opens and allows her to park. The house has some external security lighting, so I see how well a Lead Agent lives.

It's a single-story brick house with a front porch and a double rocking chair. All the window frames are white, as is the front door. It looks like something from the front of Ideal Home.

As the garage door closes, I take my travel case from the rear seat and follow Fabia into the house. Inside is like something from Dr. Who. It's much larger on the inside than it appears from the outside.

The main living area is open-plan with a lounge, dining area, and fully fitted kitchen with every conceivable gadget I can imagine. I doubt I could even figure out what some are used for.

The lounge area has three sofas in a soft fawn fabric, with a long coffee table with patterned inlays in the top. There are lamps everywhere, which must be cleverly wired as they all come on when Fabia clicks a single switch. Most of the lamps are iron and fashionably designed.

There's a wood-burning fireplace with glass front doors installed into a pre-existing chimney, with logs piled neatly in large wooden baskets to either side.

The notable thing missing is a tv. I guess she doesn't watch MASH. It seems she's more of an audio-type judging from the size of the LP collection along the right-hand wall. I hope I get a chance to listen to some of that. I wonder if she knows about Alexa?

Full-length sliding glass doors make up the complete length of the far wall, and thanks to the security lighting, I can make out a large extended porch with a brick-built barbecue area.

I follow Fabia's directions and find the guest room. It's almost as big as the apartment I'm staying in, and there's an en-suite. I dump my overnight bag on the bed, then use the washroom to change my Tampax, add a fresh panty-liner, and feel much better after I've freshened up.

I examine my face in the mirror. Thanks to the painkillers, it doesn't hurt too much, but it sure is swollen, and as the guy caught me close to the eye, the eye might be fully closed by tomorrow.

I splash my face with cold water and head back into the lounge to find Fabia putting a new filter in the coffee maker.

'Don't suppose you have anything stronger?'

'Just you wait. I have a treat for you. I'm making you one of my favorite drinks.'

While she busies herself, I look around. There's some artwork, but not much. She doesn't seem to be much of a reader, but there are quite a few framed pictures. One in particular of Fabia and a man, I assume to be her husband. It's blown up to poster size and prominently displayed in the middle of one wall. The same guy appears in several other pictures, and I ask if it's her husband.

'Gary. He died almost ten years ago,' she confirms.

'I'm sorry, Fabia. I didn't know.'

'No reason you should.'

'Do you mind me asking how he died?'

'He was a DEA Agent. Shot in a takedown that went wrong. He made it to the hospital but died before I could get to him.'

'That's awful, Fabia. I'm truly sorry to hear that.'

'Ten years ago, Sammy. It's a long time, but I still remember him every day.'

'Was he the LP collector, or is that you?'

'Both of us. He liked Jazz and Classical. I'm more of a rock chic and heavy metal.'

'You're kidding? Same as me?'

As Fabia finishes making her special coffee, we swap notes about our favorite bands and agree on most. She votes for Def Leppard. I stick with Jimi Hendrix and the Rolling Stones.

The special drink turns out to be Irish coffee. I've heard of it but never tried it. It's good. It satisfies my need for something alcoholic and my enjoyment of coffee. A winner all around. Not sure about the cream on top, but when in Rome......'

We've just put on Iron Maiden's *The Number of the Beast* but have skipped straight to the last track to enjoy *Hallowed be thy name*, which we both agree is their best track of all time, maybe even the best Heavy Metal track of all time when car lights flash by the front windows in the background.

Fabia hasn't noticed.

'You expecting anyone, Fabia?'

'No, why?'

There's a car in your driveway.'

She doesn't waste a second and shouts at me as she runs for her bedroom.

'Take cover, Sammy. Now!'

Never one to disobey an order - we'll not when it's thrown at me with such urgency anyway, I hide behind the kitchen bar and duck down low.

Just as Adrian and Dave's dual-guitar attack builds to a crescendo, the rear door entrance from the garage splinters under heavy-automatic fire.

I look around for a weapon and select a few kitchen knives from a wooden block. It's not much against a semi-automatic, but it's all I've got.

Someone kicks the door down, and four men enter, all brandishing serious firepower.

Fabia appears from her room with her sidearm and shouts

for them to drop their guns. I have to admire her calm in such a tough spot. I don't know if I would have bothered with the warning in this situation.

The guys start to spread out, simultaneously spraying bullets everywhere.

Fabia hits one of them twice, center body mass, but although it slows him, he remains on his feet.

They're wearing heavy-duty Kevlar vests.

Two more shots from Fabia attract the attention of all four men, and they open fire and destroy the wall she's hiding behind. It literally crumbles.

My only advantage is that they don't seem to know I'm there. Not much of an edge. But surprise is often the difference between life and death. I know I'll only get one chance to use it, though.

Another single shot from Fabia and one of the guys goes down with a head wound - only three left.

They continue to throw a barrage in Fabia's direction, but one of them begins to move my way, intending to come around behind her. Just before he reaches the kitchen bar, he runs out of bullets and stops to reload another cartridge.

I lean around the corner and stab one of my knives straight and hard into the guy's right upper thigh. I connect with the femoral artery at the first attempt and pull the knife back out again. I look up and see the surprise on his face, followed by the realization that blood is spurting out of his leg in jets.

He drops his semi and grabs his thigh with both hands. I don't hesitate. I thrust the smaller knife into the side of his head, and he drops like a stone.

It seems that the others still think he's reloading and hasn't noticed what's happened yet. I've probably got twenty seconds to snatch up his weapon and reload.

I get fifteen before the fruit bowl above my head shatters, and bullets fly past me.

I slide around the end of the kitchen unit and finally click the cartridge into place. I'm good to go, but the room has gone silent. I don't know where they are. If I stick my head out to find out, I'll probably lose it. If I don't, they'll probably find a way around me.

Then, I look up and find that I can see a reflection of one of them in the window. He's coming towards me very carefully.

I reach behind me, grab an orange lying on the floor, and throw it into the air.

At that exact moment, I swivel the rifle, stand up and smash it butt-first straight into the guy's face. With all the force I can muster. No hesitation.

The guy drops. Now there's only one, but again, I don't know where he is.

This time I take a chance and ease myself up until I can see over the kitchen countertop. He's nowhere in sight. I move towards the hall leading to Fabia's room, but he's not there either.

I creep down the hallway, expecting him to jump out before me at any moment, but he doesn't.

I find him on the floor in Fabia's bedroom, half the side of his face missing.

I look around and see feet protruding from the far side of the bed.

It's Fabia. She's conscious but has taken a round to the chest. I snatch a towel from the ensuite and press it to the wound, telling her to hold it while I call for help.

Even as I dial, I can hear sirens approaching fast. I guess Fabia must have called them when she came for her gun.

I sit with her, talking about music, her husband, and anything to keep her conscious until help arrives.

It's three am before I hear from the surgeon that he has successfully removed the bullet lodged close to Fabia's spine and that she's in intensive care for recovery. He thinks, barring any unforeseen complications, she should be fine.

I also ask about Mac, my roomie, and am told that he's also in recovery. His chances may not be as high as Fabia's, but the surgeon is still hopeful.

Sitting with me as we're given this news are Pat Cataldo

from the FBI and Herman Garfunkel from the CIA Cyber-tech group, both members of the inter-agency T.E.N. group, and a Senior Homeland Director, Fabia's boss, Logan Miller.

It turns out that I only know Fabia as a Lead Agent, but she's a Homeland Director. But doesn't like the title. You live and learn.

Miller, Cataldo, Garfunkel, and I agree that we need to meet as soon as possible to figure out what the hell has just happened.

Eight-thirty and I'm dead on my feet. This isn't just *monthly* dead on my feet; this is *exhausted* dead on my feet. Cataldo and Garfunkel seem fine, but apart from the obvious - they're men, I suspect they haven't fought for their lives so many times in the past week.

Still, I have my fourth strong morning coffee to keep me awake.

We've decided to meet at Homeland, in Fabia's conference room.

As well as the three of us, Fabia's Senior Director - Logan Miller - is there. He takes charge.

'Here's what we know. Director Mendez and Agent McIntyre were working with New Mexican Authorities to identify and close down a trafficking Cartel run by a man we now think is Ruben Sanchez. This cartel provides false identification documents to families in exchange for their youngest female children.'

'They what?' I ask.

'Unless you have seen the poverty people live in, in some of these Central American countries, you won't understand this, Agent Greyfox. Some houses have twenty or thirty people living in them, in maybe two rooms. None of these people will likely have work, so everyone will depend on begging or theft. Children die from malnourishment every day, and rather than have this happen, many parents will give them away, hoping they at least survive.'

'So, the cartel plays on this?'

'Yes. The most recent report I have seen from Director Mendez indicates she has identified some of the main players and a ranch being run like a Nevada brothel, only not legalized. But, whenever she discovers a specific name for the man in charge, he mysteriously disappears, and someone else takes his place.'

'Can't you stop worrying about who's in charge and just shut it down?'

'Of course, now we know it's there. But if we close it down without identifying the major players, it will simply spring up again elsewhere.'

'Try telling that to the children being abused there daily.'

Miller takes a moment and gives me a cold stare.

'Of course, you're right, Agent Greyfox. It's unthinkable that we condone these actions any longer than we must, but I also have to think of the bigger picture. We want to close this down permanently.'

'You'll never do it.'

'I beg your pardon?'

'I said, you'll never close it down permanently. If there's money to be made, as soon as you catch the people you're after, someone else will come along until you stop the demand for such a place. You can't win. We should rescue the children now.'

Pat Cataldo throws in his support, as does Garfunkel. It seems we've all been thinking along the same lines.

Miller turns to Cataldo.

'What would you suggest, Lead Agent?'

'We can run it as a joint operation, or I can take it on as an FBI op. I'm comfortable either way. But I do think we should be moving on it today.'

'Given the absence of Director Mendez, I'm happy to accept this as an FBI operation but take Agent Greyfox with you. She can represent Homeland.'

'Fine with me, Sir. If you've nothing else? I want to get started.'

* * *

With that, the Senior Director leaves, and Cataldo turns back to me.

'Did I hear Fabia correctly? You're not allowed to carry a firearm?'

My expression is all he needs by way of a response.

'Well, you better be good at report writing.'

'I can take care of myself, Agent Cataldo. I don't need a weapon to do that, and if I'm coming, I'm coming as an equal, not a report writer.'

Cataldo gives me a stare, but I can see Hiram Garfunkel smiling at his side.

We spend the next forty minutes planning the activity. The first problem is that the target ranch is outside a small town in New Mexico called Las Cruces, which is a three-hour drive south of Albuquerque.

Cataldo can arrange an FBI jet to take us to Albuquerque, but that alone will mean five hours in the air, so given time to get organized here, get to the private airstrip, and fly down there, we have to face the fact that the operation will need to be the following day.

With this agreed, we decide to spend most of the day in preparation here and fly down at night.

Garfunkel commits to finding out everything he can through his electronic sources. Cataldo will undertake to pull together the necessary people, which leaves me with some time to keep going with my own trafficking case, but also to solve something puzzling me about the previous night's happenings. The conversation I had with Fabia when I regained consciousness back in my apartment.

Deciding that my activities can wait, I drive to Langley and find Hiram Garfunkel sitting with my new cyber-buddy, George.

It's Garfunkel who speaks first.'

'You following me, Agent?'

'I smile and tell him if I was to choose someone to follow, it would most certainly be him. But that I'm actually there to meet with George.'

He laughs and tells me he's finished with him anyway, so I can feel free, then leaves.

I think I've impressed George. He's got that admiring look in his eyes. How can I talk to his God like that and escape scot-free?

Anyway, I've no time for this, so I explain the help I'm looking for.

I explain what happened at my apartment the night before and then at Fabia's home. I realize there are many ways people could find out where Fabia lives, but it wouldn't be easy to know where Mac and I were temporarily housed. Therefore, someone with inside knowledge must have leaked that information.

George gets it immediately.

But because Fabia has been leading a joint Homeland, FBI, and CIA operation, the possibilities are endless until George points out that it would be doubtful that anyone from the FBI or CIA would know such a small detail about an agent on secondment. It would be much more likely that someone in Homeland would be our source.

After that, it's an exercise in logic. The apartment is on a long-term lease, so someone had to arrange that. It had to be paid for, so someone is doing that. It had to be scheduled for Mac and me to stay there, so we add a few names to our growing list. The Human Resources people probably have some involvement. By the time we're finished, we have fourteen names on our list, one of which is leaking information. But which one?

We're puzzling over that when I have an idea. George asks what it is, but I tell him I must make a call first. I need to find out who manages the crime scene at Fabia's place.

Several calls alter; I've established that although a Homeland agent was shot, the case is being pursued by the Metropolitan Police Department of the District of Columbia - MPD. The investigating officer is a detective in the Second District - Morgan Griffin.

I find his number and call.

'Griffin.'

'Hi, this is Agent Greyfox with Homeland from last night's shooting.'

'Yeah, Sure. I remember. How are you?'

'I'm fine, thanks. Are you aware of a related incident in an apartment in District One earlier yesterday?'

'The other Homeland Agent being shot?'

'Yes. That was my apartment, and the perps knocked me out.'

'Wow. Tough day, Agent Greyfox.'

'You're telling me. Anyway, I'm trying to determine how my apartment was targeted.'

'Shouldn't you talk to my counterpart in District One?'

'No. The perps escaped up there. Whereas…'

'They didn't at my crime scene.'

'Correct.'

'So, are you investigating my case or the one up in District One?'

'Neither, Detective. I'm working on an internal security issue in Homeland, where someone leaked the address of my apartment, and I suspect that the same perps attacked both locations.'

'Okay. Got it. How can I help?'

'Have you secured cells from the perps?'

'We have from all four.'

'Have they been through forensics yet?'

'They're there now.'

'Can you have forensics forward the call logs for each phone?'

'Sure, I can ask them to do that. Where are you?'

'I'm at Langley, in the cyber-tech group.'

'Wow, you get around, don't you? Give me a number, and I'll get the info to you.'

There's not much I can do now until I hear from him, so I leave George to get on with other work while I look for food. It will be another long day, and I might as well stoke up now while I have the chance.

I've cleared the Mac & Cheese off my plate when my cell buzzes, and I see a text waiting. I quickly forward it to George and head back to the Cyber-tech Department, where he has already printed the four call logs out.

Now at this point, I would sit with sheets and sheets of paper, checking meticulously through each number, looking for one that might match the list of numbers George has compiled from our list of fourteen suspects.

But that's not how a cyber-tech works. George has written some code and scanned all the information to do a cross-reference electronically.

There's only one match, and I can't believe it.

It's three o'clock before I'm back in Homeland HQ and making my way up to an office I'm hardly ever in.

As I pass Fabia's secretary, she asks how I am, and I tell her I'm fine.

She says how awful it is that Mac and Fabia were injured and asks me if I know how it happened.

I tell her I think I know how it happened and will bring the person responsible to justice within the next half hour, as soon as I make a couple of calls.

At that, I leave her, enter my office and close the door.

I've got a pretty good idea of what's happening outside.

Ten minutes later, I get a call asking me to go to a small interview room off the main reception area at the front entrance.

I head there with a heavy heart.

Anna sits at a small table, tears running freely down both cheeks. Two burly Homeland Agents are also in the room - one behind her, the other at the door.

I pull out a chair, sit opposite, and stare at her until she speaks.

'I didn't mean for anyone to get hurt.'
'But they did, Anna.'
'I know. But still, I didn't mean for it to happen.'
'I'll pass your regrets to Fabia and Mac if they recover.'
At that, a look of sheer terror crosses her face.
'If they recover?'
'Why don't we stop worrying about them for now, Anna? Why don't you tell me what you've been up to and why?'
'They blackmailed me.'
'Who did?'
'A man. A Mexican man. I only know him as Alejandro.'
'And how did you meet Alejandro?'
'A dating website.'
'You dated him?'
'Yes. He was funny and smart. I liked him.'
'So, where does the blackmail come in?'
She's stuck. I can see it. She's also blushing, so I understand where this is going.
'You like your sex a particular way? Is that right?'
She looks as if she's been struck a body low.
'And he caught you performing on camera? Right?'
She nods.
'Was there anyone else involved?'
She nods again.
'How many?'
I have to wait so long, and I'm about to prompt her when she answers in a whisper.
'Three.'
'All male?'
Another nod.
'So you were embarrassed when he played back the four guys banging you?'
'No. That's not it.'
'Well what is?'
'I'm ashamed of the expression on my face. I'm having a perfect time, and it's obvious.'
Not much I can say to that, so I move on.

'And afterward, this Alejandro used this video to blackmail you into providing him with confidential information, such as the address of the apartment Sam and I share?'

'Yes. I didn't know what to do.'

'So, you betrayed your boss, organization, and country. Good choice, Anna.'

She actually sobs with her shoulders shaking.

'What will happen to me now?'

'I'll arrange for you to be taken into custody, where you'll be expected to reveal everything you have passed on to this man, so I suggest you start recalling the details.'

With that, I leave her telling one of the Agents to process her on my way out. I don't know if she'll be charged with treason, but her actions were treasonous for sure.

Four thirty, and I've just had time to collect my overnight bag from Fabia's house after persuading the officer guarding the crime scene that it was okay to do so and am at the entrance to Joint Base Andrews, or as I've always heard it called in the movies, the Andrews Airforce Base.

Pat Cataldo has prearranged for my name to be on a visitors list at the guard station, so I'm waved through and given directions for where I can leave my car. I follow these and am followed in turn by a jeep with two armed airforce MPs.

After parking, I'm driven directly to a lear jet already sitting outside a hanger, ready to go.

Cataldo's already there with three of his team when I climb aboard. He quickly introduces me, and we buckle up just in time for the jet to take off.

When we're in the air, Cataldo runs through the timing of the operation with us.

'We'll land at Albuquerque at ten tonight. We have rooms at the Holiday Inn by the airport. Set your alarms for two-thirty. We leave at three. It's a three-hour drive to the ranch, and I want to hit them at six before there are any signs of life. The main force will be waiting for us twenty minutes north of the ranch. It's a joint task force of FBI, Homeland, and SWAT from Albuquerque PD.'

'Do we have a layout for the ranch?'

'Yes, we do,' answers Cataldo, unfolding a map and laying it on the small table between us. 'These circles are the destination points for four PD SWAT bearcats. One at each point of the compass surrounding the property. This other circle in red is where the rest of the task force will assemble before entry.'

'I assume you're expecting some heavy resistance?'

'Yes. We'll be well armed and ready for that.'

'What about the children? How do we get them out unharmed?'

'We have a covert operation already underway. Four FBI Agents are working their way into the main building under cover of darkness. Their task is to find where the children are being kept, then secure them when we arrive until we can reach them.'

'You mean fight off as many angry gang members as come at them?'

'They're up to the task. Trust me. They're good men.'

'Anything else we need to know?'

'Only one other thing, specifically for you, Agent Greyfox. Stay out of the way. Stay safe, and that's an order.'

Five forty-five, and we've joined the main task force north of the ranch. Sun-up isn't till seven-thirty, so we've over an hour of darkness left to cover the operation. The sky's clear above, but there's only a quarter moon, so conditions are ideal. Although the temperature is forecast to be in the mid-seventies during the day, it's still barely forty at six am.

I'm glad I took the time to collect my overnight bag, and the extra sweater, combined with an FBI jacket I've been given, should keep me warm.

I see the four huge Bearcats, half a dozen SUVs, and the same number of ambulances ready to roll. I reckon we're anticipating casualties. With no time to waste, Cataldo gives the signal, and we're off, with the Bearcats leading the way.

Cataldo and I are in the first SUV behind the Bearcats, and as I look ahead, I get my first sighting of the entrance to the ranch. I'm expecting a high wooden crossbar with cow horns. Instead, I get a solid brick wall with high metal gates.

To the Bearcats, it makes no difference. The first one plows through, knocking the gates off their hinges. The following Bearcats grind the iron out of shape, leaving the way clear for the rest of us.

The remote cameras on the walls will have already alerted them we're coming, so the element of surprise is gone, and all we have now is overwhelming force.

The Bearcats split up as per the plan, and the rest of the vehicles slow up in the front courtyard of the main building, behind the one that remains with us.

SWAT members quickly spread out and take defensive positions while everyone else gathers for last-minute instructions.

The plan is to take the place head-on and hope that the FBI Agents already onsite can protect the children.

I stay as told, to the rear of the party, but I don't intend to miss out altogether. Cataldo splits his force and sends some left, some right, and leads the main contingent towards the front door himself.

The front entrance is where the best defenses will most likely be to me. So I follow one of the smaller groups to the side.

As we turn a corner, all hell breaks out behind us as automatic gunfire shatters the silent New Mexican night air. It's impossible to tell what's happening, so we keep going. There are four FBI Agents and me right behind.

The Agent in front gives us a halt command while he checks out a small courtyard at the rear of the building before waving us forward.

We're halfway across when a hail of gunfire hits us from an upstairs window. There are two shooters, and they're not messing around.

Caught midway across, three of the Agents go down immediately, and the fourth and I manage to find cover. He behind an old wooden cart, me behind a colossal water butt.

Both shooters have seen where the last Agent went, as he's receiving their full attention. I don't know how long his cart will survive the barrage.

It seems they haven't seen me. I'm his only chance of surviving, and I know I have to do something. But what?

As I'm trying to devise a plan, the shooting reduces by half. I assume one of the guys has been called to help out elsewhere.

Time to act.

I rush, keeping low, to the wall just below the window the shots are coming from, then ease myself along until I'm under a small adjacent building with a flat roof - probably a storage shed.

I climb on some wooden crates piled against the wall, stretch to my full height to pull myself onto the flat roof, and hope I still can't be seen.

I lay flat for a moment, just making sure, then run quietly towards the main building where there's an open window.

Peering inside, it's even darker than where I am, and it takes a few moments for my eyes to adjust.

I slide the window open and climb inside, standing still until my eyes fully adjust. When I'm ready, I step out of the room into a long corridor and turn left. The room with the shooter should be one or two doors along. I don't need to worry too much about noise, thanks to the background noise of gunfire and explosions.

The first door I reach is open, and the room beyond is empty. I keep going.

The next door is ajar, and I gently ease it open until I can see the back of the shooter directly ahead at the window over the courtyard.

I look around for a weapon and almost have to smile as I see a knight-in-armor standing just further along the corridor. He has the grip of a sword in his hand, and the point is resting on the ground. I doubt I could lift it, never mind use it. However, he does have something else I can use.

Two minutes later, I'm cautiously crossing the room behind the shooter, hoping he doesn't turn - when he senses me and does just that.

As he raises his rifle, I swing the Knight's helmet and connect solidly with his head, throwing him sideways to the floor.

Before he can react, I swing again, hitting the hand still holding the rifle, knocking it from his grip. I kick it further away out of reach. Step one of my plan achieved - even things up.

As the guy recovers and climbs to his feet, I realize my part one has a flaw. It didn't take into account the size of my attacker. He must be six foot six and two-hundred-eighty pounds.

I take a few steps back, swinging the helmet too and fro as if it might scare him.

It doesn't.

The man is devoid of subtlety. He charges right for me like a rampaging bull. He has two advantages over me. Strength and reach. His outstretched punch will hit me before I can make contact with him. So, I need to survive long enough to figure out how to get closer to him. That means I have to dance around a lot.

So, I dodge, bob, weave left and right - each time allowing him to use some energy throwing punches at space. It's a dangerous game. I can't afford to let him land a punch, or I'm out of the dance.

When I can see him getting frustrated, Instead of dodging, I step forward onto the ball of one foot and use it to pivot my entire weight through a kick with the other shin to the outside of his knee. This is an attack that Tarrant, my one-day survival trainer, taught me. He called it a roundhouse kick.

I let the momentum carry through until my thigh muscle is fully tensioned and use that to spring my leg back so a fraction of a second later, I'm standing where I was when I started. I've hurt him, but he's far from going down. But I've shown him I can get inside his range, and his attack slows.

As he comes for me, I do the same again, hurting him in the same place a second time.

He's getting angry and loses control. I hit him again, twice in quick succession, and he roars, throws his arms out wide, and rushes me.

Instead of backing away, I stand firm. Plant my left foot and stab my right into his stomach. This combines the momentum of his weight with the force of my kick, and this time, he goes down on his knees.

I give him another roundhouse shin to the side of the head, and he's out cold.

I go to the window and wave to the FBI Agent below.

He gives me a thumbs up and rushes towards his fellow Agents caught in the earlier gunfire. One is on his feet and already trying to help the others. I can only hope they're okay.

I cuff the unconscious shooter and then hear shouting behind me.

I lift the shooter's rifle and check the cartridge. There are three bullets left. I search him for a replacement cartridge, but there isn't one. I guess three bullets are better than none, and I'm not particularly worried about the Sheriff's no-carry issue right now.

Crossing to the door, I peer out into the corridor, but it's empty. The noise seems to be coming from somewhere to the right.

I step into the corridor and head that way until I come to an open area with a vast spiral marble stairway from the ground floor and going up to another level above me. Looking down, I can see men scampering around, running here and there. It's chaos.

Then, one of them, who seems to be in command, shouts something, and they all start up the stairs. I'm not sure what he said, but I picked up one word - *kinder*, children.

They're coming for the children on the *ultimo piso* - the top floor.

I've no choice. I have to get to them first, so I turn and run up the stairs to the second floor as fast as possible.

At the top, I have a choice - right or left. I'm about to go right when I hear someone crying at the far end of the left corridor. With no other information, I run to the left, and the crying sound gets louder.

I slow as I get to the door to the end room. It's standing open, and someone is shouting at the children to *cállate la boca,* which I guess is telling them to shut up.

I peer round the door to see two men with handguns pointed at over a dozen children huddled in a far corner, scared witless.

That's worrying, but it's the four dead FBI Agents on the floor to the right that's most upsetting. It looks like they'd been disarmed, then lined up against the wall and shot. This must be Cataldo's elite force. I remember him describing them as good men.

Fuck!

I need to concentrate.

Three bullets, two men. Shoot to kill or not?

I don't have time to think. The men behind me are running up the second flight of stairs.

I step into the open doorway and shout for the men to drop their weapons, but they react predictably by bringing their guns up and taking aim. I shoot one in the penis, and with the other, I revert to my normal practice, shoot the gun from his hand, then shoot him in the kneecap. I want these guys to survive and pay for murdering the Agents. Death would be too kind.

With both men groaning on the ground, I grab the nearest weapon and return to the door. I hear men running along the corridor toward us. They're almost here. I have no choice. There's nowhere to hide. I take up a balanced shooting stance and wait for them to come.

Suddenly, there's chaos outside in the corridor as a gunfight breaks out. A short-lasting gunfight as the task force finally fights their way to the top floor.

I shout out who I am and that the children are safe.

When the first of the SWAT officers appears cautiously around the doorway, I'm holding the firearm by the barrel, with my arms raised in the air. I have an FBI vest on, but I'm not taking any chances.

A few minutes later, Pat Cataldo pushes his way through and stops as he sees the bodies of his Agents. The color drains from his face, and I can feel his pain. He sent these men in here, and the responsibility weighs heavily on him.

I move towards him and gently place a hand on his arm. There's nothing I can say.

When he eventually pulls his look away from the agent's bodies. I see his surprise when he sees who's standing beside him.

As far as he knew, I was safely guarding the rear of the main building. Yet, here I am, the only person between the gang members and the children we're here to save.

I'm getting ready for another reaming about how dangerous my actions are when he shakes his head. I speak first.

'I'm sorry I didn't get here to help your men in time.'

'That's not on you, Sammy. You were supposed to be in the rear guard. God knows how you ended up getting even this close. Now I see why Fabia chose you. I confess it wasn't clear before, but I understand now.'

I try for innocence.

'Good looks and personality, Lead Agent Cataldo.'

Cataldo and I traveled back from Albuquerque yesterday afternoon. Although he headed into the office, I came straight to the apartment, freshened up, and collapsed in bed, where I've been asleep for twelve hours straight.

My prediction from a couple of days ago is correct. My face is swollen, and a mass of yellow and purple bruising surrounds one eye. I look like I've gone five rounds with Tyson Fury.

After a shower, I make a fresh brew and think about the day

ahead.

It seems forever since I watched Mac being shot in this very place. I can still see the blood stain on the floor. But at least the forensics people are finished, and the place is no longer a crime scene.

As I think of Mac, I need to check on him and Fabia. I put that at the top of my to-do list.

Then, I remember having Anna arrested. I've not had any time to process that. In fact, I don't think I even mentioned it to Cataldo. More important is that I tell Fabia. She was her private assistant, after all. It'll be a shock for her.

So, after I've been to the hospital, it'll be back to Homeland to try and pick up the threads of my case.

I've tracked down five or maybe six of the dozen girls, but that still leaves plenty of work ahead.

It's already eleven before I arrive at Howard University Hospital. I find Fabia sitting up in bed reading a Jeffrey Archer novel. She looks great.

She smiles and lays her book aside as I step into the room.

'So, you just can't stay out of trouble, can you?'

'Me? I don't know what you're talking about.'

She laughs, and it's a relief to see her like this. Until she was shot, I didn't realize how much I cared for this woman. We've not spent much time together, and I know very little about her personal or professional life, either come to think of it. Yet, we connect. I think it's her values and how she sees people positively while dealing with some of the most disgusting people the Human Race has produced. She gets right to it.

'So, tell me about Anna?'

I spend over an hour with Fabia. She questions me about New Mexico until I'm drained. Then, she thanks me for uncovering Anna's duplicity and for dealing with it discretely. After that, she encourages me to get back to tracking the remainder of the dozen girls I'm looking for.

* * *

Before I leave the hospital, I visit Mac. He's also doing much better, and his doctor tells me he's out of the woods and should now make a full recovery. It's funny talking with him. I feel closer than I should, given that we hardly know each other and have barely even spent time together. It probably has to do with being in danger, working for Homeland, and trying to recover trafficked children. I don't know. But, I'm pleased he's doing so well and tell him that.

I'm not overly hungry, but I know that once I'm in Homeland, the pace will pick back up, so I stop at a Dunkin Donuts on the way and refuel. I still think a DD coffee and two chocolate-glazed donuts are top-notch. Who cares about calories?

There's a new face sitting outside Fabia's office. He's in his forties, maybe, sharply dressed in suit and tie, with his hair shaved round the sides and back but lifted on top in a coif with gel.

I introduce myself and find out his name is Dominic, and he's Anna's temporary replacement. I don't need to ask about his sexual orientation, not that I would. He's openly gay and quite a character. Probably the life and soul of any party, full of entertaining views on everything from the former President to reality tv. He's a bit too much of a chatter-box for my liking, but I can probably put up with him as long as he does a good job.

In my office, there's a pile of messages for me. I slowly work my way through them, try to place them in some sort of order, and start making some calls.

'Agent Greyfox, thanks for returning my call. My name is Tima Lukic. I run a safe house for trafficking survivors. Director Mendez helped me set this place up.'

'Hi, Tima. Yes, the Director told me about your operation. How can I help?'

'I believe you have already been involved with some of the girls I have here.'

'There was a girl we recovered down in Miami.'

'Yes, that's one. But there's also one from Atlanta and another two being brought here today from St. Louis.'

'Two from St. Louis?'

'Yes. Sisters, apparently.'

'That's good to know.'

'I wondered if you are ready to interview them?'

This isn't something I've been considering, I admit. I've seen it my job to find them and someone else's to care for everything else. But saying that to this woman seems wrong. So, I ask her when she thinks might be suitable, and agree to the following morning at ten. By then, all four girls should be available.

After hanging up, I look through the message slips, and sure enough, there's a message from the Lieutenant Colonel in St. Louis.

I give her a quick call and listen as she updates me.

'The driver abandoned the two girls when the vehicle broke down on the highway. He just ran off into the woods. We're still unsure what happened between the girls after that, but one ran away, and one stayed. Perhaps the elder sister went for help. Maybe the younger one was too scared to leave. We don't know. But, after the elder sister ran away, she hid in a barn. We're not sure for how long, but it was long enough for her to get hungry, so she went looking for food. She found a couple of kids her age playing in a field. She watched them for a while, then followed them home to a small farm.'

'She must have been terrified?'

'I would guess so. Anyway, she plucked up the courage to climb onto the front porch and knock on the door.'

'That was brave.'

'Yes, it was. I haven't met the girl personally; the officer who brought her in says she doesn't speak English. So the details are a little vague. But I think the mother opened the door and saw the mess the girl was in. She took her in and fed her.'

'Why didn't she call the police right away?'

'She said, mentioning police seemed to terrify the girl.'

'So, she must understand some English?'
'Maybe the word police doesn't feel as safe in her country as here?'
'You're probably right there.'
'Anyway, the mother saw the picture you gave us on local tv and eventually called it in.'
'Have you reunited her with her sister?'
'Yes, they're both in Children's Welfare Services or at least they were. I believe they're on their way to you now as we speak?'
'Yes. I'm aware. We've established a special home for them to receive all the help and support they need in rehab.'
'Sounds like a good thing, Agent Greyfox.'
'Thanks for all your help, Lieutenant Colonel.'
'You're welcome.'

I confess I'm super-pleased the sisters are reunited. It helps emphasize how valuable the work I'm doing is. When I meet all four rescued survivors tomorrow, I'll probably get more of the same feeling.

Back to my list of messages.

There's one from my sergeant back in Naples. I can call him later. He's checking up on me.

There's another from George over in the CIA cyber-tech unit. I'm intrigued, so call him next.

After a two-minute conversation, I'm so interested I agree to his suggestion to drop by, and I'm heading for Langley.

In George's work area, he has two technicians manning separate screens, while he seems to be in overall control. I ask him what he's doing.

'Have you heard of AITSD?'
'No.'
'Artificial Intelligent Traffic Search Division. It's a new organization the FBI has funded to help track vehicles across County and State boundaries.'
'For guns and drugs and such?'

'Yes. It's a system still under development, but I've managed to get a beta copy, which is what we're running here. I'm trying to see if we can use it to track the remainder of your vehicles from the schoolyard in New Jersey.'

'How does it work?'

'The tricky part is the data from traffic cams. Some systems are owned by the Counties, some by States, and others are managed by private companies, so their software support systems are not exactly compatible.'

'They don't play well together?'

'Exactly. But, using Artificial Intelligent software, we think it will be possible to work around the difficulties and still come up with answers.'

'How?'

'Say we pick one of your vehicles. The one with Colorado plates. You recovered a girl from a vehicle near St. Louis, right?'

'The State troopers did, yes.'

'Well, let's use that as an example. We know the plate, so we load it into the system. We give the school's address, the date and time as the starting point, then ask for the end destination.'

'But how does it do that across all the different systems and boundaries?'

'Just watch.'

I do as I'm told and turn to face the large screen he likes to use for his demos. I can see a map displayed. I'm not familiar with it, but I guess it's the starting point in New Jersey. I watch a flashing dot move along various roads and onto an Interstate. It seems to work. I'm impressed. Then suddenly it stops.'

'What's happening?'

'This is the clever bit. What it's doing is checking every individual traffic cam down every possible route from where it's stuck. It's working outwards as far as a radius of twenty-five miles.'

'It's trying to pick up the trail somewhere?'

'Yes.'

'Why did it stop in the first place?'

'Remember I said all systems work differently?'

'Sure.'

Unfortunately, some are better at keeping past data than others.'

'So, when it stops. It's because the next traffic cam on the route doesn't have any information?'

'Correct. But look at the screen.'

I turn back, and sure enough, the flashing dot is back but has jumped further down the highway. George explains a downside I haven't anticipated.

'The only problem is that the more often it has to stop and search, the slower the result. So if we're tracking your vehicle to Colorado, it might take quite a while.'

'Well, it's better than any other solution we have. Can you run several plates at the same time?'

'Not on the one system. It would grind to a halt. But, I could maybe copy the beta software onto another machine and run two.'

'Twice as good as one.'

'Which locations do you want me to start with?'

'Hang on, George, can I have some paper and a pen?'

When I have these, I ask if I can get a coffee somewhere and have time to think.

He takes me to a staff break room on the next floor, and after pouring us coffees, he takes his and leaves me to my thoughts.

I have eight vehicles leaving the schoolyard. I can strike New Jersey, Miami, and Atlanta from my list, which takes me down to five.

Then as I think about the sisters recovered from near St Louis, I realize I don't know which plates were on the vehicle that broke down. I text the Lieutenant Colonel the question and return to my puzzle.

The answer to that question is important because, on that highway, they could be heading to Colorado or California.

There again, it might be the second set of New Jersey plates which turned out to be a rental, as yet unreturned and ten days late. My money's on having found the rental, so Colorado and California should still be on the list. But, with still some uncertainty, the only other two would be Chicago and Seattle. So, until I hear back from St Louis, logically, I should choose these.

There again, with the slow tracking process, maybe I should pick the furthest destinations: California and Seattle.

Fortunately, I get a text from the LC in St. Louis telling me the plates on the broken-down vehicle are from New Jersey - the rental car.

I'm confident the driver's license details for the rental car include a fake name, but it's far easier to get a fake driver's license within your home State, so I think the car was making for Kansas, and I think I know how to prove that.

But for now, California and Colorado are good choices for the ICTSG system.

By the time I've finished, the notepad in front of me has the following list.

New Jersey   Svetlana Karzikova   2 girls (deceased)
    Miami   Tony Carlotto   1 girl (recovered)
    Atlanta   Jed Clampett.   1 girl (recovered)
    Kansas (St. Louis)   John Smith (fake ID)   2 girls (recovered)
    Chicago   Arnou Chikumbutso(Chiko)   (unknown)
    Seattle   Francis Lemoine(The Monk)   (unknown)
    Colorado   Pike Clayton   (unknown)   ICTSG trace
    California   Zhan Wu   (unknown)   ICTSG trace

Having figured this out, I take my two choices back down to George. He seems happy with them, so I leave him to it.

To get some routine back into my life, I'm up at six, into my running gear, and out of the apartment by six-fifteen. I head East for a change and cross Rte29 until I reach Washington

Golf Course and run around the perimeter. This takes me past President Lincoln's cottage at the north end, down around the Basilica of the Immaculate Conception, where I cut through some smaller streets until I find the Howard University Hospital.

I take a breather outside for five, allowing myself to cool down before I enter and make for Fabia's room.

When I arrive, the room is empty.

I go straight to the nurse's station and ask, only to find out she's self-released and I've missed her by thirty minutes.

Surprised, I take the elevator to another floor and check in on my roomie - Mac.

When I enter his room, He's already wide awake and sitting up in bed. He looks so much better than when I last saw him.

He smiles when he sees me, and I'm glad I've stopped by.

We spend the next thirty minutes with me, filling him in on all the activity since he was shot. He's surprised that I became involved, even to the extent of flying down to the ranch in New Mexico and cleaning out what he described as a viper's nest.

I can also tell he's pleased we caught the guys who attacked and shot him. I would probably feel the same.

When he's up to date, I ask when he thinks he'll be out of the hospital. He says probably another week or so. Then he's heading home to California. I'm embarrassed. I didn't even know that's where he's from. I guess my people skills still suck.

By the time I leave, he's tucking into breakfast, making me hungry.

Forty minutes later, I'm back in the apartment, showered and making eggs and waffles for breakfast. I'm due at the recovery shelter in just under an hour. My chance to meet and talk with the girls I've been finding. Something I have strangely mixed feelings about. I guess having already seen the horrors some of them have been through. I don't need to know any more details. Again, if they can help me find the others, I need to do everything possible.

When I leave the apartment, it's a degree or two warmer than earlier but still cool. The sky is grey and threatening, although the weather forecast for the day doesn't mention rain.

The walk to the recovery shelter will only be twenty minutes, so set out at a brisk pace. I'm already feeling better after my early morning run, and this will be more like a warm-down exercise rather than physical exercise. Boulevard Manor is roughly halfway between my apartment and Arlington cemetery, and I'm there in fifteen, not twenty.

Climbing the half-dozen marble stairs, I stand under a portico supported by tall white ribbed pillars and ring the bell. If I were being sent to rehab, this would be the place I would choose.

The woman who opens the door looks straight out of high school and makes me feel ancient. She smiles and offers me her hand, introducing herself as Tima Luki. The voice I spoke to on the phone the day before.

Inside, she takes my wind-cheater and asks if I would like something to drink before we start. Having just had a coffee before leaving the apartment, I refuse and tell her I would like to talk with her first.

She nods and shows me into what would have been a front lounge when this building was a home. It's well-furnished and comfortable, and although it's only mid-morning, there's already a fire in the brick fireplace.

We sit at each end of a large soft sofa - the kind you sink into - and I ask her to tell me a little about herself first.

'I'm twenty-eight and was born in a small town in the suburbs of Sarajevo in Bosnia. I arrived in this country with my parents when I was a baby. We were escaping the conflict between the Serbs, the Croats, and ourselves. We have lived in Washington ever since, and I finished my education when I graduated from George Washington five years ago.'

'What did you study?'

'International relations and affairs mainly, but also political science.'

'Because of your background?'

'Probably, although these qualifications offer me many opportunities here in Washington.'

'Such as helping here?'

'No. This is simply something I have volunteered to help out with. My parents have always spoken Bosnian and Croatian, as well as some German and Russian. So, although I'm not fluent in any of these, I can get by. And when working with girls as we have here, it's probably easier for them to talk to me as I still need their help sometimes to explain myself.'

'I can see that. What about the girls? Are all four here now?'

'Yes, but only two are ready to talk with you.'

'The sisters?'

'Yes. I'm afraid it will take some time before the other two will be willing to talk to anyone. They are so traumatized by their experiences.'

'I can imagine.'

'Let me go and bring the sisters. Give me a few minutes.'

When she returns with the two sisters, I barely recognize the one I've already met. She's clean, her hair has been styled, and she's wearing fresh jeans and a sweater with a large heart on the front that proclaims love for Washington, D.C.

They're olive skinned and brown-eyed, with black hair like mine, although the younger one has this trendy new cut that is short at one side and long at the other. It looks stupid, but I'm not one to comment on fashion.

The elder sister's hair is straight and shoulder-length. She's also wearing jeans but with a simple plain yellow T-shirt.

The two girls hold hands as they sit on the sofa opposite, and Tima rejoins me.

Everything I say, I address to them directly, but it needs Tima to translate.

Their names are Safija and Tania Osmanovic, and their hometown is Visoko, half an hour north of Sarajevo by bus.

They were walking home from school one day when a car pulled up, and three men took them both by force, bundling them into the rear.

After this, the story is sadly predictable. They were moved by cars, vans, and trucks until they arrived at a port. Something neither of the girls had seen before. They managed to look through an open door in a van and see that they were in a large harbor with many ships.

I ask if they knew where they were or where they were going, but they can't answer.

After this, they described meeting other girls for the first time. Spending days in a dark, damp, cold hold on a ship before climbing down a rope net from the ship into a small fishing boat that took them ashore.

I already know everything from there, but I let them talk anyway.

One thing they can both clearly remember was passing Dracula's Castle, which confuses me for a moment until Tima explains that this version of Dracula's Castle is in Niagara Falls, along with a Hall of Mirrors, racing cars on a huge multi-level track and multi-colored lights and a constant cacophony of sound. This makes me glad I flew to Toronto and bypassed the Falls. If I want all of this stuff, I go to Orlando.

When they finish, I thank them and ask if they can look at some photographs. Pick out anyone they recognize.

When they agree, I hand them the page with photographs of the eight people I'm interested in.

They huddle close and whisper before the elder one tells me they recognize two people. One is the woman from New Jersey I already know is dead, along with the two girls she took away from the schoolyard that night.

The other is the one who took the two of them. The one who ran off into the woods when his car broke down, and a State trooper pulled up behind him.

John Smith. The renter of the Avis car from New Jersey.

Now, I have something I was hoping for. Something

actionable.

After this, we talk for a little while, but I find out nothing else. So I thank all three for helping and leave knowing what to do next.

As I step out the front door, I'm reminded not to trust weather forecasters. Rain is coming down in torrents. I call a cab and wait, giving John Smith - or whoever he is, an extra hour of freedom.

At Homeland HQ, I grab a Philly cheesesteak sandwich and seven-up from a street vendor and take it in with me.

As I pass Dominic, he congratulates me on my *excellent* choice. I smile and keep going until I'm safely in my office with the door closed.

The next twenty minutes I spend catching up with mail while enjoying lunch. I also start looking into John Smith. His name is all I know about him. Well, that's not entirely true. I also know he's not too bright. He hires a car using a fake ID but provides his actual picture on the driver's license.

I buzz Dominic and ask him to find out how I can run facial recognition on the guy, and while he's looking into that for me, I try to decide where to look next for the missing girls.

My choices are Seattle, Chicago, California, or Colorado. Six girls still to find, and I've no way of knowing where they are.

I know George is using the ICTSG software to make some progress on California and Colorado, so I'm down to Chicago or Seattle, and Chicago is closer. This seems as good a choice as any, so when Dominic calls to let me know how to run facial recognition on my unknown guy - aka John Smith- I ask him to get me booked to Chicago the following morning and make a hotel reservation for a week somewhere central.

With that done, I access the facial recognition system and enter the codes Dominic has given me, scan in the picture of John Smith, and sit back to wait.

There's a record counter clicking through at a phenomenal speed at the top corner of the screen. This shows how many faces the system is comparing to Smith. It's not the number that impresses me; it's the speed. When we do this back in

Naples, it takes forever, and that will just be the initial pass through Floridian residents.

As I wait, I look at the name the photo recognition system gave for the car with the Illinois plates. His full given name is Arnou Chikumbutso, but I'll stick with his nickname, Chiko.

I recheck that he has no criminal record, which he doesn't. So I see what else I can find from Government sources and social media.

When I'm finished, I'm not much wiser. He's fifty-one, married, with two daughters in elementary school. Originally from South Africa, but has been a US Citizen since nineteen-ninety. He's a Lay-Preacher at the Unity Cross Temple on the east side of Chicago.

I have to say, the combination of religion and having two young daughters make him an unlikely candidate for trafficking underage girls. But he was definitely at that schoolyard, and I have a photo to prove it. Why would he travel all that way and not be involved?

As I'm thinking, I remember something odd I noticed previously about this guy. Back when George was first giving me the information from the facial recognition system. The date he achieved U.S. citizenship is the same as two others on the list that came back from the facial recognition system. The others were Francis Lemoine in Washington State and Zhan Wu in California. I meant to comment then, but it slipped my mind as we were looking into driver's license details.

I give George a call and tell him what I'm thinking.

He's immediately interested and annoyed at himself for not having noticed.

I tell him I'm heading to Chicago the next day and ask him if he can look into the citizenship thing and let me know what he finds.

After I end the call, I start searching for a good contact in Chicago Police Department but don't recognize any names. On the off chance, I call my sergeant in Naples. I'm due him a return call anyway, and it's time we catch up.

* * *

We spend an hour on the call, with me telling him as little as possible about what I've been up to while keeping the conversation mainly focused on him. I've only been in Washington for a couple of weeks, but listening to Dan's voice on the call makes me feel like it's much longer. I think I'm homesick and tell him that.

He laughs and tells me I haven't been away long enough to be homesick yet. I need to stick this thing out. It'll be good for me.

When we're finished bantering, I ask him if he happens to know anyone in the Chicago Office, and he replies immediately. He worked a case a few years back with a Captain from Alabama who has since moved to Chicago. Dan's not sure what he's doing. Up there, but offers to find out for me. I accept gratefully. Even if this isn't the person to help me to start my investigation, maybe he will know who is.

After I end the call, Dominic hands me the information I asked him to set up for me. I fly out at ten thirty and arrive just before midday. I'm booked into the Hyatt Regency for five nights. That will probably be long enough, but I'm sure I can stay longer if needed.

Happy with the arrangements, I turn back to the computer screen and find I have a facial match for John Smith.

His real name is Lucas Hernandez, and he is living in a small town called Benton, to the northeast of Wichita, Kansas. Thirty-three, married with two kids. One is still in preschool, and the other at junior high - a boy and a girl.

Lucas has a sheet as long as my arm, but nothing serious. No time served, and clean for the past six years. On the surface, he looks like a lot of guys who have strayed in their twenties and sorted themselves out when kids come along. His occupation is listed as a cab driver. If that's the case, he's taken one ride too many.

I'm just looking up the Wichita police directory when I remember Fabia saying that I have FBI and Homeland resources and law enforcement available. I know she's keen that we should work together, and traditionally, the FBI would take the lead on inter-State trafficking. So, I call Pat Cataldo, who gets back to me in a few minutes with a name to contact in the Wichita FBI field office.

I place the call and introduce myself to Agent Michael Schmidt. When the introductions are over, I tell him what I'm working on and that I'm a part of the T.E.N. Taskforce. From then, I have nothing but cooperation. I give him the details I have on Hernandez and suggest he talk with the LC in St. Louis for further information on the vehicle that he was driving. For instance, if it's been checked for prints, that would help. I also tell him I'll send a copy of the photo of Hernandez taken at the schoolyard in New Jersey and a copy of the report I've written on my discussion with Safija and Tania indicating that they've ID'd him as the man who took them.

Schmidt thanks me and promises to let me know how he gets on.

This isn't helping me find more of the girls, but at least it's taking another trafficker off the streets.

Satisfied with the progress, I'm just wondering about Fabia when I get a text from Dan. It's the name in Chicago he promised me - Deputy Superintendent Lucas Horton - and contact details. I look him up in the Chicago Police Department's org chart and find he pretty well runs the show. All major operational groups report to him: Patrol, Detectives, Terrorism, and Crime Control.

He'll definitely be able to connect me, so I call him.

'DS Horton's office.'
    'I'd like to speak to the DS.'
    'May I ask who's calling?'
    Here I go again. Am I an Agent or a Deputy?
    'Agent Greyfox from Homeland Security in Washington.'
    'Ah, yes. The DS is expecting your call. I'll put you through.'
    I'm caught a little flat-footed, but I shouldn't be. Obviously, Dan would check out that it would be suitable for me to call

before giving me the DS's details.
'Lucas Horton.'
'Good afternoon, Sir. I believe you've already spoken to my sergeant?'
'Indeed, Detective. That boy never seems to be done pesterin' me. Still, he's a good boy and says good things about you, son. What can I do for ya'll?'
I notice I'm a detective again, and I admit that makes me feel better. And if my sergeant is a 'boy,' I can ignore that the DS considers me a 'son.'

I spend the next half hour telling him about the case I'm working and, when I'm finished, ask if he would be able to connect me to the best people in his organization if I'm to come up there the following day.

He's happy to help and asks me to send flight arrival details, and he'll arrange for me to be picked up. He also reminds me that Chicago isn't called the Windy City for nothing and tells me to bring a warm coat and hat.

I hang up, feeling as prepared for the next stage of my investigation as I can be.

One more thing to do before I head home. I need to call Fabia.

As I plan on staying in Chicago for a while, I've checked my bag, and by the time I reclaim it, it's gone twelve-forty-five before I exit terminal two at O'Hare International Airport.

There's a large black seven-series BMW with a blue flashing light on top waiting by the curb. I walk to it, pulling my travel case, and tap on the side window.

As it winds down, a familiar voice tells me to throw my case in the rear and get my tush out of the cold.

After doing as instructed, I climb in the front, close the door and turn to find a large black man in civilian clothes sticking his hand out towards me.

When I take hold, my hand disappears.
'If'n I didn't know better, I would swear your sergeant

picked you for your looks, young girl. My, if you ain't pretty!'

Normally, I don't stand for comments like this, but there's something so natural and welcoming about the man that I find it impossible to be upset. There's only one way I can go with my response.

'Well, it's good to see Chicago PD promote minorities to senior positions, Sir.'

At that, the DC laughs aloud and pulls out into the traffic.

'Weissman said you was saucy, girl!'

'Hot and spicy, Sir.'

'Well, ya'll will do fine here, girl. We got this cold spell down from Canada for the next few days, so you'll need all the heat you can find. Where you stayin at?'

'Hyatt Regency on the East side.'

'You wanna check in and freshen that pretty little face up?'

'I'm good to go, Sir.'

'Okay. Let's get somethin' straight first. When you'n me are alone, I'm Lucas. The rest of the time, call me DS. You got that?'

'Yes, S… Lucas. I got it!'

'Okay. I been looking into your Arnou Chikumbutso, fella. Our Chief of Detectives knows the guy, but they've never been able to put a finger on him. They call him Chiko in these parts. He's a nasty son of a bitch who lives with a beautiful wife and two sweet kids. Goes to the Unity cross Temple on a Sunday, and if'n I didn't know betta, I would say he's got God on his side.'

'Well, he may have God on his side, but he's got me up his ass, and I sting.'

'Good for you, girl. If'n you can shine some light on this sucka, we would all be eternally grateful up here. You got a picture of this guy, right?'

'Yes, I have. But I have to make clear; he's not my priority.'

'You want the girl?'

'Yes, I do. Getting her back safely is my mission. Not locking up Chiko.'

'But one could give us the other?'

'It should.'
'Okay, I can live with that. Do you have a plan?'
'I'm still working on it.'
'What do you need from me?'
'Somewhere, I can use a computer and a detective who knows Chico to work with me.'
'I can do that. Just keep me informed; that's all I ask.'

As we're driving into the city, my cell buzzes, and I ask if it's okay to take the call.

It's George, all excited.

'Remember I told you we were concerned about the possible existence of a brilliant hacker?'

'The Phantom?'

'That's the one. Well, I think you've given us another example of his work. Those three people having identical dates for achieving citizenship was doubtful, so we looked into it and found the USCIS immigration system had been hacked. And that should be impossible. Homeland Security runs it and has one of the highest security systems available anywhere. I hope I've done the right thing for you. Those three guys are no longer U.S. Citizens. I've scrubbed them from the system. They've never officially been US citizens.'

'No problem with that, and that's all great news, George. I can use it here. Can I ask you one more thing? I'm looking at Arnou Chikumbutso, and I know he's associated with the Unity Cross Temple. I'm wondering if you can dig up anything that might help me understand that connection?'

George commits to take a look and get back to me.

I update the DS as we pull into the Chicago PD HQ off Michigan Avenue, Downtown. The building is a substantial rectangular block, four stories tall, without distinguishing features. The DS gets to park outside the front door in a reserved spot. Everyone else parks in a vast carpark further back.

I show my Homeland badge at reception, and the DC waits

while I'm given a temporary access card to allow me to come and go.

Ten minutes later, we step out of the elevator on the third floor and head for the Chief of Detective's office. The door is open, so I follow the DC straight in.

The woman behind the desk stands and thinks of saluting, then changes her mind halfway.

'How can I help Deputy Super?'

I can see my presence has her stuck halfway between formal and informal. I almost smile, but that would be unkind.

The DS introduces me and gives her a two-minute brief description of my reason for being there. When that's done, he turns to me, wishes me well, and reminds me to keep him up to speed.

After he's gone, the Chief suggests we meet the person she suggests would be most interested in helping me, and I'm happy to follow.

She only walks three offices along before introducing me to Lieutenant Davina McCabe and asking her to ensure I get all the help I need.

As she's talking, I have time to admire the woman I'm being left with. Not fashion magazine front page material, but attractive in other ways. Her facial features are perhaps a little on the sharp side, giving her an unfriendly appearance, but her penetrating blue eyes, long brunette hair tied neatly back in a bun behind her head, and perfect teeth balance all of that out, and then her welcoming smile washes it away completely.

Physically, she may be an inch or two taller than me, but with a similar build - lean and muscular. Probably a jogger like myself.

When the Lieutenant and I are on our own, she asks if I've come straight from the airport and whether I would like to join her for lunch while we talk.

I'm more than happy to accept, and as we head back downstairs, I ask where we're going.

'Do you like seafood?'

'I do.'

'Well, you don't need to know anything else. Trust me.'

Twenty minutes later, we're parked up and walking half a block to a place called Joe's. I'm happy I took the DS's advice and bought a Beanie hat at the airport. It's the wind from the north that's making it so cold.

As soon as we're indoors, I'm fine. It's cozy and warm. The lieutenant has called ahead, and we have a reservation, and she's well-known here.

We have a window seat, although there's no view to talk about. At least it feels like we're in the open.

I'm told to drop the Lieutenant and call her Davina. That's fine with me, so we look through the menu, and I ask what's good. She gives me one of these looks that asks if I'm stupid. Like, everything is good, which is why we're there.

Davina orders the Fried Cod Sandwich, and I have the Alaskan Crab roll.

We wave away the wine waiter, sticking with iced water.

'So, are you a Detective or a Homeland Agent?'

I explain my secondment, and she says she thinks it's a pretty brave thing to sign up for. She's been in trafficking before in Chicago and found it very challenging.

I admit I've only been on assignment for a couple of weeks, but I've already had my ups and downs.

After this, I start telling her why I'm there, and we discuss the plan loosely forming in my head.

After lunch and back at headquarters, I wait in her office until she returns with a couple of detectives. She does the introductions.

The guys are Gino Donatello and his partner, Christian Quentin - they tell me they go by Gino and Chris. Apparently, Gino has had previous run-ins with Chikumbutso.

Gino is classic Italian, with a Mediterranean permanent tan, small wiry stature, and charm oozing out of every pore. It's already impossible not to like him. He's dressed immaculately in a three-piece suit and a bright flowery yellow tie, with polished black and white loafers and sunglasses on top of his head. It's as if he's walked straight out of a movie.

Chris is quite different. A lighter skin tone, with black hair and brown eyes. He's also six inches taller than his partner and quieter. Although a Quebecois, he speaks English with no trace of French that I can detect and is far more casually dressed.

The Luitenant tells them to hand off whatever they're currently working on and help me.

I catch a look that passes between them and know what it means. I've some work to do to get them fully on board.

When everyone is clear, Gino suggests we find a conference room, and I can catch them up with my case.

An hour later, I've laid out everything I've got on Chikumbutso, and we've taken a few moments to get some coffee while the guys think over what I'm asking of them.

It's Gino who plays it back to me.

'So, you know that Chikumbutso was at the schoolyard in New Jersey the night the girls were distributed. I agree. He would likely be there to take possession of one or more of them. His being there wouldn't make any sense if that weren't the case. Yes?'

Chris and I nod.

'Let's assume it's one girl for the moment. It makes everything easier to talk through.'

At this point, he stands and walks to the whiteboard, where we have various items pinned up.

'We know his home address and that he has a strong connection with the Unity Cross Temple.'

At that moment, before he can say anything else, my cell buzzes, and when I see it's George, I tell the guys I need to take it.

'George?'

'Hi, Sammy. I don't have much for you, but that Church you

asked me to look into.'

'Unity Cross?'

'Yeah. It seems they've just undergone a major restoration.'

'So?'

'Twenty-five million dollars worth.'

'That's some restoration.'

'That's what I thought. I can't find out anymore here, but you might like to see if you can find where the money came from. I can't see service collections delivering that sort of cash.'

'Thanks, George. I'll follow up from here.'

Turning back to the guys, I tell them what I've found out, and they're as surprised as I am. It's Chris who speaks first.

'I agree that that's too much to come from collections, so it must be from a private donor or other investors. The thing is, for that level of investment, with virtually no prospect of a return, who would be interested? Certainly not the banks or local government, and I doubt they would be successful with the State Governor, Federal grants, or a private finance house.'

'So, an individual?' suggests Gino.

'Or an organization with shady sources of income,' I suggest.

'Organised Crime?' says Chris.

'I assume you have OCGs operating here?'

'Oh, yes,' says Gino. 'Plenty of them.'

'Something we can follow up on then. The funding for the restoration,' I say.

Then switching subjects, I ask Gino what he already knows about Chikumbutso.

'Let me tell you about the Pastor at the Church first. Elder John Wright. He's been Pastor for ten years, and everything I've ever heard about him is about what you would expect to hear. He's active in the community and beyond, occasionally taking his show on the road and evangelizing across the Country. He's got a talk show slot on local radio and often speaks up for the homeless and underprivileged in society. He's married with two sons and two daughters and preaches that his first allegiance is to his family.'

'So, pretty much on the up and up?'

'Seems to be.'

'So, how does he become involved with Chikumbutso and a sum of twenty-five million dollars?'

Gino continues.

'Now, Chikumbutso appeared on the scene here around ten years ago. Every time I've been involved with him, he wriggles free with the help of a fancy-suited attorney.'

'What have you been looking at him for?'

'Some GBH and possibly a couple of homicides. The rumor on the street is that he's a fixer for a gang that died in the late nineties but has reappeared. They call themselves the Black Disciples.'

'You know who these people are?'

'Some of the low-lives, yeah. But we've no idea who runs it.'

'But you think Chikumbutso is a member?'

'Well, someone is paying his attorney big bucks. And no lay-preacher salary's going to do that.'

I stand and write Black Disciples on the whiteboard with a question mark.

'So, how do you want to proceed, Detective?' asks Chris. 'What are you thinking?'

'I think all we've got is a connection to the Unity church and maybe the Devil's Disciples. So, all we can do is put on surveillance. Follow Chikumbutso around. Find out where he's going and who he talks to, then see if we can fit something together. Do you guys have the budget for a surveillance operation?'

'I can ask the Lieutenant, but given that she's already said we should help you, I don't see it as a problem.'

'Can we do it with just the three of us?'

'If it's daylight hours only, sure. We can handle it. If it ends up being late at night, we'll have to bring in another couple of guys.'

We stop at that point, all agreeing that the surveillance will start at six am the following morning. Gino offers to take the first post as his home is in Chikumbutso's area. I thank the guys and head downstairs to reception to collect my travel bag and call a cab.

While waiting, I realize I've just blown the weekend for Gino, Chris, and their families. I'd forgotten the following day is Saturday. This is a habit I seem to have developed. Focussing on the case and not thinking about others.

Saturday went by entirely uneventfully. Each of us took five-hour shifts, with me finishing last at nine o'clock at night before crashing back at the hotel and sleeping like a baby. I think the past week, in particular, has been creeping up on me, and I needed to catch up.

Sunday, after I've had breakfast, I get a text from Gino saying he's followed Chikumbutso to the Unity Church if I'm interested.

I grab a cab and am with him twenty minutes later outside the church. I spot him easily, open his car door and climb in.

I hand him one of the two coffees I brought with me. I'm guessing he's a straight black drinker like myself, and I'm right.

As we sip, I take my first good look at the Unity Church across the way from where we're parked.

This is one strange church.

There's virtually no ornamentation. No marble colonnades, no huge cross, or stained glass windows. It looks more like something a child of three might draw when asked to imagine a prison.

It's a tall square block, with each side identical in length. The stone looks like sandstone, but I'm not a stone expert. Anyway, it's a light creamy color.

The only windows are high along each wall, maybe twelve feet up and only a few feet in height. It must be almost pitch dark inside. I can't find anything else to say about the place. It's the most austere religious place I've ever seen.

As we watch, plenty of people make their way into the

entrance, presumably for a Sunday morning service.

'They're both in there,' says Gino.

'Both?'

'Chiko and the Pastor.'

'Makes sense. How many services do they have, do you know?'

'I looked the place up on the web, and there's this one and another at seven-thirty tonight. The rest of the week, the place seems to stand empty.'

'What about normal social activities? Bake and buy sales. Coffee mornings. Feeding the homeless, the things you say the Pastor is keen on?'

'Not mentioned on the website.'

At this stage, I've gone quiet, and Gino notices.

'What're you thinking, Detective?'

'I think we need surveillance on this place every night. No one would spend twenty-five million on a building and let it stand unused for six days every seven.'

'Yeah, I see what you mean. You want me to pull in another couple of guys?'

'I don't think we have a choice, Gino. Unless we can set up remote surveillance?'

'We can ask, but I suspect that if anyone ever finds out the police department is running twenty-four-hour surveillance on a house of worship, there would be a hell of a stink.'

'Still worth asking. Why don't you leave that one to me.'

'You're welcome.'

After that, we sit quietly until the congregation starts coming out and dispersing. Chris arrives to take over as we're waiting and is surprised to see us both there.

'What's up?'

Gino tells him we're waiting to catch sight of Chiko and the Pastor, who seems to have stayed behind after the service.

He tells Gino to go home, but he wants to wait this out. It's clear both our minds are working along the same track, and it's not long before Chris catches up.

It's a full hour before the church door opens, and the Pastor appears, climbs in his car, and drives off. Thirty minutes later, Chiko exits, locks the door, and drives away.

I announce I'm going to have a look around the church.

A little while later, I'm none the wiser. There's the front door we've been watching and a rear door where the trash cans are. But, as I noticed already, the only windows are up at the top of the walls, and I can't see a thing inside.

Back at the car, we decide to call it a night, and Gino drops me off at the Regency.

When I get to my room, I get another call from George.

'Not too late for you, am I?'

'Never, for you, George. You're my main man.'

I hear a laugh at the other end.

'Just found a little more out about your Unity church funding. The funds are routed through a Bahamian Bank, which for a church restoration is suspicious, to say the least. I can try to get more info for you through unofficial channels, but for now, that's all I've got.'

'Thanks, George. That helps.'

'Night, Sammy.'

I undress and climb into bed, still puzzling over the pieces slowly coming together. I know Chiko was in NJ, and he likely returned to Chicago with at least one girl. I know his US citizenship is false and that George has deleted it. Something Chiko doesn't yet know.

He's heavily involved with the Unity church, which has just undergone a massively expensive restoration, and the funding source is dodgy. I also know that Chiko has some likely involvement with the Devil's Disciples, and has avoided prosecution several times, so he's a slippery character.

Then, there's the church itself. Something about the design of the place is bothering me, and I know what I need to do about that.

There's also Chiko's connection to the Elder John Wright

and how involved the Elder is or isn't.

When I turn off the light, I have my actions lined up for the next day.

After a restless night, where details of the case circled round and round in my head, I get up, put on the running gear, and head out. This morning my route takes me down by the Shed Aquarium, around the outside of Hutchinson Field and Grant Park, then across Michigan Avenue back to the hotel.

I shower, stop at the Urban Counter for a breakfast sandwich and coffee, then walk the twenty-five minutes to Headquarters.

When I arrive, I head straight for the DS's office and find him already in a morning briefing with his staff, including the Chief of Detectives. I help myself to another coffee and sit down to wait.

When everyone starts to leave, I ask if I can have a moment with the DS and the Chief, and I'm waved into the same conference room they were using.

'How ya'll this morning, girl? You solved this case o'yours yet?'

'No, DS. That's what I want to talk with the two of you about. I want to use imaging equipment on a surveillance operation.'

'Sounds okay to me. You see a problem?'

It's the Chief who responds.

'It's on the Unity church, Sir. I already discussed this with Gino and Chris. There's no way we can get approval for surveilling a house of worship. The press would have a field day with us.'

'Now, calm down there, Chief. Don't you go getting' het up around the collar.'

With that, the DS turns back to me.

'I assume you have a mighty reason for asking' for this?'

'How long do you have, Sir?'

I run through everything I have on Chiko and the funding of

the building and the fact that he and the Pastor seem to stay pretty late at night at the church.'

'So, you're thinkin' something is goin' on in there. Something that shouldn't oughta be?'

'Yes, Sir.'

The DS looks at the Chief, who shrugs.

'I'll see what I can do. Now get outa here. I got a busy day ahead.'

'Thank you, Sir.'

As I leave, the Chief follows me out.'

'That's a ballsy call, Detective. I hope you're right.'

'So do I, Ma'am.'

My next stop is to do a little more online research on the Unity church, so I head downstairs to the office the lieutenant has provided me and log on to the computer.

Looking at the church's website, I find it was originally an African Methodist Episcopal Temple built in the early nineteen hundreds. Looking at old pictures, although it has had this expensive restoration, the exterior of the building looks just as it does now. Same blank walls, high windows, and lack of any defining feature.

There are also a few pictures showing the inside of the building, and it's not like any church I've ever seen before. The building is perfectly square, and the Pastor's lectern is on a raised platform in the middle. The seating is arranged all around, with the rear rows slightly higher than the front. So, wherever you might be sitting, you're looking at the people directly opposite you, beyond the Pastor.

Apparently, this building design is so unique it achieved recognition in nineteen-seventy as a National Historic Landmark.

The church can hold four hundred people.

There's a tab on the website exclusively for details of the restoration, and in there, I find a copy of an application to the local city council. This gives me an idea, and I print it, fold it, and put it in my pocket.

After this, I focus more on Chikumbutso. Only one organization can help me with the information I'm interested in, so I do something I've never needed to do before; I look up how to contact Interpol.

We learned a little about Interpol at the academy. Enough to know that it isn't a law enforcement agency. It's more of a cooperative framework that allows and encourages different international liaisons between police forces and security services. I'm looking for a starting point, and I end up with a number in Lyon, France.

After this call, I know where to call next and admit it isn't one of the first countries I would have thought about. First, I check the time and see that it's already after seven in the evening, where I'm about to call, but I decide to give it a shot anyway.

I place my call to the African Union branch of Interpol in Ethiopia - only started in two-thousand-sixteen, mainly as a response to trafficking and online child sexual exploitation - and it's answered almost immediately.

The woman at the other end of the line listens patiently as I explain who I am and what I'm trying to achieve before asking me how specifically she can help me.

I give her Chikumbutso's name and the details we have on file for him and ask if she can see if he had a record in South Africa before he moved to the U.S.

She promises to find out what she can and get back to me as soon as possible. She also warns me that things don't always move quickly in Africa.

After I end the call, I pack up, grab my coat and head back out into the cold northerly wind for a third time. This time, I'm heading for City Hall.

I decide to take a slightly longer route which takes me along the Lake Michigan shoreline, where I find a place called the Fountain Café in the center of Great Park en route. Where better to stoke up for the day ahead.

I manage to find a seat by the window, I can't see the Lake, but the park is still interesting enough. Although it's bitterly cold, there are lots of people around. I guess that's a big city for you. I don't know if I would ever get used to it or if I would ever want to.

I'm good to go after a freshly ground coffee and a blueberry muffin.

Finding the correct department at City Hall takes a little longer than it might have if they had better signage. Still, I eventually find the department responsible for archiving all information relating to construction in the city.

When I ring the small bell at the reception area, a glass panel slides aside, and a young woman asks if she can help.

I tell her I'm interested in the recent restoration work on the Unity church and hand her a copy of the restoration approval certificate I copied from the website.

She asks if I would like to wait or have the information posted.

I tell her I'll wait and sit on an empty hard wooden bench. I'm sure this is designed to put people off waiting. It won't be getting any design awards from me, that's for sure.

Twenty minutes later, she's back with a puzzled expression.

'I'm sorry, Detective. We don't appear to have any documentation relating to the application you gave me. Maybe they applied for approval but withdrew it again?'

'What about the stamp in the top corner? Do you recognize that?'

'Why, yes. That's our department's stamp, alright. But I've searched the adjacent files on either side in case it was misfiled, but there's nothing there. I don't know what to say.'

'What about your electronic files?'

'Hang on. I can check that here.'

Two minutes later, she confirms the same result. There's nothing in the system for any restoration application.

'You do have schematics for the church building on record?'

'Oh, yes. We have drawings for every building in the city.'
'Can you let me see what you have?'

Another twenty minutes later, the woman appears at a door along the hallway and asks if I would like to come and examine what she has.

Inside, I'm standing in a vast long room with four isles disappearing out of sight. Each aisle is lined with shelving, and each shelf is packed with cardboard boxes, files, and drawing tubes filled with architect's drawings and construction details.

There's a ten-foot-long, leather-inlaid table in front of me and a pile of drawings and documentation waiting for me.

The woman returns to the reception area and leaves me to it with the encouraging words….knock yourself out.

I spend the next hour sorting through masses of schematics, all shapes and sizes, with accompanying documentation, until I come across a recent interior schematic. Attached with a paper clip, but to the rear of the drawing, is a single sheet of paper describing a proposed amendment as adding a storage facility to the boiler room.

This proposal isn't reflected on the schematic, nor is there any other reference to it.

I knock on the door to reception and ask the woman if she has any idea why I can't find any further details, but she's unable to help.

Another thing that I've learned is that there's no significant difference between the most recent schematic and the older versions, making me wonder what they spent the twenty-five million dollars on.

At that point, I'm convinced there's been a colossal cover-up operation here but that I'm unlikely to learn anything else in the records. I ask if she has a facility to copy the sizeable interior schematic, and she has, but it will cost me.

By the time I get back out onto the street, it's late afternoon, and hard sleet is peppering everything and everyone. I've got a cardboard cylinder with the interior schematic under my arm, and I feel deflated. I was hoping to find out more about whatever restoration work was done. But at least I have some good questions for future use when we bring in Chikumbutso.

Given the weather, I grab a cab to headquarters, where I make for my temporary home, spread the schematic out on my desk, and start examining it in detail.

Something that's been bothering me suddenly becomes clear. There's nowhere else besides where the congregation sits and the Pastor preaches. It's like an empty shell. Actually, it's more like a football arena with a minuscule playing field. Each of the four groups of seats has an access way down each side which will allow attendees to enter and leave.

There's no closet. No chamber for the Pastor to prepare his sermon or receive parishioners. Nowhere for heating or air-con if they have any; you couldn't even hide a broom here without someone tripping over it. Presumably, that's why there was a proposal for a basement extension.

I'm still mulling this over when I get a call from the DS telling me I have approval for three days of surveillance.

I call Gino and let him know.

He offers to book out the equipment, and we agree that we'll both cover the late shift at the church.

Ten-thirty that night, and we're beginning to think watching the church is a waste of time. Then, a car pulls into the car park at the side of the church, and Chiko enters the front door.

A couple of minutes later, the rear door of our vehicle opens, and Chris joins us. He's been following Chiko.

Gino is fussing over a laptop on his knee, and I'm holding the drone, waiting for instructions to release it. It's equipped with both thermal imaging and night vision lenses.

When Gino gives me the thumbs up, I step out of the vehicle and place the drone on the ground where Gino can see it.

As I stand back, it lifts in the air, hovers for a few seconds, then takes off across the road heading for the church.

I'm glad to get back into the warmth.

Gino is piloting the drone, and Chris and I are watching the split-screen images on the laptop. The left side is the night vision image, and the right is the thermal image.

Outside, the drone climbs to the height of the church windows, and when it gets there, Gino holds it in position.

We stare at the screen, but there's nothing to see.

Gino starts to move the drone around the building, so we're still looking inside, but from different sides. Still nothing, There's certainly no sign of Chiko.

'Where do you think he is?' asks Chris.

'No idea. How long can you hold the drone there?'

'Only a few minutes, then we'll need to bring it back and change the cells.'

'Okay, let's take a chance and do it.'

The moment Gino lands the drone back beside our vehicle, the church door opens, and Chiko exits, locking the place behind him.

'Damn. Bad luck,' mutters Chris.

I collect the drone as Chris takes off to follow Chiko, although we're pretty sure he's heading home.

'We need to be smarter using the drone, Gino. We need to be watching as soon as he arrives.'

With nothing planned for the day, I spend the day thinking ahead. After I finish up in Chicago, I've three remaining locations to follow up on. Washington State, Colorado, and California.

I at least know something about Francis Lemoine in Washington State and Zhan Wu in California - thanks to George, they're no longer legal U.S. citizens. That could prove very useful.

The details from the facial recognition search show home addresses for them in Seattle and San Fransisco, which makes sense.

The third guy, identified from his driver's license, is the odd one out. No record. No known connection to organized crime.

And he doesn't live in a major city - he lives in a small suburb outside Denver called Parker.

The difference with this last one intrigues me. If he has no apparent connection to organized crime or record of involvement in trafficking, he's unlikely to be on the FBI's radar. That means I'll be contacting the mile-high city PD for their help on this one.

Parker is in Douglas County, so I decide to start at the local level and see what turns up. I call and ask to speak to the Sheriff, Marc Beavers.

After explaining who I am and what I'm doing, the Sheriff says that he's seen the picture of the twelve girls but that no one in his force has seen them.

I ask him if he's aware of any trafficking in his County, and he tells me the same thing I hear every time. That there's always trafficking going on, but in Douglas County, it's mostly Mexicans or South Americans coming up through Mexico.

I mention Pike Clayton, the guy I'm interested in, and the Sheriff knows who I'm talking about.

'He's a farmer, like most folks around here, but we've been hearing some rumors about him these past few months.'

'What sort of rumors, Sheriff?'

'Nothing definite, but we think he's running some illegal gambling ring. Not on a grand scale, so we've been looking the other way his way. The farming folks like their entertainment and work hard to have their fun. We tend to leave them alone unless they cause trouble.'

'Nothing to do with trafficking then?'

'Don't think so. But I can ask around if you like?'

'I'd appreciate that, Sheriff. When I'm finished here in Chicago, I'd like to come down your way if that's good with you?'

'Glad to have you, Detective. Let me know when you're coming, and we'll throw out the welcome mat.'

'Thanks, Sheriff. I'll do that.'

I'm about to start thinking about the remaining two cases

when my cell buzzes, and I answer to find myself listening to a strongly accented South African voice.

Ten minutes later, I know much more about Arnou Chikumbutso than I would ever want to. He's now most definitely a key person of interest, and I have one more lever I can pull when I eventually bring him in.

First, I need to find where he's holding whoever he brought back from New Jersey, and my only option at the moment is the Unity church.

I'm restless the remainder of the day, anxious to get the surveillance on the church going again, and this time to find out where Chiko disappears to when he's inside the building.

So it is that at ten o'clock that evening, Gino and I are sitting outside the church again. But this time, Chris has already warned us that Chiko is on his way.

The drone is fully charged and over the road on the ground to the side of the church, waiting for instructions.

While waiting for Chiko, another vehicle pulls into the car park. It's the Pastor.

He opens the church door but remains outside, presumably waiting for Chiko.

Chris tells us he's still ten minutes out when another vehicle pulls into the car park, and four men climb out and shake hands in turn with the Pastor before going inside. The Pastor remains at the door, presumably still waiting for Chiko.

The next call from Chris confuses us. He reckons that Chiko isn't making his way to the church but is heading downtown.

So, who's the Pastor waiting for?'

We don't know, so we wait. He waits. We wait some more until the door opens, and the four guys come back out of the church.

'Fuck!' I say out loud.

Gino looks at me.

'You don't think…?'

'What else do you think just happened? And we sat here

and watched!'

'Hang on; you could be wrong.'

'You're kidding, Gino. You're thinking the same as me. I'm going in.'

'You can't. We don't have a warrant. Besides, the Pastor has locked up and just pulled out.'

I sit back, frustrated and feeling helpless, which is not a feeling I like.

We're thinking about what to do next when Chris calls to say that Chiko has dropped off his kids and is heading to the church.

We don't have long to wait before he arrives, parks, and enters the church. By the time Chris climbs in the rear, the drone is already up at window level, and we can see Chiko on both sides of the screen. Thermal image and night vision both show him up clearly.

He's making his way toward the preacher's central area.

When he gets there, he suddenly disappears from both sides of the screen.

'Where's he gone?' I ask. 'What happened?'

Gino is tweaking the drone controls, but both sides of the screen remain blank.

'He must have gone behind something screening both video and thermal signatures.'

'But there's nothing there,' says Chris. 'We've studied the schematics.'

'Yes, but remember the planning amendment that was misplaced? I'll bet I know what it was for.'

We all say the words at the same time.

'A basement extension!'

'And that's where he's holding her.'

'Or them,' corrects Gino.

'Right, I'm definitely going in now,' I tell them, climbing into the freezing night.

'But you have no....'

* * *

By now, I'm no longer listening. I'm across the road, up the path to the front door, and inside before I can blink.

There's an eerie light from night security lamps inside, and it takes me a moment for my eyesight to adjust. When it does, Chikumbutso is walking straight towards me with a puzzled expression.

'Can I help you?'

I realize now that Gino is right. I might blow the whole thing if I reveal what we're doing without proper approval. I need a quick about-face.

'Sorry. I saw the door open.'

'Isn't it kind of late to be checking out a church?'

'Yes, I'm new in the area and looking to join a church, so when I saw the open door….'

'Well, we're over-subscribed here already, so maybe you should try St. Mary's or St. Nicholas's?'

'Yes, thanks for that. I'll take a look at them.'

With that, I about turn and leave him to lock up.

By the time he gets into his vehicle, I've hidden away in our unmarked, kicking myself for having almost blown the investigation.

After he pulls away, I open the door again and ask if they have a tire iron in the trunk.

'What are you going to do now? asks Chris. 'I thought we just agreed to do this by the book?'

I give him a steely stare.

'What do you think happened to whoever is in that basement tonight? Tell me that.'

When I get no answer, I pop the trunk and remove the tire lever.

'Cover me and let me know if anyone comes.'

I go back across to the church door, and it only takes a matter of minutes before I have it levered open, and I'm in the dimly lit interior.

I open the torch app on my cell and start going down to the rostrum area of the vast empty room, my footsteps echoing as I go.

When I'm at the center, all I know is the imaging signals disappeared when Chiko was right where I'm now standing, so I start to look around. If there's a cellar, it's well concealed.

I'm even down on my hands and knees at one point, feeling for a doorway, and it's only because I'm so low that I see the red button under the Pastor's lectern.

I reach up, press it and move away just in time as the floor opens up almost exactly where I am.

I shine my torch down into the gloom below.

There are wooden stairs leading to a dusty concrete floor.

I climb slowly down, looking around as I do. A large boiler stands dark and cold to one side. Cleaning materials are stacked on a shelf with a couple of brooms and an electric floor polisher in a far corner. Elsewhere, one tall set of shelves is filled with what looks to be mainly boxes of Bibles.

Other than that, the place is empty, and I'm feeling foolish.

Then, I notice scrape marks on the floor against the far-away wall.

They're forming an arc. An arc that tells me there's a hidden doorway behind an empty rack. I go to move the rack but find it's attached to the wall. Down on my knees, I shine the light between the shelves and discover a concealed barrel bolt. I slide it open and stand to look for a second at the top of the shelves. Finding it, I slide it open, and already I can feel the shelving move slightly as the section of wall they're attached to swings free.

I stand back up, gently pull the racking until the hidden doorway is fully exposed, and shine my light inside.

The room within is too deep for the light to penetrate, so I step through the dark doorway and tense as I hear a sound in the furthest recess. Just a hint of movement, but enough to tell me I'm not alone.

Step after step, I cautiously proceed until the light picks out the wooden frame of a small bed, and on it, a young girl is sitting, with her arms up over her eyes, hiding from the light.

She has long, stringy dark hair hanging over her shoulders,

hiding her face. She's wearing a flimsy nightdress and a wooly sweater, many sizes too large.

As I get closer. She doesn't move. She's frozen with fear, and even my soft words of encouragement don't help.

I crouch down so that I'm at her height and show my badge, but she refuses to look.

I don't want to go any closer and frighten her, and am undecided about what to do when the door behind me creaks, then slams shut.

I rush towards it and hear the barrel bolts slide back in place.

I bang on the wall, but no one answers.

I check the signal strength on my cell, but it's virtually zero. There's no way I can make a call. My battery indicator tells me I've got around ten minutes left, so I cross back towards the girl, get down on the floor, lean against the bed, and switch off my cell.

I get an understanding of how scared this young girl must be. The darkness is absolute. It's also cold. All I can do is wait until Gino or Chris come looking and hope they can find me.

I don't know how long I sit there, but it's long enough for me to start shivering. I've just started doing some simple exercises to regain my circulation when I hear the bolts sliding back and the door opening.

The sudden light completely blinds me, and I don't see the baseball bat coming until the last second; then, it's too late.

When I come to, there's blood congealed down one side of my face, and I have a splitting headache. There are several lights in the room, and I slowly grow accustomed to them. Someone has propped me, sitting up against the wall. My hands are tied, but my feet aren't.

Men are talking in whispers. I try to make out what they're saying, but all I get is the tone of their exchange. They're arguing. I guess about what to do with me.

I see one of them holding my Agent's badge, so they know

I'm Homeland Security. I don't know if that's a good thing or not.

I focus on the men. There are three of them; the one holding my ID is Chiko. I have no idea who the others are, but they're all big guys. If my hands weren't tied, I would give myself a five percent chance of overcoming them, but like this, it's not even worth thinking about. All I can do is talk to them.

'You know I'm a Homeland Agent, don't you?'

They stop whispering and turn towards me. Chiko answers.

'A foolish Homeland Agent.'

'I'll give you that. Coming in here initially on my own wasn't very smart.'

'What do you mean initially on your own?' one of the others asks.

'We didn't have sufficient ground for a search warrant, so I'm the sacrificial lamb. I come in first to see what's here, then the rest of the team come in when I say so.'

'Rest of the team? So where are they then? You've been in here for over an hour.'

'She's bluffing,' added Chiko. 'Don't listen to her.'

'They'll have seen you coming in after me. They'll be here any minute now.'

The three go into a huddle again, then, without saying anything, back out the door and slide it shut, leaving me in absolute darkness again.

But they've made two mistakes. And I spotted both of them before they left. The baseball bat is on the floor to one side of the door, and my cell is where I must have dropped it when they struck me down. I crawl across to collect the cell first, then to where I remember the baseball bat, and feel around until I find it. Although my hands are tied, I can still get a good grip on it with both hands. It feels good. Maybe my chances are up as high as ten percent now.

The problem I will have is that when they next open the door, I'll be blinded just as before, and that will take away the initial moment of surprise I'm hoping for.

I need the girl's help.

I stand, and by keeping one hand on the wall, I work around the room until I'm back at the bed. The girl isn't saying anything, but I can feel her presence.

I switch on the light, turn the intensity down to a minimum, and shine the light on the wound on the side of my head. I want her to see that we're in this together.

After this, I lay the cell in front of her and lean away from it.

Initially, she doesn't move, then slowly reaches out, lifts it, and shines it on her face.

There's enough light for us to see each other, and I touch my hands to my chest and tell her my name.

She tells me her name is Mia.

I ask if she speaks English, and she nods.

The next twenty minutes are spent with a mix of English and sign language as I try to explain my plan to her. When I think she understands, I hold out my hands, and she stares at them but then reaches out and struggles with the knots. Her hands are small, and her strength is significantly reduced, but eventually, she manages to work me free.

I rub my wrists and thank her.

My chances are now all the way up to fifteen percent.

I reach out and ask for her hand.

She's reluctant, and I get that, but I need her to move.

She eventually takes my hand with more encouragement and slides off the bed to stand beside me.

I lead her across the room so we both stand where the door will open.

My battery power is down below five percent, but I turn the brightness to max, switch it off and hand it to Mia.

In the dark, I make sure she's holding the cell the right way around and knows where to switch it on. I have the baseball bat at the ready. Now all we have to do is wait.

This is where we get lucky. Only a few minutes after this, we hear movement outside, and Mia switches the cell light on to allow my eyes to adjust.

Then the bolts slide back, and the moment the door swings open, I hit out, aiming for a kneecap and hit a bullseye, first strike.

The guy curses and shouts as he falls back onto the ground holding his knee.

In that fraction of a second, I'm through the doorway and swinging higher, this time at my second target.

He's not so easy. He's seen what's happened and steps back just as my swipe passes his head.

I reset, the bat held up to one shoulder, ready to release.

If I give this second guy too much time, he's strong enough to overcome me, so I pretend to swing at him, but at the same time kick out with my opposite foot catching him in the groin.

As he grunts and doubles up, I bring the bat down on the back of his shoulders. I don't want to kill the guy; just incapacitate him.

He falls to the floor face down, unsure what to hold first. I bring a foot down heavily on his right hand and hear bones crack. He wriggles to his feet, and I poke him hard in the gut with the bat, taking the wind from him, and down he goes for a second time. This time he's staying down at least for long enough for me to help Mia up the stairs.

But just as we're almost free, the floor entrance up above slides closed again, but this time we're no longer alone and have some very unhappy company.

I push Mia up to the top of the stairs and place myself between her and the two injured guys.

Down below, only one of the two torches they were carrying is working. It's lying on the floor, not far from the guy I winded.

The one with the smashed knee is in real pain, and I don't see him causing any more trouble, but the other is slowly getting back to his feet, and he looks angry. Real angry.

Angry is good. Angry and stupid usually go together well,

especially in a fight. I also have the high ground and the only weapon. My confidence level is soaring.

That's when he pulls his gun.

I've no time to think. If I think I'm dead. I throw myself at him from the top of the stairs.

As I make contact, I push the gun to the side with one hand and rake my nails down his cheek before my weight knocks him down, with me landing on top of him.

He's cursing at the damage to his face while I roll off him, grab the bat once more and hit the hand holding the gun with it.

The gun flies off into a far corner as he brings one set of broken fingers to hold the others.

I swing the bat again, and although he sees it coming, I connect with the side of one knee, and he goes down, writhing in agony.

I collect the gun and torch, then climb back up to Mia and examine the hatch covering. There must be a way to open it from the inside and from above, and it only takes a few minutes to find a button on the outside of the stairway.

I press it and stand with Mia behind me this time, not sure what's waiting for us up above.

Two faces appear, looking down. Gino and Chris. It's Gino who speaks first.

'You having fun down there, Detective?'

'Yeah, sure. A laugh a minute. Where the hell have you guys been?' I ask, climbing out into the church and looking around.

The place is crowded. There must be at least a dozen officers and half a dozen men secured in handcuffs - one of which I'm glad to see is Chikumbutso.

I turn round and help Mia up out of the basement. She clings on to me and is as frightened as she was when I first saw her down below. I hold her close.

'This is Mia,' I tell the others.

Gino lowers himself to her height, holds out his hand to her,

and turns on his full Italian charm.
'Hi, my name's Gino.'
To my surprise, Mia reaches out and shakes his hand.
'Do you like ice cream?'

I stand back in amazement as Mia takes Gino's hand, and they leave the church together.
I can see Chris is as surprised as I am. We look at each other and just shrug. Some people have it, and others haven't.
Officers and medics are already going into the basement in the background when I notice an empty coffin on a gurney off to the side.
'What do you suppose that's for?' I ask.
'Your final journey, Detective. And you nearly took it.'

I'm shocked when I arrive at Northwest Memorial Emergency Department. The Ambulance paramedics drop me off, and I notice the time is three am. I must have been in the church a lot longer than I thought.
A nurse cleans up the wound on my head, and I have a scan to check there's no lasting damage, but it comes back clear, so they release me with painkillers and instructions to take it easy for a few days.
It's six-thirty before I climb into bed back at the Regency and fall asleep in minutes.

Midday and after a long soak in the shower, I have an all-day cooked breakfast delivered to the room and tuck in. I'm famished. I can't remember when I last ate anything.
As I eat, I wonder where Mia is, but I feel sure that if Gino is taking care of her, she'll be somewhere safe. I imagine she'll already be with Child Welfare Services.
So, one more girl recovered. I should feel good, but the past few days' events and the pain in my head have taken the edge off that. Besides, there's still something I have to do here. Something I'm looking forward to.

* * *

Two pm, and the DS is waiting for me in his office. I phoned ahead, and he cleared time for me. Lieutenant Davina McCabe is also already there when I arrive.

I'm pleased to see coffee is available and help myself to a cup before joining the lieutenant at the DS's desk.

'So, young missy. You've stirred up a whole pot of trouble in this here city of mine since you arrived.'

'Yes, Sir.'

'I would appreciate your telling me bout what's been happening.'

It takes almost an hour for me to go through everything that led up to the events in the church the previous night. When I'm finished, I sit back, waiting to see where the DS will come from. After all, I did break into the church without a warrant. At least a couple of charges are pending against me for that alone.

'Well, I would be lyin' if I didn't say that some influential people would like to see you strung up and swinging in the wind, missy. But I'm not one of them. So you can quit your worryin' on that front.

'Good to know, Sir.'

'The thing we haven't quite tied up yet is how Elder John Wright fits into all of this if he fits in. Needless to say, he and the black community are all shouting about his innocence from the rooftops. And I would surely be interested in knowing if he has any involvement in the Devil's Disciples OCG. You wouldn't know nothin' bout that, would you?'

'I might be able to help you there, Sir. Has Chikumbutso been interviewed yet?'

'I've had a preliminary interview with him, but I've been waiting for you,' says the lieutenant. 'Do you want to have a go at him?'

'You've read my mind, lieutenant. That's exactly what I want.'

'Can I ask,' says the DS. 'Is the girl you recovered one of yours?'

'Yes, she is, Sir.'

'So, mission accomplished for you. Are you sure you want to stay involved with Chikumbutso?'

'Definitely, Sir. I'm not finished here until he's been dealt with. The man's a monster and needs to be locked away.'

Later that afternoon, I'm in an interview room sitting beside Lieutenant Davina McCabe and opposite Arnou Chikumbutso and his expensive attorney.

The lieutenant starts the interview recording with the time and names of those present, but as soon as she's finished, the attorney speaks first.

'My client is innocent of all charges you may present against him and will be bringing his own charges against this organization for illegally breaking and entering a place of worship and causing significant damage to said property. I also object most strongly to my client being shackled to the table. He represents no risk to anyone here, and this whole thing is dehumanizing for him. Under my advice, he will not be obliged to say anything today.'

The Lieutenant thanks him for clarifying their position and turns the interview over to me.

I look Chiko directly in the eye and ask him where he was born.

The attorney begins to object, but Chiko answers the question.

'Johannesburg.'

'South Africa?'

'Yes.'

I pause briefly to keep him wondering where I'm going next.

'In the Soweto township, I believe?'

He's quick to hide his surprise but not fast enough to hide it completely. One point to the good guys.

'Husband to Chantelle and father of Niclaas and Gideon?'

The expression on his face is now stoic. He's not giving anything else away.

'So, you see Arnou....do you mind if I call you Arnou, or would you prefer Chiko?'

'Whatever.'

'Okay. Arnou it is, then. So before we start today, I would like to show you something,' I tell him, removing a single page from a folder before me, turning it, and pushing it across the table towards him.

'What's this?' asks the attorney.

'It's a letter of confirmation from the register of United States Citizenry, stating that Arnou here is not actually a U.S. Citizen.'

'But that can't be true. According to the certificate I have on file, he has been a U.S. citizen since nineteen-ninety.'

'Well, that's the thing, because according to the report I have in front of me, Arnou was still in South Africa until ten years ago. Isn't that right, Arnou?'

Chiko and the attorney exchange glances, but neither is prepared to speak. I continue.

'In fact, when Arnou here was in his home township ten years ago, he discovered his wife was having an affair. Isn't that the case, Arnou?'

Although Chiko remains silent, his discomfort is growing. Sweat beads are forming on his forehead. I carry on.

'So, what did Arnou do about that? Talk it out with her and swear to be a more attentive husband. Ask her to choose between himself and the other man. No, that wasn't Arnou's solution, was it?'

Again, I'm making direct solid eye contact with him across the table.

The attorney interrupts.

'If you're going somewhere with this, Detective, can you please get on with it and leave out the amateur theatrics?'

I ignore the attorney completely, refusing to release Arnou from my gaze.

'No, Arnou's solution was much more elegant. After removing his wife's lover's head with a machete, he dragged his wife into their yard and tied her to a wooden chair under a tree. He then carried his crying two-year-old son out, strung a rope around his neck, threw the other end over a bough of the tree, pulled the son's body up into the air, and watched him writhing in front of his mother's eyes as she screamed.'

I'm still staring at Chiko. His attorney has gone strangely quiet.

I don't relent.

'Following this, he brought out their other son - six-month-old Gideon and repeated the process. Only the baby's weight wasn't sufficient for him to die, so Arnou disemboweled him and let the fresh hot entrails spill into his wife's lap.'

The silence in the room is now complete. Everyone is holding their breath.

'After what must have seemed forever to his wife, he slaughtered her. Not quickly with a single stroke, but slowly and painfully. When the police arrived, the ground beneath her chair ran red with blood.'

The room is no longer simply silent. There's a complete absence of sound - something different altogether. Something tangible.

The expression on Chiko's face is now a complex mix of anger and resignation, but I know, at this point, he's ready for the next step.

'So, Arnou. Given that you are most definitely not a U.S. citizen, I would like to show you another document,' I tell him, repeating the earlier process with another single page.

'This is an International Warrant for your arrest and repatriation to South Africa. This is good news for you, Arnou. You get to go home.'

'The fuck I will! I ain't going back there. I'd die there. It's against my Human Rights!'

'Good try, Arnou. But, you gave up your Human Rights when you gave up being Human - a sentiment that I think your wife would understand.'

'You can't revoke his citizenship,' the attorney interjects half-heartedly. I reckon even he is shocked by Arnou's history.

'I'm sorry. You misunderstand. We're not revoking

anything. According to the Registry, Arnou here has never been a citizen and is therefore subject to immediate deportation.'

'But we have a certificate?'

'I don't know who you bought it from, but it's not worth the paper it's printed on.'

Chiko's agitation is growing now, and his voice is getting louder as he claims that sending him home is as good as giving him the death penalty.

At this point, I look at the lieutenant, and she nods. We agree. Now's the time to talk about an offer.

'So, if you don't want to go home, Arnou. Maybe we can work out a deal for you here?'

'What do you want?' Chiko replies, silencing his attorney.

The attorney doesn't give up.

'Please ignore my client. It's time we take a break. I need time to consult with him.'

'I don't need your consulting, asshole. Don't you see? I'm fucked. I deal or die. So, shut the fuck up and let me hear what they want from me.'

'You really should not say another word.'

'Out! Just get the fuck out of here. Now!'

'I must advise against this....'

'I don need no fucking attorney anymore. Get out!'

With that, the attorney makes a grand show of packing up his notes and closing his briefcase dramatically before rising and leaving the room.

'So, what do you want?' asks Chiko.

It's seven in the evening before the Lieutenant, and I repeat the process with Pastor John Wright.

I start the conversation by asking if he prefers Pastor or Elder, to be told that either is suitable but that most people use Pastor. With this cleared away, I thank him for coming in so late to discuss the events the previous night at his church.

This time, I decide to go straight for the jugular.

'So Pastor. You claim to know nothing about the young girl being held captive in the church basement. Is that correct?'

'Yes. What a terrible affair, and to think it happened in a place of Worship, it's hard to credit.'

'As is your claim to know nothing about it, Pastor. Do you seriously expect us to believe that's true?'

'As God is my witness, it's true.'

'Well, it's nice to know you have God on your side, Pastor, as I'm sure that will allow you to have a much easier conversation with him when you eventually meet him in person. But for now, I would rather stick with reality.'

'I object to both your tone of voice and implications for my client,' interrupts the attorney sitting across the table. An attorney that the lieutenant has already told me is the most expensive in Chicago.

'Objections duly noted. Can you please tell us who the Pastor was during the recent restoration work undertaken in your church? It was you was it not?'

'Yes, but I don't see what that has to do with anything. Many people were involved, architects, structural engineers, and others.'

I take a page from my folder and pass it over the table.

'Do you recognize the signature on the bottom of this application document? An application for the recent major restoration work carried out on your church. An application which turns out to be for an additional room in the basement.'

The Pastor remains quiet and passes the page to the attorney.

'There's no need for you to confirm the signature, Pastor. We've already identified it as yours from other documents found at the church and your home.'

'My home?'

'Yes, Pastor. We have a full forensics team going through your home as we speak. Who knows what additional information we may find there, but let's see what we already have, shall we?'

I don't wait for a response.

'Can you identify this?'

I pass him a certificate.

'It's my Masters in accounting. So?'

'Accounting,' I repeat. 'To a layman like myself, that's a bookkeeper, right?'

The Pastor says nothing.

'So, we already know you knew there was an extension to the basement in the church where the girl was being held, and now we know that you understand bookkeeping, so perhaps you can tell us what this is?' I ask him, taking a small black book from my folder and laying it before me.

Still, the Pastor remains silent and unmoved, but the attorney is getting decidedly twitchy.

'This,' I explain. 'Is a set of accounts. But as you can see, all the entries are in code. Perhaps, as we found this in your concealed basement, you can explain the code to us?'

No response.

'Let's move on, shall we? You recently spent twenty-five million dollars on restoring your church. The only restoration I've detected, other than an additional room in the basement, is that you have changed the seating. Is that where you're twenty-five million went? New seats?'

Still no response.

'No matter, Pastor. Rest assured. We'll find out where the money went. And I'm sure your parishioners will be impressed. Pure speculation on my part, but if I wanted to launder a large sum of cash, that would be an excellent way of doing it.'

'That's an outrageous speculation on your part, Detective. You've no grounds for making such a suggestion,' interrupted the attorney. I switch tack but keep the pressure building.

'Let's leave this for a moment. You've already told us you know nothing about the girl found locked in your concealed basement. That the person responsible must have been your lay preacher, Mr. Chikumbutso, and how he could do such a thing is abhorrent to you?'

Still just the stoney face of denial.

'Well, it may surprise you that Mr. Chikumbutso has given us a full confession, explaining how he obtained the girl for you through your connections with an OCG organization in Brooklyn. Transported her across the country, delivered her to you, and even helped you lock her in the concealed basement. He also told us you were aggressive with the girl and the cause of most of the injuries the girl is now being treated for. And that you were also renting her out to selected congregation members. A fact which we are now able to corroborate independently.'

'This is all nonsense, Detective. My client has already told you he knows nothing of this girl, and as for all these stories, they are boundless lies.'

'If that's the case, I'm sure the good Pastor will be more than happy to give us a DNA sample,' I tell them, placing a DNA swab kit on the table.

'Oh, and by the way. The girl we have been discussing says that the Pastor here prefers anal action. So we knew exactly where to look for your presence, Pastor.'

At last, I can see the resignation in his eyes. It doesn't mean he won't fight in court, and I'm sure his expensive attorneys will make lots of cash defending him, but he knows he's going down. I can tell.

I can't resist a final comment.

'Incidentally, the girl is recovering well; thanks for your concern, Pastor. It may take her a while, but she'll enjoy her life again before you will.'

I catch a flight back to Washington on Thursday morning and head straight to the apartment. It seems that I'm working twenty-four-seven on this assignment. Fabia told me this would be challenging work, but I could not have predicted everything that has happened to me in three short weeks.

I change into my running gear and pound the streets for the next hour and a half, returning for a shower and a change of clothes. I'm feeling too beat to bother looking for somewhere to eat, so I order a pizza and Diet Coke online from a place I've found called DC Pizza. The Pizza's a three-cheese blend with red onions, bacon, and Pepperoni.

By two o'clock, I feel ready to hit the office. It's only been a few hours, but I feel much better than I did this morning.

At Homeland, Dominic is fussing over his boss, Fabia, who's in her office. I knock and enter.

The expression on Fabia's face tells me I've arrived just in time.

She cuts Dominic off and asks if he can bring us some coffee.

When he's gone, I sit and ask her how she's feeling.

'I'm okay, Sammy. I probably should still be resting at home, but I've been so bored. I thought, at least sitting behind my desk, I can be doing something useful.'

'You've got some color back in your cheeks anyway.'

'Yes. If I don't breathe too deeply, I can even laugh.'

At that point, Dominic brings the coffee, then leaves us alone.

'So, Sammy. What have you been up to?'

An hour later and I feel like I've been through a wringer. Fabia wanted to know everything. She's like a sponge for details.

Seeing how I feel, Fabia crosses to the door and asks Dominic if he would mind refreshing our coffees.

As she returns behind her desk, she asks me where I'm looking next.

'I'm not sure. I've three locations left. Washington State, probably Seattle. Colorado, where it looks like my guy is a hick farmer in the boonies south of Denver. Or California, most likely San Fransisco.'

'So, if you have to pick?'

'Well, I've already contacted the Sheriff in Douglas County, south of Denver. So I might as well start there.'

'A hick farmer sounds like an odd recipient for one of your girls?'

Dominic interrupts delivering our coffee then leaves us again.

'I agree. The Sheriff says he's asked around, and other than he might be involved in some gambling with other farmers, he seems pretty clean.'

'But you know otherwise, Sammy. You've got the picture of him in the schoolyard in Queens. Looks can be deceiving in this game, as I'm sure you've already discovered.'

'I guess a rich retired financier in Miami and a Pastor in Chicago support that. You're right, of course. By the way. How's Mac, my roomie?'

'He's going to be fine, Sammy. In fact, we've already moved him to a hospital in San Fransisco where he will continue his recovery closer to his family.'

'Maybe I can visit when I'm out there?'

After this, I'm back in my office checking for messages and going through emails when my cell rings.

'Detective Greyfox.'

'Hi...Detective. Are you Agent Greyfox with Homeland?'

'Yes, sorry. I'm a detective but on secondment. I guess I'm not sure what I am at the moment.'

I hear a laugh at the other end of the line.

'I work in homicide, and I feel like that most of the time. I'm Detective La Costa, by the way. Seattle Criminal Investigations Unit, homicide department.'

'Hi, Detective. What can I do for you?'

'You put out an APB on twelve under-age girls you are tracking down?'

'I did. Have you found one of them?'

'I'm sorry to say we have. We fished her body out of the Duwamish Waterway yesterday. She's the third down on the left-hand side of the page you sent out. She's in the morgue as a Jane Doe right now. I hate having Jane Does. Do you know her name?'

'Sorry, Detective, I hardly know any of their names, but if I find out, you'll be the first to know.'

'Thanks for that. She's with the Coroner right now, and we'll have more details of how she died later today, but we already know she's been dead for around three days before being dumped in the waterway.'

'Can you send me a copy of the autopsy results when they're available?'

'Sure, no problem.'

'I'll do everything possible to get you a name, Detective. I agree with you. Going into the ground as a Jane Doe is such a sad ending for anyone, never mind for a young girl.'

'Thanks for that.'

' Stay in touch.'

The call from Seattle has floored me again. Maybe I could have saved her if I'd started there instead of Miami. There again, I did recover the girl from appalling conditions in the financier's pool cave. Save one, lose another. Is that what this is all about? I know I can't save everyone, but each one I lose hurts more than I could have imagined. This roller-coaster ride is brutal.

I now need to update my list on the whiteboard.

New Jersey	2 (deceased)
Miami	1 (recovered)
St Louis/Kansas	2 (recovered)
Atlanta	1 (recovered)
Chicago	1 (recovered)
Seattle	1 (dead)
Douglas County?	
California (SFO?).	?

So, I'm still looking for four girls. Four more girls who may be in dire circumstances, and that fires me back up again. I lift the phone and call Sheriff Marc Beavers in Douglas County. I need him to know I'll be there the next day.

My eight-fifteen flight from Reagan lands in Denver two hours later thanks to moving from Eastern time to Mountain time - a two-hour difference.

Denver Airport is a different experience from anything I've

seen so far. The construction is like thirty or more massive Native American teepees combined over a multi-story structure. Inside, the high teepee roofs give an open-air feeling to the place and let in the maximum natural light.

Passing through the terminal to collect my baggage, there are so many stunning multi-colored murals everywhere. In the baggage area itself, there are two enormous examples. One apparently symbolizes environmental destruction versus environmental healing; the other depicts war versus peace. According to a fellow traveler I wait with, these two pieces are believed to show that Denver Airport is part of a giant conspiracy centered around a group known as the New World Order.

I don't know, but it seems like some people have too much time on their hands coming up with stuff like that.

I'm happy to collect my bag and get out of the place.

Outside, it's a couple of degrees cooler than Washington but still pleasant enough to have my lightweight wind-cheater unzipped. I'm glad I've brought my sunglasses. The sky is clear, and the sun is blazing.

I exit door 520 on the terminal west side and follow the Rental car signage, where I take the Avis courtesy bus to collect my car.

I drive from the airport at midday with my sat-nav set for Castle Rock, Douglas County, around an hour south.

I stay east of the city, choosing the smaller highways and bypassing all the built-up areas, but I can see the mountains in the distance beyond the city on my right. The country I pass through is primarily flat and rural. I understand why there might be a lot of farmers in the County.

As I get closer, I see the main I25 highway passing on my right, but I can make it into Castle Rock, staying on the more minor roads.

The town looks like a small town anywhere in America. I pass the County school, a couple of cafes, a barber shop, pizza house and keep heading south until I hit third and hang a left.

The Sheriff's office is down on Perry Street opposite an open space with a farmer's market in full swing.

I park around the rear but enter the front of the building, show my ID, and ask if the Sheriff is available.

I'm told he's out for lunch, but I can find him if I head over to Granelli's Pizzeria.

I follow the directions, and five minutes later, I've found who I'm looking for.

The Sheriff has just started a giant pepperoni pizza. If he eats the whole thing himself, I'll be mighty impressed.

I introduce myself, and he tells me to grab something for myself and join him.

Ten minutes later, my slice of Hawaiian Pizza looks minuscule in comparison, but I have an extra large coffee to make up for its inadequacy.

Eating doesn't seem to slow down the Sheriff's conversation, and I do well to dodge pepperoni spoilers flying my way from time to time.

'So, Detective, you asked me if your man Pike Clayton is involved in anything more severe than gambling, and the word I'm getting back is that his gambling issue involves Cock fighting.'

'Cock fighting? That's a Federal crime now, isn't it?'

'Technically, it is. But as I told you the other day, these farming folk live hard lives, much harder than most folks. If they need to blow some steam and not harm anyone, we tend to leave them be.'

'Don't these Cock-fights usually lead to more trouble? Fights, drugs, guns, and such?'

'Maybe somewhere's, but they haven't round these parts.'

'Not yet?'

I've succeeded in stopping the Sheriff from chomping while he gives me a stare.

'Look, Detective. You say you can prove that Clayton was in a schoolyard when some underage girls were being distributed. Is that right?'

I nod.

'Do you have any proof that he took any of them?'

'No, Sir. I don't.'

'So, without you having proof that he's done anything wrong, you can see why I might be reluctant to stir things up around here?'

'What about the Cock-fighting? Surely the Humane Society must be knocking on your door?'

'Not if they don't know about it.'

I can't believe what I'm hearing. This guy is wilfully ignoring a Federal crime taking place on his patch because he doesn't want to stop local farmers from having their fun.

'Well, Sheriff. As you say, the Cock-fighting's not my issue, but getting an explanation from Clayton about why he was at that schoolyard is.'

'Now there, I can agree with you, Detective. I've already spoken to a couple of my deputies, and they'll take you out to Pike's place to chat when you're good and ready.'

After this, the Sheriff tells me about Parker, the town closest to Pike Clayton's ranch. The people in the town itself are almost exclusively white, with maybe ten percent Latino and Spanish. People are either retired or Denver commuters.

He says house prices have been soaring, and it's still almost impossible to find a place below five-hundred-thousand dollars. So, a wealthy neighborhood.

I finish my pizza slice ten minutes before the Sheriff and wait until he's ready. Then he puts on his hat, and we head back to the station.

There's no sign-in process at the door. No security badge issued. Nothing. I walk past the duty reception area unchallenged.

I'm feeling really uncomfortable about how things are being run down here.

On the way into his office, he asks a secretary to find the patrol officers he told me about while he then sits behind a huge old wooden leather-topped desk and puts his boots up.

'Take a seat, Detective. It shouldn't be long. I asked them not to leave the building.'

As I sit, I take a moment to look properly at the man across from me. I would guess he's around fifty, with long silver hair combed straight back and falling over the open collar of his uniform shirt. He's well-tanned; that's probably true for virtually everyone in Colorado. It goes with the climate. He has unhealthy skin, especially on his bulbous nose. The pores are too large, and there are pock-marks, maybe from childhood measles.

I notice an ashtray on his desk with the remains of a cigar stubbed out, but he shows no inclination to strike up while I'm there, which is good. I detest cigar smoke. But the fact that he smokes indoors is another black mark in his book, as far as I'm concerned.

A knock on the door behind me disturbs my thoughts, and I turn to see two deputies enter the room. The first looks like he's eighteen years old. Tall and stringy with a long thin drawn-out face to match. The other is a woman roughly my age, a little smaller and more compact than me, with round features and blonde hair tied back in a bun. She speaks first.

'You ready for us, Sheriff?'

The Sheriff points to me and introduces me by name, telling me that the young man is Officer Dylan Reed, and the other Officer is Maria Delores.

I stand and shake hands with each of the new arrivals. Then thank them for offering to take me out to the Clayton place.

'So, if there's nothing else,' says the Sheriff. 'I'll let you folks get along.'

Outside, Delores asks if I've had lunch and is disappointed when I say I have. But, I say I'm happy to keep them company while they catch me up. With that, their mood improves considerably as we head to the small in-house cafeteria they have.

I order a coffee and sit by the window while I wait for them to be served and join me.

We chat for a while, doing the get-to-know-you bit while

they eat. Then Reed asks me how old I am.

The question takes me aback, and I don't quite know what to say when his partner jabs him in the gut, tells him to mind his own business, and apologies to me.

'He's always like this. No idea of social niceties, I'm afraid. You'll get used to him.'

Reed has gone sullen, and I'm betting I won't hear much more from him.

'So?' I ask. 'Tell me what you've found out about Clayton?'

Delores wipes her mouth with a napkin, then opens her notebook.

'Clayton, fifty-three. Single. Never married. No children. Parents both deceased. His father left the farm to him. He has half a dozen farmhands, probably Mexican, but I don't know. I doubt they'll have papers. He tends to live on the edge.'

'But sometimes crosses over?'

She gives me a quizzical look, then gets it.

'The Sheriff's told you about the Cock-fighting and illegal gambling.'

'Yeah, well, I have an update on that for you.'

'What's that?'

'He has a fight set up for tonight after dark.'

'At his ranch?'

'Yeah. Nine pm. I was wondering if you might have a time in mind to visit him?'

I smile, knowing this isn't what the Sheriff intends me to do.

'Well, I'm pretty tired right now, so I'll look for accommodation and put my head down for a while. How about we talk to Clayton later?'

'Sure, sounds good. How would eight-thirty suit you?'

'Perfect. Any idea where a good place to stay would be?'

'If you want a little home comfort, I've got a spare room you're welcome to. You can save your expenses.'

'I don't want to put you out.'

'Nonsense. Now I know we're working tonight. I'll clear it with the sergeant and take some time off. You can follow me.'

'If your sure it's no trouble?'

With that, I'm told to stay where I am while they talk with their sergeant.

Thirty minutes later, I've dropped my travel bag on Delores's spare room floor and am back in the lounge area where we're relaxing. The local radio plays sixties rock in the background, and I love some of the tracks the DJ chooses.

We've dropped the surnames and are now Sammy and Maria.

'I'm sorry again about Dylan. He's had a lot of learning difficulties growing up, and the Sheriff has taken him on to give him some focus, but I'm not sure it will work out. I like the intention, but you need your partner to have your back, and I'm not sure I have that with Dylan.'

'Is there much serious crime in this area?'

'Not really. If you think Castle Rock itself, there's less than one in a thousand chances of you being involved in a serious crime, whereas, in Colorado, it's more like four times that. Most of the crimes here are property crimes with the chances being round one in seventy versus one in forty for the State.'

'So, while having your back is important, and I won't argue that with you. At least the chances of you being involved in something where you need that are pretty low?'

'Sure. But have you heard of Murphy's Law?'

I laugh.

'Not only have I heard of him, I've met him personally quite a few times. Tell me. You live here on your own? No, Mr. Delores?'

'No. I did have a partner, but she moved out a year ago. Been on my own since then.'

'It's probably hard to find someone new in a small place like this, is it?'

'Tell me about it.'

After that, we spend the following few hours swapping stories, mainly about the job, sometimes about our personal lives. Maria makes us simple cheese and mushroom omelets, which we enjoy with a glass of red wine we allow ourselves. The time flies by. She's good company. Easy to talk with.

At eight-thirty exactly, Officer Reed knocks on the door.

Maria says that this is one good aspect of her partner. He runs on time every time.

We agree that it's probably better to use my rental rather than a squad car, so Maria gets in front of me, and Dylan sits in the back.

The road out is quiet, and it only takes fifteen minutes till I see the entrance to a ranch up ahead, and Maria indicates that it's our end destination.

I pull through the overhead hanging sign, which tells me I'm now on the Ponderosa, which I think sounds like a grand name for a small farm. Still, who cares.

As we approach the farm, I can see there are several buildings. There's a main farmhouse, a couple of large barns, a water tower, and several distributed sheds of various sizes, but none of these are what catch my attention and cause me to come to a halt.

Up ahead, there must be well over a hundred vehicles parked around the farmhouse and the barns.

I look at Maria, but she's as surprised as I am.

'I thought the Sheriff said this was a small local thing that the farmers do for fun?'

But Maria shrugs.

'Look at the plates on some of these vehicles. You've got Arizona, New Mexico, Kansas, and even Texas. This is no small farmer's get-together. Do the Feds have an office in Denver?'

'I think so. I don't know.'

I get out my cell and place a call hoping that George is still working at Langley. He picks up immediately.

'Sammy? Where are you?'

I take the time to tell him exactly where I am, suspect that some significant intra-State organized criminal activity is taking place and that I need serious backup ASAP. He listens carefully, and when I'm finished, he promises to do what he can. I end the call wondering what we should do next.

'We should call the Sheriff,' suggests Maria.

'Probably not a good idea. Besides, he won't have the kind of resources we need. If there's serious money involved here, and there's bound to be. There will be plenty of firepower. More than the entire Sheriff's office would be able to handle.'

'So, what are we going to do?'

'What *you're* going to do is sit tight with Dylan while I look around. Do *not* come after me. I want you to stay here where I know you're safe.'

'I should come with you.'

'No. I'll be less likely to attract attention alone.'

With that, I pull forward and park the car where Maria will have a good sight of at least the parked vehicles. There's no way I can get close to the farmhouse.

As I open the door, I feel the tension in the air. Something big is going on. It's not that there's a lot of noise. It's more like there isn't. It's the apprehension I'm sensing.

Maria comes round and sits behind the wheel, ready for a quick exit if we need to make one. I remind her to stay put once more and start walking through the parked vehicles making my way toward some figures I see huddled around the double doors to a barn in the distance.

At first, I'm surprised how close I get without being questioned, but then I realize that's because whatever is going on inside has everyone riveted. No one is looking my way.

I look around, trying desperately to figure out how I can find out what's going on when I see some bales of straw piled high against the outer wall of the barn. These have likely been removed from dry storage to make space for whatever is happening inside.

I climb one bale at a time, stopping to position them from time to time until I'm at the top, and by turning my head sideways, I can peer through a gap between the wooden wall and the corrugated concrete roof sheets.

All I can see is a crowd of people. They're excited and talking over one another. Several are taking wagers, most are drinking, and quite a few are armed. There are a few women there, but it's mostly men.

I change position and lean my head the other way. Now I can see what looks like a fenced-off boxing area. There's no canvas or anything, just the barn floor. But ropes are there to mark a space for action. I assume the Cocks are about to be released. I can't believe people travel these distances and pay good money to watch these birds slash and tear chunks out of each other.

If I move a couple of bales, I can move along and see more of what's about to happen. Unfortunately, I lose balance trying, and without meaning to, I shout aloud as I tumble bale over bale back down to the ground.

Shaken, I'm standing and brushing myself down when a man shouts at me.

'What are you doing here?'

He has a rifle slung over his shoulder. At least he's not pointing it at me.

'I fell.'

'Fell from where?'

I point up the stack of bales.

'Have you paid?'

'Not yet.'

'Well, pay up or clear out. What's it going to be?'

'I want to watch, but I don't have any money.'

'Well, you're fucked, little lady.'

'Unless you accept a different form of payment, I say,' opening a couple of buttons on the front of my shirt.

'You offering what I think you are?'

I can see the desire in his eyes as I pull my shirt tail out from my jeans and sit provocatively on one of the bales of straw.

'Have we got time before the show starts?' I ask.

'If'n were quick. Looking at you, I don't think that'll be a problem.'

As he walks towards me, he lays his rifle aside, unbuckles his belt, and starts to drop his pants.

I lead him on by opening my shirt, revealing my bra.

By now, he's barely seeing straight as he shuffles towards me, pants around his ankles. He's so focused on my breasts; he doesn't see my roundhouse coming.

It's not about strength or force. It's more about precision, and my strike is pure, right against the soft area at the side of his forehead.

He drops like a stone and stays down.

I quickly tuck my shirt back in and do some buttons up, then search the guy and find what I'm looking for - an entry ticket.

It's nothing fancy. Just a piece of card with the address and time stamped on it, but it's all I need.

I work my way back around to the front of the barn and make sure I'm holding my ticket where it's visible; I wriggle through the crowd, slowly working towards the front.

I get a few annoyed looks, but no one stops me.

When I'm still a couple of rows back, a man steps into the center of the cleared ring and welcomes everyone to another fun evening, at which point there's a roar from everyone.

The man raises his hands and waits until everyone quietens down before announcing the event this night is something no one has seen before. It's a double fight, where the opponents will fight two against two.

Again, there's another roar.

When it quietens, he introduces the contenders.

'From New Mexico, we have Francisca and Rosa.'

Judging from the noise, there's quite a traveling support group for these two Cocks.

'And, from our home State, we have Emelia and Sofia.'

There's obviously more support for the home State, and it takes some time before the noise quietens.

'As you know. The fight will be to the death. If both survive on either team, they will be expected to fight each other. There will only be one winner, so place your bets now.'

Suddenly there's a flurry of activity with everyone shouting and cash changing hands. They didn't know about the final twist, where only one winner would be allowed.

I use the betting distraction to improve my position, squeezing past several more people until I freeze as I see the contenders for the first time.

They're sitting on two wooden benches on opposite sides of the cleared area - two per bench. They're young girls dressed in virtually nothing. They should look terrified, but they don't. They're drugged up in some way. Almost hyper. One girl is scratching her arm so badly it's raw and bleeding. They look feral and dangerous.

I don't recognize either of the girls on the far bench, and the ones in front of me have their backs to me, but I'm guessing that one or both of them are the girls I'm looking for.

I'm in here on my own, four feral girls about to take each other apart, I'm surrounded by a hundred or more excited spectators, many of which are armed, and I've lost my license-to-carry.

Suddenly, there's a loud explosion from outside, and someone shouts. Still, the crowd waits, assuming someone else will worry about whatever has happened out there.

Then there's a second explosion and a loud whoosh, and more people are shouting this time. Word spreads. Someone is blowing up their vehicles.

Another loud explosion and the crowd begin to stampede towards the door.

Another explosion, and people are shouting over each other, guns are coming out, and I'm left with the guy running the show and two helpers holding chains from collars the girls have been forced to wear.

I reckon Clayton is the organizer. He's now shouting for the men to take the women back into the house. He hasn't noticed me at all.

I look around for anything I can use as a weapon and see a pitchfork against a far wall. I rush over and grab it, then turn to find Clayton pointing a rifle straight at me.

'You might like to lay that backdown, little lady. And tell me why you're not outside with everyone else?'

'I was just going but didn't bring a gun, so I grabbed the pitchfork. I don't know what's going on out there, but I'm not going without something.'

He stands studying me momentarily, weighing my story before asking to see my ticket.

I step towards him, holding it out, and as soon as he reaches for it, I kick the rifle out of his hand and follow that with a straight knuckle jab to the throat.

Unfortunately, the momentum of losing the rifle moves him back out of my range, and the jab falls short.

We stand staring at each other until he lunges straight at me. No subtlety, just sheer aggression.

I sidestep and bring my knee into his groin as he stumbles past me. I'm not entirely on target, but close enough to mean he's slowly getting back on his feet; I grab the rifle and smash it down on the back of his shoulders, laying him out flat.

I don't have time to congratulate myself before someone grabs me in a bear hug and squeezes the air out of my lungs. I remember to fight my instinct to try pulling his hands away and concentrate on getting my hand under the smallest finger on one hand and bend it back until it cracks. I feel the pressure release, but it doesn't go away; I grab a second finger and do the same. This time it has the desired effect, and I'm free to take a deep breath and turn to face my attacker.

I failed to break either finger, and he's snapped them back into place. Safe to say, he's not happy with me, though, and he's now more cautious.

We circle each other, Both hesitant to take the first move.

Eventually, I see him ready his right arm and know he's about to throw a punch, so I balance my weight such that as soon as he swings, I can step back out of his reach, then when his fist is passed, I step inside his defense, dance round him and strike him hard in the kidney, repeatedly.

By the time he's figured out where I am, he's damaged so severely that a high kick to the head and he's out of the fight.

I'm breathing heavily but still alive.

I turn to look for the girls, but they're gone. The other guy must have taken all four. I look around, find the rear exit and follow them out. I can see him still short of the farmhouse, struggling with four girls who don't want to obey him.

As I run towards him, he loses it with one of the girls and punches her so hard she goes straight to the ground. But, as she's chained to one of the other girls, he now has another problem, which is when he sees me coming.

Seeing no option, he throws the chains down, turns, and starts to run.

I let him go. I don't think I can handle another fight.

As I reach the girls, I slow down and take my badge from my pocket.

'Do any of you speak English?'

The girl chained to the one on the floor is terrified but can't move. She stares at me. The other two rush towards me.

At first, I think it's relief that they're being rescued, then I see that feral look in their eyes again, and when they open their mouths to scream, I see their teeth have been ground to sharp points. These are not young girls; these are attack dogs.

I'm larger and stronger than they are, but there are two of them, and they're prepared to fight to the death, something I'd forgotten.

I've no choice. I must defend myself.

I open my stance so that I'm balanced and let them come. The first to arrive is taller, although she's not even up to my shoulders. I jab her hard once straight on the chin, and she goes down, out cold. This doesn't stop the other girl who throws herself on me before I can prepare, and I find myself rolling in the dirt, trying to keep those teeth from tearing into my neck.

Although she doesn't have my strength, she makes up for that with ferocity, and she rakes her sharpened nails down the side of my face.

I scream aloud and react with a solid blow to the side of her head, knocking her off me. As I stand up, so does she, but I don't give her another chance. I hit her again under the chin with an uppercut, knocking her clean off her feet and backward, where she lands in the dust, dead to the world.

I put my hand up to my face, and it comes away, covered in blood. There's not much I can do about that right then. My first task has to be to secure the girls.

I first drag the two who attacked me over to the house's front porch, then go back and carry the other unconscious girl while the one chained to her walks beside her.

When they are all together, I take out my handcuffs from a rear pocket and cuff all four of them to the porch rail.

Only then do I sit down and look around.

I haven't realized it, but there are at least a dozen blazing fires in front of the barn, and people are running around like headless chickens. I don't think anyone knows what's happening. It's chaos on a grand scale.

I hope none of them come looking for me.

Then I see the lights coming up the road to the farm. There's a convoy of vehicles, at least a dozen, perhaps more. Some have blue lights flashing on the top. I'm guessing George has come through for me again, and the FBI has arrived just in time to stop everyone from escaping.

Sometime later, I've given preliminary statements to the FBI, explained about the girls, and confirmed that two of them were ones I've been looking for. Then, given the bruised state of my body, and the mess my face is in, the Lead FBI Agent agrees I can get fixed up but expects me to show up at the Denver office the following day.

So it is that, at midnight, I'm back at Maria's place, with her tending my wounds.

She says the scratches on my face are not too deep and should heal without leaving any scars, but she's worried when I show her my bruised body.

She runs a hot tub for me and helps me in.

It's heaven, and I relax for the first time in hours.

She brings a couple of glasses of red wine in and sits on the loo beside me, filling me in on what happened outside the barn.

Having seen the fight outside the barn, she realized I was heading into serious trouble as I worked my way through the crowd at the entrance, so she and Dylan started siphoning petrol from some of the vehicles and filling beer bottles that were left lying around.

When they were ready, they started fire-bombing the vehicles one at a time until everyone rushed out of the barn; at this point, they hid out of sight.

Maria says that Dylan had more fun than she had. He could also throw the bottles much more accurately than she was and couldn't stop laughing while doing it.

We talk until the bath is cold, then I climb out to find I'm still aching all over. Maria helps rub me dry, then wraps me in a warm dressing gown and leads me to bed.

Monday morning, I say goodbye to Maria and thank her for taking good care of me. She kisses me and tells me I'm always welcome in Colorado.

Saturday morning, she had to go into the station and explain what happened at the farm to the Sheriff, who wasn't pleased with her. She didn't care.

For my part, I called the FBI Lead Agent in Denver and told him that I had suffered more than I initially thought and would be unavailable for a debrief as I would need the weekend to recover from my injuries fully. He wasn't happy, but I didn't care either. I had something much better in mind to do with my weekend.

However, the reality catches up on me as I take I25 north to Denver, then pick up I70 Eastbound to the Sandown interchange. As I swing off the interchange, I see a large Drury's hotel on my left and recall it only being a fortnight since I stayed at one of their hotels, only that time it was in St. Louis. That seems like a lifetime ago, but it's only a few weeks. It's strange how time passes. In some senses, I've been to so many places and done so much in that two weeks, but at the same time, it has passed in a flash.

I work down to the FBI District Office on 36th and Ulster. A colossal granite block with the FBI logo on it tells me I've arrived at the Denver division. I pull my rental into a visitor's space and go to the reception.

The building is four or five stories tall, enclosed entirely in reflective glass. The flat concrete roof extends to one side in a massive overhang supported by a rectangular column. I can't figure out why it's there for the life of me. Probably some architect's vision is being realized. To me, it's a waste of time, effort, and public funds.

There are three receptionists at the front desk. I present my Homeland creds and ask to speak to Lead Agent Greg Wallace.

As I wait, I notice a large poster on the FBI wanted noticeboard and cross to look at it. It has pictures of over forty individuals gathered from many different cameras. During my absence, these people have been involved in a violent protest in Washington. I try to make out what happened, but the poster lacks enough detail. All I get is violence in the Capital and vandalization of Federal property. I guess I'll find out when I get back to Washington later in the day.

Next, I take a look at the most-wanted pictures. Everyone in law enforcement sees this regularly, but I use the time to refresh my memory.

There are only two I don't recognize. Robert Fisher wanted for killing his wife and two young children in Arizona. It makes me think of Arnou Chikumbutso up in Chicago.

The other is a white Hispanic male. Forty-year-old Arnoldo Jiminez from Texas who killed his bride less than twenty-four hours after marrying her. He's believed to have fled to Mexico.

At this point, a twenty-something woman smartly dressed in a two-piece jacket and tight-fitting skirt introduces herself as Lead Agent Wallace's assistant and asks me to follow her.

Wallace's office is on the top floor with a clear city view. Unfortunately, there's a storm blowing in, and the ordinarily blue sky is dark and gray.

The PA takes my order for a coffee, strong and black, and

disappears, leaving me with Wallace.

'How are you feeling, Agent Greyfox?'

I can either respond to the words or the innuendo. I choose the former. I've no skin in having a pissing contest with the guy. He has a job to do, just like me. He's annoyed it's taken me three days to get here. I get that, but I still don't regret it.

'I'm good now, Sir. Still a little shaken up, but well on the mend.'

'Glad to hear that. How about we sit over here,' he suggests moving from behind his desk to an area with more comfortable seating and a coffee table just as his PA brings the coffee. I see he takes his the same as me.

When we're seated, he asks me to go through everything, starting with why I found myself in Colorado in the first place. I do as asked, beginning with the vehicle in the schoolyard up in New Jersey.

He mostly lets me talk, asking a few questions here and there for clarification, and when I'm finished, he surprises me.

'I confess, Agent Greyfox. I was expecting some half-assed excuse for getting into a situation way above your pay grade. But the opposite is true. You deliberately put yourself on the line against unbelievable odds to rescue some underage girls you don't even know. That's truly astonishing.'

I don't know what to say. So I sip my coffee instead until the uncomfortable moment passes, and I can ask questions.

'Can I ask what's happening to the girls, Sir?'

'They're in a poor state, I'm afraid. They were inconsolable and violent at the scene on Friday night, so they had to be constrained and transported to the Pediatric Mental Health Clinic here in Denver.'

'I doubt you had any choice. I saw how dangerous they were for myself.'

'Yes. I see that from the scratches on your face. Did one of them do that?'

'Yes, Sir. She was scared.'

'She was more than scared. She was pumped full of steroids and a relatively new drug we see more and more called

Flakka.'

'Flakka?'

'Yes. Its full name is α-Pyrrolidinopentiophenone, usually shortened to alpha-PVP, or on the street, it's called Flakka.'

'It's a stimulant?'

'Yes, it's associated with hallucinations and aggressive, angry behavior. The steroids just made it worse. These girls were ready to fight anyone, anywhere. You were lucky we got to you when we did.'

'Have you checked on them since they were brought in?'

'I checked this morning, and they've all started detox, but the doctor I spoke to says he's not hopeful. There may be too much internal damage due to overheating as a side effect, which can cause internal organ failure.'

I find that a lot to take in, so press on, knowing I'll have to deal with everything later.

'What about the people you rounded up? Did you get the guy running the fight? Pike Clayton.'

'And here's where we scored, Agent. Big time.'

'How do you mean, Sir?'

'We have sixty-three people in custody, including your Mr. Clayton. But more importantly, over half of them have existing warrants out for them across five States, and best of all, we've captured someone we thought we'd lost to Mexico. Someone on our most wanted list.'

'Arnoldo Jiminez, the bride killer.'

'Excellent, Agent. I see you keep up to date.'

'So, a good night's work, Sir. I'm glad everything worked out.'

'And I'm glad you survived, Agent Greyfox. You just committed the craziest stunt I've ever seen or the bravest. I'm not sure which. But I'm glad you're still here for me to thank you.'

With that, he offers his hand, and we shake.

Before I leave, I tell him about the special facility we've set up for helping the trafficked girls through rehab and pass him Fabia's contact details. He assures me he will get in touch and keep her informed about whatever progress is made with the girls.

I have enough time at Denver International to grab some lunch, so I choose Aviator's Sports, sit on a stool at the bar, and order a full American breakfast and a Corona. The Steelers are playing the Cincinnati Bengals on the screen nearest to me, twenty-two to seven up in the third. It must be a replay from the previous day.

It's a good game, but my mind won't focus.

I'm back when I first see the girls come for me. The horrific sight of their bared teeth sharpened to points and the absence of humanity in their eyes. At that moment, I thought I would die, and even now, recalling it makes me shudder.

Apparently, I'm not hiding my fears so well, as a guy beside me interrupts and asks if I'm okay.

I thank him and tell him I'm fine, which is far from the truth. I'll see those teeth in my nightmares for some time.

I'm saved from further thoughts as lunch arrives and helps distract me. The Bengals have pulled back to a one-point deficit going into the fourth, so I force myself to pay attention as I eat.

The flight home is uneventful. I arrive around seven-thirty on a cold evening, with a sprinkle of snow blowing in the air. I collect my rental and head for the apartment.

When I open the door, I suddenly feel so lonely.

This place is more comfortable than I've ever experienced, but it isn't home. It's soul-less, and I see that all signs of my roomie have gone, which doesn't help.

Just the previous night, in Maria's home, everything felt so different. I felt welcome and that I belonged. Here, there's no one to welcome me and console my aches and pains and my troubled inner self. Troubled by all the things I've been forced to witness in such a short time. I don't know how much more of this I can take. Or whether I should even try.

I'm dead tired, so I change into my sweats, make myself

Mac & Cheese, pop a Corona, and lounge in front of the box watching reruns of MASH. It's not much, but it feels like all I've got.

Against all odds, I sleep well and wake with the alarm at six, put on the running gear, and run for ninety minutes. When I return, I shower, get dressed, demolish some toasted bagels, then set out for Langley. It's time I move on to find the two remaining girls, and George is my best hope.

There's no doubt George is pleased to see me. When I enter his office, he's up from his work area and hugging me before I can react. I stand like a plank of wood, caught off guard.
  'You're alive?'
  'Yes, George. Well spotted.'
  'I was frantic when I received your call from that farm. You sounded like you were in real trouble.'
  'I guess I was, George. And I'm here to thank you for what you did for me. Getting that support pulled together so quickly couldn't have been easy.'
  'Not as bad as you think, Sammy. Remember Fabia, Pat Cataldo, and my boss are trying to roll out the T.E.N.S. mission across all States. I'd already started with Colorado, so I had an in.'
  'Nevertheless, thanks, George. You really saved my bacon.'
  'I'm just so happy your safe. Now, tell me all the details. I've heard some from Denver, but I'd rather hear your version. Let's get some coffee.'

We're back in George's work area an hour later, and he's showing me how the two ICTSG searches are going. This reminds me of the call I had from Detective La Costa in Seattle homicide, telling me they had found one of the girls in the waterway. I'd forgotten to pass that on to George and am bothered that maybe I've wasted his time.
  I tell him right then, but he tells me not to worry.
  I'm confused and say so.

'Firstly, you don't know how many girls were transported to Seattle. Correct?'

'Yes. But that alone isn't enough to take any action on. The guy's attorney would have him free in thirty seconds.'

'Yes, but you do have a photo ID of the guy you think is responsible at the school in New Jersey.'

'Sure.'

'Well, what if we can add an end-destination through an ICTSG search?'

'Yes, but I asked you to focus on Colorado and California?'

'But, what if I ran three copies of the ICTSG software and included Seattle?'

'You're kidding, right?'

'No, I'm serious. I couldn't just leave a location out of the search because I didn't have sufficient hardware.'

'And you're looking for an end destination, which will give sufficient grounds for a search warrant?'

'And who knows what forensics might turn up?'

'Good thinking George. How close are you to the address?'

'Funny you should ask, Sammy. We already have it. Look at the screen.'

I look at his large screen and see the familiar flashing dot. It's stationary over a street in a city; I assume it is Seattle.

I get the address from George, call Detective La Costa straight off, and give him the good news.

He thanks me and asks if I'm any further forward with a name for his Jane Doe, but I tell him I'm not. He promises to stay in touch and ends the call, leaving me worried about not knowing who these girls are that I'm searching for.

I discuss this with George, who offers to contact Interpol for help. We know the name of the freighter which delivered the girls from Europe, but the only other information we have to go with is the passport photographs and a few names of the girls we have already secured here in Washington. And that gives me an idea, but I need one more thing from George first.

'How about the other ICTSG search - tracking Zhan Wu to California? How's it going?'

'We're almost there. It's a three thousand mile trip, so the fact that we're still following him is pretty impressive.'

'Can you show me on the screen?'

'Give me a moment.'

As I watch, a second dot appears on the screen, and I ask where it is.

George expands the scale and points out Carson City to the south of the flashing dot.

'We're almost at the Nevada-California border.'

'How much longer to the end destination?'

'End of play tonight or early tomorrow would be my best guess.'

'Thanks again, George. This is fantastic work.'

'It's been a good trial for the beta version of this ICTSG software, so I reckon the FBI will be pretty grateful as well.'

Outside Langley, in the car park, I call Tima Luki, the woman responsible for running the rehab center in Boulevard Manor. When she answers, I ask if I can visit with the girls, and she agrees.

Twenty minutes later, I'm frustrated. I'm driving around the block in circles, unable to find a parking space. Eventually, I decide to make for a multi-story three blocks away when I see a car pull out in my rear mirror. I stop, trying to indicate that I intend to reverse in, but someone beats me to it.

I punch the steering wheel, and my frustration level rises even further.

Twenty minutes later, I'm back at the rehab center; the walk from the multi-story has given me time to calm down. I'm still annoyed at myself. It's not like me to be so irritable.

Tima opens the front door and welcomes me before inviting me into the same room I've been in before. This time, there are five girls present. And I'm pleased to see they all look a lot better. This place seems to be working for them. Just seeing them makes me feel proud of what I've achieved. And when I think of the terrible conditions they were surviving in, I know deep down that finding the remaining girls is something I need to see through. Beyond that, I don't know.

Tima starts the conversation by introducing each girl, beginning with Safija and Tania, whom I already know. Next up is another girl who looks to have the same olive skin and dark hair but has a leg in a cast. This girl is from Ljubljana in Slovenia, which Tima explains is in the Eastern European area, not too far from where the first two girls are from. I recognize her as the girl I found in the Church basement in Chicago. Her name is Eva Kovač. She speaks no English at all, but Tima has learned she was taken from her bed in the middle of the night and explains that her home is in an impoverished part of the city, where many people sleep where they can.

The next is different in appearance. Although skinny and underweight, she has a sturdier build, white skin, which is almost unhealthy to look at, and blond hair tied in two ringlets, one falling at each side of a pretty face. Her name is Karlotta Bauer. She can speak French and German, but as I speak neither, it's down to the fantastic multi-lingual talents of the host to explain what she knows about the girl.

I can only recognize her as the girl I found beneath the wealthy financier's pool in Miami.

'She's from a small town called Gollin in Austria, near Salzburg, close to the border with Germany. She was taken from a play area in an outdoor market when her mother was distracted by someone stealing her handbag.'

The final girl is also blonde but either malnourished or naturally rakishly thin. Given what she's been through, it could be either. This girl I recognize from the raid South of Atlanta. One of the girls being hot-cotted out to wealthy men for up to seven hours a night. I can't imagine what this has done to her mentally. I can only hope she has the resilience of youth on her side.

Tima tells me her name is Anna Schneider, and she's from a small village in the countryside on the outskirts of Cologne in Germany. Whoever took her used the same trick by distracting the mother, only this time, it was making her believe she had knocked someone off their bike. As she left the car to see if he was okay, someone else took Anna from the rear of the empty vehicle and bundled her off.

When the introductions are complete, I ask Tima to pass out copies of the pictures I've brought showing all twelve girls and ask them what they know about the others.

Initially, the girls are reticent, and I reckon that's because the pictures remind them of where they've been and what happened to them, but they slowly come around, and I gather all the information I can.

Afterward, I'm pleased. I at least know a little about most of the girls, even if it's only their first names in some cases. By the time we finish, I'm keen to return to my office and lay out everything I know.

I thank the girls and Tima for their help, and then before I can leave, Safija, then her sister, rushes me and hugs me. They're still there when all the others join in, and I'm blown away. I'm only vaguely aware of Tima smiling in the background.

I intended to head straight to the office at Homeland, but after what happened, I decide to first stop for coffee and a donut at Dunkin Donuts.

Sitting on an uncomfortable plastic seat in the window, I can't believe how emotional I am. I'm all over the place. I'm pleased with the girls' hugs, but there's more going on than that. More that I don't know how to deal with.

Later, back at Homeland, I'm pleased Fabia's not in her office, and I can sneak past Dominic and close my office door behind me.

I don't need people around me right now. I need to focus.

First priority. I call Detective La Costa up in Seattle and give him what I have on his Jane Doe. Her first name is Lotte, and having listened to the girl's description of where she was picked up, it sounds like she may be Dutch. I tell him I'll be passing the information along to Interpol along with his contact details.

In turn, he tells me that getting a search warrant for Francis Lemoine's place was straightforward, and the forensics team is there right then.

I thank him for the update, and he thanks me for the girl's name. There maybe was a day when I would have been surprised that he would be so affected by something so simple, but not now.

Next, I need to sort out my thoughts, but first, I need a map.

I buzz Dominic in and set him the task. The map needs to cover both East and West Europe, and while he's looking for that, I review what else I've learned about the girls.

After passing the girl's name to La Costa in Seattle, six other girls are left to consider.

There are two down in the Mental Health clinic in Denver. They are Džana and Una, from the same country as Safija and Tania - Bosnia.

Then there are the two who died in an incident in New Jersey that Fabia told me about. Something that was related to a different case she was working. Even with Tima's encouragement, the girls couldn't remember their names but thought they both came from Northern Italy. I make a note to pass on my information to Fabia, who can get it to the correct people in New Jersey.

And finally, there are two girls I have yet to track down. I hope that they're both in California somewhere and that there isn't another of them floating in a waterway up in Seattle. One of these girls is German, but the girls weren't sure of her name. They called her Soppy. I'm guessing it would be Sophie or maybe Sofia. The last is another Dutch girl, stolen from her mother the same day as the girl who died in Seattle. Her name is Mattie.

So, I now know what the two girls I'm still looking for look like and their names and nationalities. Interestingly, they're both white Western Europeans, and I wonder if that's telling me anything about west coast preferences?'

While I wait for Dominic, I call Lead Agent Greg Wallace in

Denver and tell him what I've discovered about two girls he has in the Mental Health Clinic. He thanks me and promises to pass the information along. I can only hope knowing their names and where they come from will help their treatment.

When Dominic returns, I have him help me open the map on the floor and find where the girls were taken, starting with the furthest south in Bosnia.

I draw a red line starting there, where four girls were taken in Bosnia, before picking another up in Slovenia, then two in Italy. The line then extends through Austria and Southern Germany and up to Holland, where the Dutch girl, Lotte, is picked up, as well as the last two I have yet to find. One is from Northern Germany. The other is also Dutch.

The red line is virtually straight and indicates that the trip was well organized in advance. These aren't random kidnappings coming together. This is a well-organized operation, undoubtedly run by an Eastern European OCG.

In less than twenty-four hours' drive time, twelve girls have been collected and transported over a thousand miles through half a dozen countries. So much for the so-called advantages of Europe's border-free travel initiative.

I fold up the map and ask Dominic to have it hand-delivered to George over at Langley. With that done, I follow up by sending an email with all the details I've collected, including the name of the freighter that transported the girls over the Atlantic, the date of arrival in New Jersey Harbor, and all the details I now have about each of the girls. I request he passes everything along to Interpol.

After this, I spend the rest of the afternoon report writing. I start back in Chicago and end up in Denver. This takes me till close to seven in the evening, and I'm drained when I finish.

I'm about to put on my coat when Fabia knocks on my door.

'Hear, you've been having some exciting times in Colorado, Sammy.'

I think the raw scratches on my face and my expression tell her I don't want to talk. She picks up quickly and tells me she's looking forward to reading my report before wishing me a good night.

I breathe a sigh of relief, put on my coat, and make for the exit.

As I leave the front of the building, a mix of rain and sleet lashes across the car park, driven by the strong northerly wind. I pull up my collar and dash for it.

By the time I get into my rental and slam the door, I'm cold and wet. And that does nothing to lift my sinking spirits. I suddenly feel the weight of responsibility for finding the remaining girls on my shoulders. Here I am, moping because it's been a tough few days, and I'm cold and wet. What must they be going through?

I deliberately don't set the alarm for the morning and manage to sleep until eight. I decide against a run and settle for a shower, fresh coffee, and a couple of toasted Bagels with cream cheese.

I'm not exactly running on all cylinders yet, but I feel more positive. My eye is fully open again, but my face is still pretty badly bruised, and the nail scrapes are only just beginning to scab over, so I still look a sight, but there's nothing I can do about that. Otherwise, I have a few bruises elsewhere around my body, but they're healing and don't feel too uncomfortable.

Given the odds I was up against in Colorado, I think I've come out in pretty good shape.

I check my cell, and there's a simple message from George saying, 'Eureka!'

I guess the ICTSG system has produced a result in California. It looks like I should pack a bag again.

With my travel bag in the trunk of my car, I park outside Langley and find George in his usual place, hunched over a laptop.

'Morning, George. Got your message. Have you got time to show me?'

'Morning, Sammy. Sure. Look at the screen.'

I can see the blue flashing light is stationary.

'So, where is it?'

As he did before, he changes the map's scale until I'm looking at a major city just to the south.

'That,' he tells me. 'Is San Fransisco. And the end destination for the vehicle that left the schoolyard in New Jersey is somewhere in the Napa Valley.'

'Wine country?'

George grins.

'So, if you need any help on this one, I could be available, Sammy?'

I laugh.

'Thanks for that, George. I'll bear your offer in mind.'

I move closer to the screen before asking my next question.

'So, is there an actual end destination address, or is it an area?'

'Unfortunately, it's only the area. We run out of traffic cams in the Napa Valley.'

'So, I've still got work ahead of me?'

'Looks that way. But if you're heading to San Fran, you can hook up with Pat Cataldo. He's working another case out there, so there is no reason why you shouldn't meet up. He can probably introduce you to some folks over there that might be able to help.'

'Good idea, George. Do you happen to know where he's staying?'

'I'll send that to you when I find out. By the way, I've forwarded everything you sent me yesterday to Interpol, and they were more than interested. You may have revealed one of the main trafficking routes across Europe.'

'Yeah, well, I wish I'd found it earlier.'

'Better late than never. If Interpol can close it down, maybe that will reduce the number of children being moved?'

'For a little while, maybe. But you know how this goes, George.'

'Sure. Well done, anyway. Now, if you've nothing else…'

'Thanks, George; I'll tell you where I am in San Fran.'

Lost souls

* * *

From Langley's reception, I call Dominic and tell him my latest plans. He asks me to wait while he checks flights, then comes back to tell me there isn't a direct flight until the evening at six thirty-five. It's a five-hour, forty-five-minute flight time arriving just after nine in the evening Pacific time. If I accept a stop, I can leave a little earlier, at four-thirty, but the arrival time is virtually the same, so I tell him to book me on the direct flight. Before I hang up, he asks if I have a preference for hotel accommodation, and I tell him I'll leave it up to him to negotiate the best deal.

Since it's only past midday, I have four hours to decide what to do with. I call Fabia and see if she's busy.

She has some free time and has read my report on what went down in Colorado, so she's keen to meet with me. We agree I should drop my car back at the apartment, where she'll pick me up, and we can head out for lunch together. Then she'll drop me at Reagan International afterward.

An hour or so later, were sitting opposite each other in a lunch venue of her choosing. A place called Marcel's. Fabia knows this place well and tells me a little about it.

'The Chef and proprietor here started as a dishwasher and now is a Michelin-star Chef with eleven restaurants, many of which are here in Washington. He's a classic rags-to-riches story and a nice man. And before you say anything about the prices in here, Sammy. This lunch is on me. Not Homeland Security. Me. So you can choose whatever you want, and we'll also have a decent glass of wine.'

'You don't need to do this, Fabia. It's not necessary.'

'No, you're right, it isn't. But I want to. You've been through a lot in the month since you came here, and I don't want to lose you like I have so many others. I want you to talk to me.'

We're interrupted as a waiter talks us through the menu. We both choose Chef's tasting menu, which includes Prince Edward Island Mussels, pan seared Scallops, New York strip for me, and Herb crusted lamb for Fabia, then a choice of ridiculously over-indulgent desserts.

A server pours iced water and disappears, leaving us alone.

I have no idea how to start, but I feel tears forming as I even think about it.

Fabia reaches across and lays a hand on mine.

'Sammy, whatever you're feeling, I will understand. I've been doing this work for several years, and it never gets any easier. Just take your time and tell me what's going on.'

I wipe my eyes with my hand and take a few deep breaths.

'I don't know how to explain it, Fabia. I feel like I'm on a monster roller-coaster ride, and every time I think I'm rising, something drives me down again. I've been through some tight experiences in homicide, but this is something else.'

'It's because of the children, isn't it?'

I nod.

'They're so helpless and vulnerable, and I don't understand how people can do the things they do to them?'

'People can be cruel, Sammy. You know that.'

'But to defenseless children?'

'There are many reasons why people act like this. For some, they are acting out some sexual desire; for others, it can be one of many other things.'

'Like what?'

'Repressed emotions, a need for status that they are unable to achieve in their lives, sometimes they gain pleasure out of hurting someone else, and other times it's a perverse need to be close to someone.'

'I thought it was all about power and control?'

'And for many, you're right. Have you ever heard the story of a Senator being honored with a banquet and he asks a waiter for another pat of butter for his bread roll?'

'No. What happens?'

'The waiter refuses, and the Senator tells him he's a very powerful man and the banquet is in his honor.

So, the waiter explains that he has power too. He's in charge of the butter. One pat per person and walks off.'

I laugh at that, but I get her point.

'But surely there's a big difference between needing to feel powerful and abusing vulnerable children?'

'If you look at the past lives of most people who sexually abuse children, there are issues either in their childhood which lie behind the behavior, or they are compensating for some shortfall in their current lives.'

We stop momentarily as the first of our dishes arrive, then Fabia continues.

'So, for example, someone growing up and suffering domestic violence can believe treating others the same way is okay. Their childhood experience normalizes these behaviors. Then there's the way the media sexualize power and aggression, while many mainstream television programs dramatize manipulation, coercion, and pornography.'

'So your saying abusers are either often abused themselves or misguided into performing abusive acts by the media?'

'The first is true, and many case studies support that. The effect of the media on rational, balanced thinking beings is minimal. But for someone who has not achieved that sense of balance and control in their lives....'

'They're vulnerable?'

'Exactly.'

'It's the same with drugs. Users have either had bad breaks or met the wrong people when they're most vulnerable.'

'So, you get it?'

I nod again while I push my plate away, having enjoyed both the Mussels and the Scallops. But, we're to be offered no reprieve. The dishes are cleared as soon as we finish, and the next course is served. My New York Strip looks magnificent. I would guess it's around eight ounces and sliced into thin strips with the tender meat pink, not bloody, just as I like it. It's accompanied by a couple of crispy roast potatoes and pepper sauce on the side. Simple presentation. Beautiful.

Fabia seems just as pleased with her lamb, and as we eat, she gets back to asking me what she wants to know. How I'm doing?

I start with the highest high. When the girls ran toward me and hugged me. As I tell her about this, the tears appear again. This time I wipe them away with my napkin.

Then I start to run through some of the lows, and there are many more of these.

As we eat, Fabia comments now and again, sometimes sharing some of her more difficult experiences but generally listening to everything I tell her.

By the time we've finished the main course, I've brought her more or less up to date.

That's when she asks me the question I knew was coming.

'Are you going to stick around, Sammy? But before you answer, I need to say there's no penalty box if you don't, and I, for one, will think no less of you if you say you're heading home to Florida.'

I stall for a bit but eventually have to come out with the truth.

'I honestly don't know, Fabia.'

She sits back in her chair and considers this carefully before giving me an answer I'm ill-prepared for.

'Good. At least you're still thinking about it. When I read the details of your last assignment in Colorado, I feared I'd already lost you.'

'So, *don't know* is a good result?'

'Right now, *don't know* is the best I could hope for.'

As promised, Fabia drops me at Reagan International, and I'm waiting in the departure lounge when I get a text message from George giving me the contact details for Lead Agent Pat Cataldo and where he's staying in San Fransisco. I can only assume he must have spoken with Dominic, as we're both staying in the same hotel - the Hyatt Regency.

My flight leaves on time, and I have over five hours to get my head back in the game before I land in San Fransisco. Whether I stay or go after this trip, I need to focus and finish this job.

* * *

When I exit the hotel foyer at six-thirty the following morning for my run, it's a wet and windy day, although the temperature is pleasant. I stop briefly at the waterfront down at the Port to admire the Oakland Bay Bridge before putting it behind me and heading north up past the piers at the Embarcadero.

I'm surprised at how busy the ports are, even at this time of the morning. I've heard how people tend to start early and finish early on the West Coast, so I guess this is why some of the inbound ferries are already crowded.

It's a twenty-minute easy jog up to Fisherman's Wharf, where I pause to take in Alcatraz out in the Bay through the mist. A solitary two-story stone building with a water tower and a tall lighthouse on a rock, isolated and forbidding. Not a bad place to lock away some of the people I've been coming across in the past few months - but sadly, it's no longer available.

When I'm ready, I continue my run staying as close to the water as possible until I reach Crissy Field, where I can admire the Golden Gate Bridge before turning and heading back to the hotel. An hour and fifteen, all told.

After I shower and dress, I have a quick breakfast at the hotel, then leave my rental in the hotel's underground car park and walk to my destination.

Knowing Pat Cataldo is here, I'm confident he'll connect me with the local FBI field office later, so I head for the San Fransisco police department's Investigation Bureau and present my credentials at the front desk.

I ask to speak to whoever is responsible for trafficking and take a seat to wait.

Twenty minutes later, a woman introduces herself as Sergeant Shiela McGovern, the Chief of Detectives' assistant. She asks me to follow her.

We take a lift to the top floor and step out into a hallway with perhaps twenty glass-walled offices. The Sergeant leads me to the furthest away and shows me in.

The man behind the desk is one of those people who look naturally fierce, and I momentarily regret not having asked to talk with a detective. Still, when he stands and offers his hand, he smiles, and his whole demeanor changes at that moment.
'Welcome to San Fransisco, Agent Greyfox.'
'Thank you for seeing me, Sir.'
'Not at all, Agent. Your reputation precedes you?'
'I'm sorry, Sir. What do you mean?'
'I had dinner with someone you know last night, and he mentioned you would be coming.'
'Lead Agent Pat Cataldo?'
'Correct. He's here for a couple of reasons, and one of them involves my team. He had quite a lot to say about you, though.'
'I'm sure he exaggerated, Sir.'
'Maybe, maybe not. Anyway, what can I do for you?'

In the next thirty minutes, I explain why I'm in San Fransisco, leading up to my picture of Zhan Wu leaving the schoolyard in New Jersey. He listens to my story and only reacts when he hears the name. Even then, he doesn't interrupt until I'm finished.
'So, you would like some help figuring out where Wu has your girl or girls? Is that right, Agent?'
'Yes, Sir. And the use of an office somewhere would be good.'
He rises, crosses to the door behind me, and speaks to his PA before returning.
'I think you may be interested to find out what we're already working on here, Agent Greyfox. And, the person you are about to meet is heading up the operation.'
At that moment, we're interrupted by a knock at the door as a petite Asian woman, dressed casually like me in jeans and a shirt, enters and asks the Chief if he's looking for her.
The Chief introduces her as Lieutenant Su Huang. I've no idea of her age, as I always find gauging Asians very tricky. I reckon she's somewhere between her mid-thirties and fifty.

She's petite in all dimensions, yet she compensates by being tall and straight. I think back to one of my favorite stars - Bruce Lee, in the old black-and-white movies and wonder if she's also a martial arts student. I know I shouldn't think like that these days, but hey, ho. Lee was dead long before I was born, yet when I first saw him in *Enter the Dragon*, I had to watch all of his other films. To this day, I still think of him as the best fighter I've ever seen.

The Chief asks her to see if she can help me in a case I'm working here in San Fransisco, and to find an office I can work out of, then leaves us to get to know each other.

Shortly afterward, we're in the Lieutenant's office. I have a coffee; she has a sparkling water. Before I even start to explain why I'm in San Fransisco, she asks me how I come to be working for Homeland, and I explain that I'm a homicide detective but on secondment for six months.

She smiles at that, and I ask her why.
'Because you feel like a detective, not an agent.'
'You can tell the difference?'
'Oh, yes. It's the same with the FBI.'
'Ah, but that's easy. They all wear suits and ties.'
She laughs, a light tinkling sound.
'So, Detective. You would like some help?'

I start with Zhan Wu this time and work backward into the story. She also knows Wu but is prepared to hear me out before commenting.

When I finish the update, I show her my pictures of the two remaining girls I'm looking for.

She looks at them and tells me she recognizes them from the APB a few weeks ago, but other than that, she has nothing to add.

'I will have this recirculated to all agencies in the city and the surrounding Counties. You never know. Someone might have seen them.'

'You don't sound too hopeful.'

'Have any of your other girls been seen shopping or in play parks, Detective?'

I have to give her that.

Her interest level goes up when I explain ICTSG and how the CIA cyber-tech group has helped me locate where Zhan Wu was last seen when returning from New Jersey - Napa Valley.

At first, I think she's interested in the new capability of ICTSG, but then I realize she's more interested in the Napa Valley destination. It seems like this is on-target for her in some way.

'Okay, Detective. I can see that your investigation and something we are already working on are somehow connected. So, I suggest I introduce you to the team and get you someplace to work. How does that sound? But first, let me arrange a security ID so you can come and go as you need.'

With that, she makes a call, and I wait with her until someone from internal security comes and takes my picture.

With that done, she leads me down two levels to the Homicide Division but passes through until she arrives at a small separate room with four people.

'This,' she says. 'Is our trafficking team.'

She introduces all four people in the room to me and asks them to see what they can do to help me, then leaves us to it.

This is better than I could have hoped for. Four detectives. It's just like being home again.

The sergeant asks me to tell them what I'm working on, and I'm beginning to wish I had a recording ready to playback. Nevertheless, I run through everything one more time with the same result. They're interested in Zhan Wu and the Napa Valley location.

When I'm finished, I ask if they think they can help.

'Why don't we tell you what we're working on?' suggests the sergeant. 'Ling. Bring her up to date while we order lunch. You okay with double cheese pizza, Detective?'

'Works for me.'

***

With that, the room empties, leaving Detective Ling Yú and me alone.

'You seem like quite a tight group?'

'Yes, we are. We've worked together on and off for nearly ten years, but we're on our biggest case so far, and it sounds like you are as well.'

'I'm intrigued. Tell me more.'

'We are investigating a group of people we believe are trafficking Chinese children. What is unusual about this case is that we don't believe an organized crime gang is involved. We think that this is a small but highly professional, family-oriented gang. They've remained undetected by being small and operating outside the normal crime channels until we got a lucky break.'

'What happened?'

'A private investigator was stabbed entering his hotel and left for dead. Luckily for him, the doorman saw what happened and called the paramedics immediately. That probably saved his life. It was Homicide who first talked to him, but as soon as they heard what he was working on, they passed the case to us.'

'Trafficking?'

'Yes. He had been hired by the parents of two young children that had gone missing in Hong Kong. He followed the trail as far as San Fransisco and is convinced they're being held somewhere north of the Golden Gate Bridge. He gave us the name Zhan Wu as someone he believed to be involved. Unfortunately, everything he could tell us was all circumstantial.'

'So you couldn't approach Wu?'

'No. We don't have anything specific to charge him with, and we don't want to tip him off.'

'Okay, so when I mentioned Napa Valley as the destination for Wu, does that fit with the information from the PI?'

'Yes. But it's still vague. We're currently running a surveillance operation on Wu, but so far, he hasn't crossed the

Bridge. Can you tell me exactly where the ICTSG trace led?'

'Sure. Wu was heading into San Fransisco on the I80 but never made the Oakland Bridge. So the technician backed up until he found Wu leaving the highway around the Solano County Fairground. He told me that at that point, either he had reached his end destination, or he would be turning north up Rte 37 into Napa county.'

'He couldn't go any further?'

'No, no more traffic cams. But there's one other piece of information that might be useful. On such a long trip, the technician thought there would likely be two drivers. So he checked at the fuel stops en route and pulled a picture of the second guy. The quality is too poor for facial recognition, but I can show him to you if you give me a minute. I have it on my cell.'

When I find it, Ling Yú recognizes the figure immediately.

'That's Wu's right-hand man. Hou Jiang. He's a second one of the gang we're watching.'

At that point, the others appear bearing lunch, and we take a break while the pizza and soft drinks are dispersed before Ling Yú brings the team up to date.

'So, we are working the same case?' says the sergeant.

'It depends?'

'What do you mean, Detective?'

'We might be working on the same case, but are our objectives the same?'

They all stop eating for a moment and give me puzzled stares.

'Say more.'

'My mission is to recover the last of the girls on my list, and if we can roll up your gang simultaneously, that's great. But my priority is finding the girls. You're trying to close down a trafficking operation, and that's not good enough for me. I don't just want the culprits locked away. I want the girls found.'

'So, you want us to watch and wait?' suggests Ling Wú.

'Yes, but with a twist.'

When we've finished lunch, I ask if there's a desk I can use, and the sergeant tells me there's an empty desk one flight down in Narcotics. He takes me down and gets me settled. I ask if I can review everything they've got on file so far and spend the rest of the day working my way through hours of surveillance details and reports, making some of my notes as I go. I come across only one slight oddity about a particular location that turns up in one of the surveillance reports, so I note it and carry on.

By five o'clock, I'm entirely up to speed and ready to implement the plan I agreed with the team earlier in the afternoon.

Given that they already have Zhan Wu under surveillance, I can go straight to him.

He's settling in for an early supper at Chef Hang's restaurant in China Town, accompanied by two other suspected gang members, including Hou Jiang - the second driver.

The restaurant has a large bright canopy over the doorway with the name emblazoned in bright red, making it easy to find. At the front is the ever-present wrought-iron gate to protect the premises at night, but now it's standing open, and I enter a room that could be a Chinese restaurant anywhere in the world. Tiled floor, polystyrene flat false-ceiling undoubtedly concealing a myriad of wires and pipes for heating and air conditioning, all supported by fake marble columns. Plain pink table linens, with circular glass protective coverings and uncomfortable wooden chairs. This is a place designed not for comfort but for fast turnaround.

Zhan Wu and his cohorts are sitting in the furthest corner, the table in front of them piled high with assorted dishes. They're talking animatedly, chopsticks used to annunciate highlights in their conversation.

I make my way across the room, heading straight for them. As they notice me coming, they stop talking and turn toward me to check me out. The two who had their backs to me decide I'm no threat, so they turn back and continue eating. But Zhan is no such fool and can recognize trouble when he sees it.

As I stop at their table, I confirm I'm talking to the right man.

'Zhan Wu?'

'Maybe. Who's asking?'

I flash my Homeland ID and return it to my pocket.

'I would like to ask you about this,' I tell him, handing him the picture of the two remaining missing girls. 'I believe you might be able to help me?'

Zhan glances at the picture on the table, his expression revealing nothing, but his eyes become cold and deadly as a snake's.

It's just after eight when I enter the Fog Harbor Fish House.

When I spoke with Lead Agent Cataldo earlier, he said he already has a reservation as it's somewhere he eats every time he is in San Fransisco and said he would call and change the reservation for two.

Scanning the room, I quickly spot him sitting in a window booth at the far side. Although I met him when I first joined Homeland, I haven't spent time with him, so other than knowing he's a high-flyer within the FBI, I know nothing about him. I reckon this is my chance to find out.

He stands as I arrive at the table and waits until I'm seated before he does likewise - a gentleman.

'Glad you rang, Detective.'

'Whoa, right there. I'm off duty. It's Sammy.'

Cataldo smiles and tells me to call him Pat.

From there on, we get along fine. He's an attractive man. Married with two children, all back in Washington. His eldest is starting college the following year, and the other is still in high school. When I ask him what he does for fun in his spare time, he laughs.

'When the job doesn't have me tied up, my wife always has things she wants me to do or places she wants me to take her, and the kids can be a full-time job all on their own. There's basketball and soccer practice for the younger son, and the elder one will be on a football scholarship, so you can guess how many hours Mary and I have to spend running him around.'

'Not a lot of spare time then?'

'There isn't anything below absolute zero, is there? How about you, Sammy? What do you get up to in your spare time?'

'Homicide detectives don't get much spare time either, at least not when we're on a case. If I do have time, I spend it visiting family. My parents mainly, but I also have an Uncle I'm close to.'

'You're not married then?'

'Nope. Not even close.'

'But you want to be?'

'I'm not sure how to answer that. I guess if I ever meet the right person, I'll know. But otherwise, I'm happy as I am.'

As we talk, we share a bottle of Cabernet Sauvignon from a local Napa Valley producer and order food from a fantastic menu. If the food tastes as good as the aromas from the kitchen, I'm in for a treat.

When we're more relaxed, Pat asks me why I'm in San Fransisco, and I repeat the story. Only this time, he already knows the background and has been reading my reports, so only the California update is needed.

I mention that I've hooked up with a local trafficking team, and they're already working on what seems to be a related case.

As we work through our meal, I tell him about Zhan Wu and the probability that not only is he responsible for bringing the last two girls across from New Jersey, but he may also be involved in trafficking underage Chinese girls.

Pat's interested and asks intelligent questions. I must admit it's nice to be with someone so smart, and I enjoy his company. Pity he's married and firmly in a no-go area for me.

When I'm finished, it's his turn, and he tells me what he's

doing in San Fransisco.

It turns out to be two things. He's expanding the T.E.N.S. initiative to California and meeting with most of the bigwigs across the State. But he's also following up on details of a case that involves Human Organ Trafficking, something I know very little about. I ask him to tell me more.

'There's a non-profit organization called Organ-Watch which tries to uncover illegal trade outside the official system, and the founder, the Chair at Berkeley for Medical Anthropology, recently contacted me to suggest a hospital here is involved in supplying Human tissue and organs illegally.'

'Is this big business, Pat?'

'You bet it is. It's a huge business. The thing is, it's like all commodities, which means that demand will determine the price. In this case, though, it would be more accurate to say that he who has the most money will get the product.'

'How does that work?'

'They usually run a dark-net website similar to eBay, only you don't have a week to enter your bid. You have a few hours. If the buyer is lucky, he will be the only one asking at that time and pay the minimum bid. If he's unlucky, the price can go through the roof.'

'No maximum price?'

'Correct. And other sites allow a buyer to place an order for a specific date. In this case, several suppliers may bid to fulfill the order, so the cost is often lower. But more recently, these companies have been getting together and refusing to bid against each other.'

'Keeping the price high?'

'Yes. But, in this case, it also means that the successful supplier will be looking for a particular organ for a specified date, and they're not normally easy to come by.'

'Isn't there a problem with organ compatibilities and such?'

'Yes, but the procurement process defines all of that.'

'This is a sophisticated operation, Pat.'

'Yes. And you can see why someone in a hospital could become involved.'

* * *

I take a moment to finish my meal while thinking it will never cease to amaze me how low people can sink - literally stealing an organ from one Human being to sell to another for profit.

'How much will an organ cost?'

Pat pushes his plate away and sits back.

'The most valuable organs are the liver and the lungs. A single lung or liver can fetch a quarter of a million easily. A heart, something similar but maybe a little less, A kidney is around a hundred grand.'

'And this is all illegal?'

'Yes. Although many people in poorer countries are willing to sell their organs to feed their families, that becomes a whole different case if it comes to court. The World Health Organisation claims that Daesh was selling victims' organs through the dark net, which caused all kinds of complications and diseases for unsuspecting recipients. A few years back, there was a major political storm in Brazil where mothers deliberately allowed children to die, sometimes even hastening the death to earn a hundred dollars from wealthy Americans.'

'For a hundred dollars, that's awful. And you think a hospital here in San Fransisco is involved in this somehow?'

'That's what I'm here to find out, so the Jury's out on that right now.'

'Can I ask? Is it a particular hospital?'

Pat hesitates but then shrugs and tells me.

'It's the Pacific West Medical Center.'

'But that place is huge and famous.'

'Yes, but you're probably unaware that the FBI has already successfully prosecuted major hospitals in New York, Chicago, and Washington, DC. All major well-acclaimed hospitals. It's often a few particular people, though, and not the establishments themselves.'

At this point, we fall silent.

The meal is finished, and Pat calls for the check as I consider how desperate donors and recipients can be and how the unscrupulous operators in the middle can force the prices up and the costs down.

We walk back to the hotel together, and Pat heads for bed. I make for the bar. I need a Corona or two.

I sleep particularly soundly and suspect the Cabernet Sauvignon, followed by a couple of Corona in the bar, have helped. It doesn't seem like the time difference between Eastern and Pacific time is having any effect.

I shower, get dressed, and, having eaten so late the previous evening, skip breakfast and walk to the office. As I walk, something is buzzing around in my head from the conversation with Pat Cataldo the last evening, but I can't pinpoint it. It'll probably come to me later when I'm not trying.

As I show my new credentials at the front desk, my cell buzzes, and the team upstairs asks me to join them. I tell them I'm on the way up but will collect a coffee first. Ling tells me not to bother. They've got that covered.

When I reach their small conference room, I see what Ling means. There's fresh coffee and a dozen Dunkin Donuts on the table.

I'm told to help myself but that my turn will come.

The team members are joshing around as I choose a Boston Creme to go with my coffee.

The sergeant, Ron Myers, is a bulky individual. Not fat, but widely built. I suspect he's been a defensive linebacker at college. I wouldn't want to try knocking him down, that's for sure.

On his left sits Danny Torres, a Latino who has lost control of his arms. He can't speak a word without throwing them around and gesticulating. I'm guessing he's from an Italian background.

On the sergeant's other side is Win Taylor. He's the quiet one of the bunch. He only speaks when he's spoken to. Probably some Brit in him. Stiff upper lip and all that stuff. He's wearing a wedding band, so I know he's married. I wonder if he has kids like Pat Cataldo.

Finally, there's Ling Yú. Small but feisty. She can hold her own in a room full of guys. She's no wet lettuce, that's for sure.

When I eventually tune in to what they're talking about, the sergeant is complaining.

'We've been told our surveillance op is costing too much. We're switching to electronic surveillance whenever possible. But before you all start grumbling, I know it's not as good, but we have to cut our costs, and yes, that means less overtime. The Chief's on the warpath, and I have no choice.'

'So, does that mean cameras and listening devices?' I ask

'You wish,' says the sergeant. 'We're talking basic electronic tagging of vehicles, so at least we'll know where the key players are. And whatever personal surveillance we can provide inside normal working hours.'

'That's it?'

'Best we can do. The good news is, as you know, we already started last night when you went to see Zhan Wu. We planted a device on each of their three cars. And guess what happened this morning?'

'They went to Dunkin Donuts like me?' Laughs, Torres.

'No, smart ass. Zhan drove out of the city, across the Gate, and into Sonoma County. He went to a specific winery - the Black Juggler.'

'That's the first time he's been out of the city since we started tailing him,' adds Ling Yú.

'He's wine tasting in the morning? Very classy.' says Taylor.

But I'm sure I know better.

'No. He's visiting the same place he went to when he returned from New Jersey. He's gone to where he delivered the girls.'

'You think that's where they're being held?' asks Torres.

'It's just a guess. But I think I got to him last night when I confronted him.'

'And he's run straight to his boss?' adds the sergeant. 'I agree with you, Sammy. I think you've rattled him.'

'Where is he now?' I ask.

'Let's take a look,' says Torres, opening up a laptop and typing before turning the screen towards us. 'He's still there. The Black Juggler.'

'What about the other two you tagged?' I ask.

'They haven't moved, or at least their vehicles haven't. They could be traveling with Zhan.'

'Yeah, that's a possibility,' answers the sergeant. 'Let's see what we can discover about this Black Juggler Winery.'

At that point, the meeting breaks up, and I ask if I can spend more time reviewing the files.

'Knock yourself out, Sammy. I'll give you a shout if anything turns up.'

Back down at my desk in Narcotics, one or two of the guys at least smile some level of recognition at me as I pass through. But no one talks to me, and that suits me just fine.

I start much the same as I did the previous day, at the beginning, going through everything - one report after another convinced the devil is in the detail.

By the time I roll out of the place, the sun has already disappeared, and I regret thinking that the time change hasn't affected me. I'm feeling a lot sleepier than I should.

So, I head back to the hotel, order a BLT with a couple of Corona for my room, and relax on the bed, watching a stupid film on an action-for-men channel. Like women don't like action! It doesn't matter how often I watch tv. I'm always upset with the sheer volume of ads. Especially when the frequency picks up as whatever you're watching comes toward the end.

I don't get advertising. I mentally switch off and ignore it, often channel-flicking for a while to see what else is on. Of course, it's incredible how many channels show ads when you do this. So many it's hard to find an actual program.

My head is on the pillow by ten-thirty, and I'm asleep shortly after.

Saturday morning, and I allow myself to stay in bed till eight. The last thing I do before getting up is look at the weather forecast and see it's a foggy start to the day, but it should clear by lunchtime.

The team is taking turns monitoring the surveillance tags and has agreed to get together at three to see if there's any progress.

I'm pretty happy to have the time off. I want to wander around the city and take in some sights.

I wear denim cut-offs and a cool blouse with my windcheater on top, and when I'm ready, I head out to find some breakfast.

I buy a coffee at Proyecto Diaz and walk down to Ferry Park, where I sit on a bench for a while, watching the Ferries come and go.

I'm joined by an older man, probably in his eighties. He's wrapped up for winter with several layers under his long, thick coat.

He has a nose that's been in the ring at some point, badly bent out of shape, and a French-style beret on his head. Like me, he has a coffee and is doing pretty much what I'm doing, watching the Ferries.

We get talking, and I tell him I'm from Florida, just in the city for a few days. Never been before.

He tells me he's the son of Jewish immigrants and has lived in the city all his life.

As we chat, he points out the various Ferries to me. The Bay Ferry that travels the farthest down from Vallejo up in Solano County. Then there's the Golden Gate Ferry from San Quentin, California's oldest prison.

I tell him I've heard of it, and he tells me I probably haven't heard the half of it.

'It's got the only death row in the State. Holds up to near-enough four-thousand men, and around seven hundred will be on death row.'

'You seem to know a lot about it?'

'I should. I was a guard there for thirty years fore I retired.'

'Do they still perform executions in California like we do in Florida?'

'Not anymore. They used to gas them, then switched to lethal injection, then the damned liberals took over the State, and it all stopped in the late nineties. You guys got it right over in Florida.'

'So, you were in favor of the executions?'

'There wasn't any other answer for some of the monsters they got locked up in there. Some are so bad; we had to split death row into three areas to keep some from killing others.'

'Why three areas?'

'One for the ones that don't cause any trouble. Another for those that might, and the third for those that don't know any other way to live. We called the last one the adjustment block. It had solid doors with slots for food delivery. We would never go into a cell unless we believed the inmate was genuinely ill. Hard to tell, so four of us would go in together.'

'These inmates were in solitary then?'

'Yes, but we weren't allowed to call it that. I worked that block for three miserable years. I still got nightmares bout some of these guys.'

We talk a little more before I thank him for his company and move on.

I recall one thing he told me was that when he started work in San Quentin, he believed he would be helping inmates rehabilitate. But by the time he finished, he was one of the strictest disciplinarians.

I can't help but wonder what that's telling me about what working in child trafficking might be doing to me.

Instead of following the waterfront today, I cut inland through the city streets. I'm looking for a couple of places I've seen on tv. First up is Lombard Street, often seen on *The Streets of San Fransisco*. Its nickname is the most crooked street in the world because it's built on such a steep hill that the architects decided the road needed to zig and zag for safety reasons.

As I stand at the bottom and look up, it's pretty astonishing. It's not a huge hill, but there are eight tight bends in the short distance. There's no way you can speed down this.

The designer obviously achieved his purpose.

Next, after this, my must-do is to ride the famous cable car. I don't read many books, but I've read a few of Michael Connelly's and love his Detective, Harry Bosch. When Netflix started making the books into a series, I watched every one of them. This cable car is in several of these.

The Lombard Street stop isn't far from where I am, so I buy a ticket and ride the green line back to Union Square.

I can imagine a body being discovered on the trolley and Bosch and his long-suffering partner trying to find the killer.

By the time I get off, I'm floating on air. The experience has been fantastic, and I feel truly relaxed for the first time.

I have time for lunch, then head into the office to meet the team.

The weather forecast turns out to be pretty accurate, so it's a bright sunny day outside. However, the tinted glass windows on the SFPD building, combined with our location inside, about as far from a window as possible, makes it gloomy.

As I make my way through the office, it's virtually empty, and the lights are off other than in the area around our small conference room.

Three o'clock and the team are all there.

The sergeant kicks off the update.

'From the surveillance yesterday, Zhan Wu stayed at the winery for around an hour, then returned to his home, where he has remained since. So nothing for us there. What about the Winery, Torres?'

'Taylor and I have been looking at that. Let him tell you some of the background.'

This is almost the first time I've heard Taylor speak.

'Do you know the Russians planted some wineries in Sonoma county almost two hundred years ago?'

'The Russians. You're kidding, right?' said the sergeant.

'No. It's for real. But since then, so many others have been involved. Missionaries, Hungarians, French - anyone who knew anything about growing vines. Do you know how many wineries are now in the greater Sonoma area alone? Take a guess?'

I don't think any of us want to seem foolish, so we remain silent until he answers his own question.

'Over seven hundred.'

At that point, Torres starts flailing his arms around and picks up the story.

'So, our particular winery has been there, in its current form, for nearly thirty years. A Hispanic family privately owned and ran it until three years ago, but due to ill health, they sold it to a company called OFS.

OFS has registered a DBA under this name and submitted articles of incorporation as required. According to the California State Secretaries website, the registered owner is Qui Chang.'

'Chinese, again,' says the sergeant.

'Yes, and a woman. Qui is an immigrant, having achieved U.S. citizenship on 11/1/90. She's unmarried, with three sons, all of which work with her running the winery.'

'So, what do we do now?' asks Ling Yú. 'Plant trackers on vehicles at the winery?'

'We can't justify it based purely on a visit from Zhan Wu. No, we'll have to be patient. Keep an eye on Wu and see where else he might lead us,' replies the sergeant before he turns to me.

'I'm sorry, Sammy. It doesn't seem like we're being much help to you. You probably feel a sense of urgency about finding your missing girls, but I'm still not even a hundred percent convinced we're even working the same case.'

'Don't worry, Sergeant. I can be patient. And by the way, I *am* convinced. But I still need to prove it. I'm going to go back over all the past surveillance details again. I can't help but feel there's something in there I've missed.'

Back down one floor, all the desks are empty, and I have to find the lights.

On the way down, an idea has worked its way into the front of my mind, and my objective is to find out if what I'm thinking is true or not.

So I set about my task with a new sense of urgency and skim through the masses of reports until I come to a surveillance report from following Zhan Wu over a week before.

Sure enough, scanning through the details, I'm right. One of the locations visited by Wu was the Pacific West Medical Center. This could be one giant coincidence, but Wu visiting the same hospital under investigation by the FBI seems highly improbable.

As I think about the implications of what I've just discovered, I can't help but wonder if Wu has delivered the girls to the hospital to have their organs removed. Surely not. There again, having heard the lengths people will go to in the organ-supply business, maybe this happened.

Perhaps he takes them to the winery to recover before moving them elsewhere for other use.

That sounds possible, but then why not take them directly to the hospital in the first place? Why did he turn off I80 and head up to Sonoma County? Was something happening to the girls in the winery before they were taken to the hospital? Was the Black Juggler more involved than just as a pass-through recovery center?

Too many questions and not enough answers. Trying to think what best to do next, I worry about revealing the FBI case to the team, so I can only talk with Cataldo.

I call him, but he's tied up the rest of the day and for dinner. We agree to meet in the bar back at the Regency around nine-thirty.

I'm good with that as I have more work I want to do first.

I start by returning to the beginning of my case, where I found out I would be looking for twelve underage girls, and read my reports. I'm onto something, don't ask me what yet.

I find nothing of interest until I come to the initial report from ICTSG giving me the details of the drivers they were able to ID.

***

Name: Arnou Chikumbutso
  Nickname: Chiko
  Born: South Africa
  DoB: 6/19/69
  US Citizen from: 11/1/90
  Location: Chicago
  Family: Married with two sons.

Name: Francis Lemoine
  Nickname: The monk
  Born: Quebec
  DoB: 2/9/66
  US Citizen from: 11/1/90
  Location: Seattle
  Family: None

Name: Wilson Clampett
  Nickname: Jed
  Born: Atlanta, Georgia
  DoB: 3/22/75
  Location: Atlanta
  Family: Wife deceased, one daughter.

Name: Zhan Wu
  Nickname: None
  Born: Shanghai, China
  US Citizen from: 11/1/90
  DoB: 5/15/79
  Location: San Francisco
  Family: None

As soon as I see this, I call Ron Myers upstairs with a question and confirm my suspicion. I tell him I'll explain in the morning.

Ending the call, I immediately make a second and hope George in Cyber-tech is working the weekend. I'm not disappointed.

'Sammy? How's sunny California?'

'George. What on Earth are you doing in the office at eight o'clock on a Saturday night?'

'Another project. Saving the World, of course. How can I help you?'

'Remember you said you had a Phantom hacker who changed the immigration status for some of the people I've been chasing down?'

'Sure.'

'You removed the legal status for Chikumbutso in Chicago. Did you do the same for the others?'

'Certainly did. Immigration should be calling on them in the not-too-distant future.'

'Can you check another name for me?'

I give him the name I'm interested in, and he's back within a few minutes to confirm my suspicion. He asks if he should delete the citizenship status, and I approve this.

When I end the call, I'm sure the two cases are joined together. The girls brought down from New Jersey, and whatever is happening at the Black Juggler. Now when I meet with Cataldo later, I'll try to find out if his case is also tied in.

This is all becoming tricky.

With still a few hours before I meet Cataldo, I decide to call my sergeant back home. He should be off duty and sinking a cool one.

'Sammy, is that you?'

'Hi, Dan. Am I disturbing you in flagrante delicto?'

'You mean, am I having wild sex? No. But it sounds like fancy Washington's rubbing off on you, Sammy. Where did you learn about flagrante delicto?'

'A girl never tells, Dan.'

I hear Dan laugh, and it's a good sound. It makes me miss not just him but everything. My parents, my uncle, the weather, beaches. Florida.

He asks me how I'm doing, and I try voicing out loud for

the first time what I think is happening in San Fransisco.
He listens, not interrupting until I'm finished, and then I ask him what he thinks.

'I think I'm glad you're there, and I'm here, Sammy. You've got a tiger by the tail if you're right. You better be super careful how you proceed from now.'

'That's my plan, Dan. You know me, Super-careful Sammy.'
He laughs again.

'Tell Cataldo everything you've told me. He's a good man to have on your side.'

'Meeting him in a couple of hours.'

After that, we generally catch up on more minor matters, me telling him I'm homesick, and he is telling me about a new dog he's given his niece. Little inconsequential things, all of which I miss.

Back in the hotel, I freshen up and eat at the bar downstairs. Hot spicy chicken wings with a blue cheese dip and a Corona. Perfect.

An hour later, Cataldo arrives and suggests we move to a table rather than sit at the bar. He orders a Sauvignon Blanc for himself and a Corona for me. I follow him to a corner and tell him I'm impressed that he knows what I drink.

He laughs and admits that he had seen the server behind the bar remove an empty just as he entered the room.

'I am a Detective, you know,' he whispers across the table. 'So, what's with the clandestine late-night rendezvous, Sammy?'

I'm glad I used Dan Weissman as my sounding board beforehand. The whole story comes out much more connected than it might otherwise do.

When I finish, I ask him what he thinks.

'I think you're probably right, Sammy. Yes, everything is circumstantial, but I've built cases on a lot less in the past. So tell me, what do you want to do from here?'

When I explain that I would like to introduce him to the SFPD trafficking team, he's okay with the idea but mentions that the local FBI teams and SFPD haven't always been the best bed partners. This is one of the reasons for his visit here in the first place.

Before we finish, I call Ron Myers and confirm that the next team meeting is set for noon. I tell him I'll be bringing someone to join the discussion. He agrees without asking who it is.

I'm happy with that.

Another foggy morning and the air is drizzly wet, but when I'm running, I don't care.

I push myself a little harder, working on strength rather than stamina, and by the time I get back to the hotel, I'm soaked in sweat.

I head straight for the in-house gym and do some cool-down exercises before going to my room.

The equipment in the place is obscene. Rows of everything. Cross trainers, treadmills, weights, and these running machines where you can choose the route you run on a screen in front of you. You can even choose who to run with - a top athlete or a networked friend. This is not something that has interested me before. I like the loneliness of running and being outdoors. But this looks like a different kind of fun.

An hour later, I'm showered, changed, and waiting in reception, where I've agreed to meet Cataldo. We might as well travel together.

I suspect my jaw drops when I see him. He's not in a suit. He's wearing a Redsocks T-shirt with trainers over a pair of track bottoms.

I've just never seen him out of a suit before.

He smiles at me.

'I may be FBI, but I don't have to look like it. Come on, we've got some detectives to meet.'

I already offered to supply the munchies, so we stop on the

way to the office and buy some fresh croissants.

When we get to the conference room, the team is already there. They have that *I-don't-want-to-be-here-on-a-Sunday* air about them, and I can't blame them.

They're curious to find out who I've brought with me.

Before I say anything, Ling Yú asks us how we like our coffees, then pours them for us while I open up the box of croissants and let the buttery smell waft into the room.

The next thirty seconds are like watching the seagulls swoop on your sandwich when you're momentarily distracted on the Ferry.

It seems I've made a good choice.

When seated, I introduce Cataldo and tell them he's an FBI Lead Agent I know from Washington.

I think the mention that he's from Washington helps, implying that he's just hanging with me and passing through, as they readily accept him.

I get him started by telling the team about the T.E.N.S. initiative and that Cataldo is one of the program's founders. I know they've heard of it, but hearing about it from Cataldo will be different for them. They're curious, so I hand the conversation to Cataldo and leave him to talk.

It ends up a lively discussion, with the team asking many questions and sharing some of their less favorable interactions with the FBI. Cataldo is impressive, though. He doesn't hide from the past and readily accepts that, in many cases, the FBI should have acted differently.

The more he talks, the more I see the team coming around. I hope I'm right because I'm about to thrust the FBI into our investigation, bang in the center.

When the conversation comes to a natural pause, the sergeant asks if there's any other reason I have requested Cataldo to join us. No fool, is he?

'Funny you should ask,' I reply. 'You're not going to believe this, but as well as promoting the T.E.N.S initiative here, he's also working the same case we are.'

'Trafficking Chinese children?'

'Not exactly,' says Cataldo. 'I'm working on an illegal Organ-trafficking case.'
'And that relates to what we're doing; how?' asks Ling Yú.
I interrupt.
'I'll take that one. Remember when Torres was following Zhan Wu, at one point, Wu visited a hospital?'
'Pacific West Medical?' says Torres. 'I remember.'
'Well, guess which hospital the FBI is looking into for organ harvesting?'
'The same one?' says the sergeant.
'Correct,' I tell them. 'So, I know it's a stretch, but what if the trafficking operation and the harvesting of Human organs are both part of the same case?'
Cataldo interrupts.
'I should just mention that children's organs fetch much higher prices.'

At this, the room falls silent for a moment as everyone weighs up what they've just heard. It's Torres who speaks first.
'It makes sense to me. When I followed Zhan to the hospital, I thought it was strange. So when I finished my shift, I swung around there and asked some questions at reception. They were initially reluctant, but I used my natural charm to persuade them to let me see who he had registered to visit.'
The team laughs when the natural charm is mentioned. Apparently, there's a history there.
'Anyway, you jokers. He was registered as visiting a Dr. Xiao Liang.'
'Another Chinese connection,' adds the sergeant before Torres continues.
'I google the good doctor afterward, and guess what? He's a surgeon in the transplant unit.'

This is the moment that I will look back on later and realize that any possible organizational boundaries have just disappeared. From this moment, we're united with a single aim.

When we reach this point, I propose my two alternative scenarios for what may be happening. Either the children are being taken to the hospital to have organs removed, then being allowed to recuperate at the winery, or else they are being held at the winery for other reasons that don't need to be explained before being sent to the hospital later.

Cataldo offers a slightly more sinister version which is the girls are being used at the winery until there is demand for a specific organ.

'Like us ordering Pizza?' suggests Torres.

We spend a while debating what we consider to be the most likely scenario without coming to any conclusion. We need to start following up on all fronts and figure the details out as we go.

Cataldo says he'll focus on Dr. Xiao Liang, whereas the rest will concentrate on Zhan Wu and the Black Juggler winery.

I haven't mentioned that the owner of the Black Juggler is in the Country illegally. I want to follow up on this before I say anything.

After we break up, Cataldo says he has another meeting over dinner, so I head back to the hotel and order room service.

While I wait, I call George.

When he answers, I'm surprised. There's the sound of children running around in the background. Sunday night, and he's home with the family. What am I thinking?

Before I can apologize, he thanks me for saving him from defeat at Monopoly.

Still, I do apologize and offer to call again in the morning, but he won't hear of it and insists I tell him what I'm looking for.

He listens quietly, obviously intrigued, and tells me he'll get back to me when he's found the right person to talk with.

I finish the call just as room service arrives and sit down to enjoy my burger and fries as the Black Panther movie is just starting on the tv.

***

I'm only halfway through the movie when a text arrives from George telling me he's forwarding the information I asked for, but I might want to look through it on a desktop rather than my cell.

I'm too impatient and not really into the movie, so I start opening attachments and scrolling through the information he's sent.

The Hong Kong and Shanghai police departments have forwarded their files on Qui Chang, the Black Juggler's owner, and they make for fascinating reading.

Born to a low-income family in the mid-nineteen-sixties, Qui Chang grew up in the paddy fields outside of Shanghai in the Yangtze River basin. While growing up in a male-dominated culture, as an attractive teenager beyond her years, she took advantage of her looks. She deliberately pursued a married man, withholding her charms until he married her. He assumed that once she had what she wanted, his polygamy would go undetected, but he had underestimated her need for wealth. His wealth.

Over the five years, they remained together, Qui Chang slowly amassed significant sums, which enabled her to divorce her husband while threatening to reveal his polygamy.

Her next move had been to woo a wealthy businessman from Hong Kong and further build her private wealth; However, that still was not enough for her insatiable appetite, and she soon discarded him in favor of another he had introduced her to.

Intrigued, I read that she married none other than Zhou Jianghong, the enforcer for a prominent Hong Kong Triad mainly dealing in drug trafficking and counterfeiting. Under her influence, the Triad shifted into illegal online activities, initially targeting healthcare fraud.

This immediately fits with our thinking about possible organ trafficking.

***

According to the Hong Kong police, her husband fell out of favor over missing cash and ended up in the Yangtze. Qui Chang avoided the same fate by offering to return the missing money from her fortune if they allowed her to leave the country with her three sons and live peacefully. This brought her to California just over three years ago.
Not as her immigration status indicates - back in 1990.

Thinking through what I've learned that might be useful, the health scam background is circumstantial again, but it's one more clue that we're on the right track. Then there's the fact that she's an illegal immigrant, and I've already taken care of this with George's help. Finally, perhaps the most helpful thing is that I know she will not be welcome back in Hong Kong.

It's almost eleven in the morning when our small convoy of vehicles leaves SFPD, heading north over the Golden Gate Bridge into Sonoma County.

With help from Pat Cataldo, the Chief has given us extra resources, and we plan on positioning vehicles strategically along the route so that they can tail anyone heading back south from the winery.

I'm traveling with Ron Myers. Ling Yú and Taylor are in the car behind. The plan is that they will play tourists but will be backup if we need them. Torres is back in the office monitoring the trackers to give us early warning if Zhan Wu or his two cohorts come our way.

It's a spectacularly clear, warm day, and I enjoy my first trip over the Bridge. I know it carries traffic for Rte 101 and the fabled Rte 1, or the California Freeway as it's known, from one-hundred-eighty miles north of San Fransisco, down to Capistrano Beach south of LA.

I'm familiar with the route as it's one of those drives I've promised myself I'll take one day, preferably in an open-topped convertible.

Once we're over the bridge and through Sausalito and San

Rafael, we stay on Rte 101 until we head east on Rte 37 towards Vallejo, where one of the Ferries I watched the other morning starts its southbound journey. After that, we pick up Rte 29 and finally drive into Napa Valley - wine country.

I would say that the wineries are good at signposting, and it isn't long before we find the Black Juggler. We turn into a long driveway that meanders through fields heavily populated with straight rows of carefully cultivated vines.

   When the Hispanic family originally built this place, they spared no money. The main building has a Tuscan feeling - individually crafted-stone walls, inlaid with arched windows and all beneath a dark-red tiled sloping roof. There's also a square tower block of twice the height overlooking a cobbled courtyard.

   We work our way through a car park seemingly large enough to hold every vehicle in San Fransisco at the height of the season, with half of the parking space devoted to Coach parking for wine tours.

   Between Ron and I, we've agreed that I should be upfront as I'm the one who rattled Zhan Wu at the Chinese restaurant.

   Pushing open the door to the obligatory shop, I take a few moments to let my eyes adjust as I look around. Not only do they sell wines, but charcuterie, cheeses, homemade pickles, and other produce from local suppliers. There's a wine-tasting bar set up to my left. A great slab of polished tree trunk on top of a row of wooden wine casks with glasses and a selection of local wines to sample.

   I suspect I might indulge myself if I weren't here in an official capacity.

   As I approach a salesperson behind the main counter, I show my ID and ask if I can speak with the owner - Qui Chang, on urgent police business.

   I see the hesitancy in the woman's eyes while she weighs up the best response and wonders if she should come up with some excuse or other.

   But she doesn't. She asks if I have a car.

Having told her I do, she tells me to drive around to the rear of the building and follow the track up into the nearby foothills. This will take me straight to the owner's house.

As we drive, I call Ling Yú in the car behind and tell her where we're going. They agree to hang around at the shop, sampling some wine as long as possible. Not a bad backup duty, I think to myself.

I agree with her that when we get to the house, I'll call and leave the line open so they can hear what's happening and come to our aid if need be.

It's not a brilliant backup plan, but hopefully, we won't need one.

As we crest the hill, I get my first view of the destination. It's very much in keeping with the shop down below, hand-crafted from the same chiseled pale stone.

We pass between two rows of tall willowy trees, which lead to a circular driveway surrounding an ornamental pond with a single water spout shooting fifteen feet in the air.

Ron pulls in alongside a pale cream Bentley Continental, and I can only wonder if this reflects the lifestyle afforded the owner by running a wine business or something else altogether.

Before we leave the car, I call Ling and place the cell back in my pocket.

As I step up to the front porch with Ron right behind me, one of the largest African Americans I've ever seen opens the door and stands to one side.

We enter what I can only describe as a richly appointed home. The style is still very Tuscan, with tiled flooring, pale walls with tapestries here and there, and brass lamps of all shapes and sizes. I think the owner is a lamp collector - maybe searching for Alladin's lamp. Who knows?

I follow in the giant's footsteps, or more accurately, I follow him using many more footsteps than he requires, outside the rear of the house and onto a verandah overlooking a large outdoor pool.

He stops and indicates the woman sitting by the pool under the shade of an umbrella, reading a book - or at least pretending to do so. Obviously, the woman in the shop has already called ahead, and we're expected.

Qui Chang is not at all what I expect. I'm stupidly expecting another version of Ling Yú - petite and classically Asian in appearance.

This woman is not like that. For a start, although she's sitting, her long legs stretch out under the table. She's undoubtedly a good six inches taller than me. She's also more shapely than Ling, with a fuller figure up top yet a slim waist.

Her hair is silver and combed back into a long woven ponytail that hangs over one shoulder, but her eyes are the most surprising. They're pale blue, like a Husky.

Besides the silver hair, there's hardly anything else to suggest that this woman is seventy years old. If she's using anti-wrinkle cream, I want some. Damn it, I have more wrinkles than she has.

She doesn't stand or offer her hand, but she does wave us to take a seat and ask if we would like some cool lemonade, but I decline.

Our plan here is simple. Get in, rile her, and get out. Then see what she does.

'Thank you for seeing us so promptly, Madam Qui.'

'It's a pleasure. How may I help you, Detective?'

'Can I just confirm that you are Madam Qui Chang, the owner of the Black Juggler Winery?'

'Yes, Detective. I am.'

'In which case, I have a couple of things which may be of interest to you,' I tell her, taking the page with the photos of the two remaining girls I'm still looking for from my pocket, unfolding it, and passing it to her. 'I'm looking for these two young girls and wonder if you might be able to tell me where they are?'

Qui Chang's face is a mask of inscrutability. She's giving nothing away. She takes the proffered page, studies it carefully, then hands it back to me.

'I'm sorry, Detective, I can't say I recognize these girls. But, I do wonder why you would think I might. Young girls of this age tend not to spend much time in wineries.'

'I'm asking a lot of people. Anyone who seems to have an interest in under-age children in any way and the SFPD thought I should talk to you.'

She's still unperturbed, or at least very good at appearing to be.

'So, you're on a fishing trip, Detective?'

'No, Madam Qui. I'm searching under every possible rock to find these two girls, that's all.'

'And you think I might populate such a place?'

'It's astonishing the people you find under rocks, Madam Qui. It never ceases to surprise me.'

I'm expecting some admonishment, but she mentions that I said I had a *couple* of things that may interest her.

'Ah, yes. Thank you for reminding me. There's this other detail I want to let you see.'

With this, I remove another sheet from my pocket and do the same as before, handing it to her.

'What is this? she asks.

'It's an official letter from the U.S. Immigration Registry, saying that at my request, they have checked your immigration status and found that you are in the country on falsified documentation. In other words, Madam Qui. You're an illegal immigrant.'

'What is this? Some trick? I've been a U.S. citizen for many, many years. There must be some mistake.'

'No, I don't think so. The only mistake was obtaining your citizenship fraudulently, which I believe the U.S. Immigration and Customs Authorities will follow up with you within the next forty-eight hours.'

'This is ridiculous. I'll have my attorney take care of this.'

'Good luck with that, Madam Qui,' I tell her, rising from my seat. 'I hope you enjoy becoming reacquainted with some of your friends and family back in China or Hong Kong. Oh, by the way. I might have mentioned you're coming to them. I believe they're already rolling out the welcome mat for you.'

The calm mask is gone, replaced with barely contained rage.

'I think we'll be leaving now. Enjoy your journey home, Madam Qui.'

In the car, Ron turns to me and tells me he hopes never to cross me. I reckon that's his way of saying well done - you've got her riled.

By mid-afternoon, it doesn't seem like my visit to the Black Juggler has had any effect - at least not with Qui Chang.

The surveillance operation is still in place, so it's too early to give up hope.

Ron, Pat Cataldo, and I are in the cafeteria back at SFPD. It's Cataldo who has the most exciting update.

'I've spoken with the Dean of Pacific West Medical about my concerns, and I admit to being impressed when he doesn't immediately deny any wrong-doings in his hospital. When I mentioned this to him, he had already heard of similar things happening elsewhere, so at least he was willing to hear me out.

'So, is he willing to help?' I ask.

'Yes. He already has. He called the Facility Manager responsible for the entire complex, who brought some schematics of each of the main buildings with him. It turns out they closed an entire wing down a few years back because of increasing maintenance costs in what was one of the original buildings.'

'A surgical wing?' asks the sergeant.

'Yes, it was. So, I asked him if he thinks it could still be in use, and although initially, he doubted it, he asked if I wanted to visit and see for myself.'

'Not a good idea,' I say.

'No. I agree. I explained that I didn't want to tip our hand if something was going on and asked him if there was any other way he could check?'

'Power usage.'

'Excellent, Sergeant. Each building has its power feed, so he checked to see if power is being used. Bottom line. The old wing has been drawing power for the past two years and still is today.'

'So, what does that mean?' I ask.

'It means, if we're correct and there's organ trafficking going on in there, then it's not being done ad hoc. It's ongoing. So there are either people in there undergoing surgery every day....'

'...or there are people in there being cared for?' I finish.

'God, do you really think that's what's going on?' asks the sergeant.

'I don't know,' says Cataldo. 'But we can't wait around to find out.'

At that moment, the sergeant's cell rings, and he answers it. Cataldo and I remain quiet, digesting everything we've just discussed and thinking about what to do next.

When the call ends, we get an update.

'That's the surveillance team. They've been following Zhan Wu all day, and he's just arrived at the Black Juggler. They've also traced another vehicle up there, belonging to Qui Chang's attorney.'

'So, they're making plans?' suggests Cataldo.

'More likely, the attorney is confirming Qui Chang's lack of official U.S. citizenship. It would only take him a single phone call.'

'Well,' says the sergeant. 'If the guy's any good, he should be telling them to pack up and get out of the Country before ICE get to them. They might be arrested for using forged documentation rather than being deported as an illegal immigrant. I suspect jail time in a U.S. Pen doesn't sound too good to them.'

'They won't want to leave any incriminating evidence

behind them at the winery,' I say.

'I was just thinking that,' adds Cataldo. 'So, if she's holding young girls there, she'll have to move them.'

'To the Pacific West hospital?'

'That would be my bet. Remember, she doesn't know we've discovered the hospital part of the operation yet.'

At this point, The sergeant excuses himself to help coordinate the surveillance operation. This leaves Cataldo and me figuring out the next steps.

'Pat, when you met with the Facilities Manager, did you discuss how they might get in and out of the closed wing?'

'Yes. If they use the old theatres there, they can't bring people in and out of the main reception or the emergency area. So he suggested they must be using the old docking bays at the rear.'

'What are you thinking, Sammy?'

An hour later, after much discussion, Cataldo tries to sum up what we think needs to happen next.

'First. We can't delay raiding the hospital. So even if Zhan Wu does not go there today, we go in tonight at the latest.'

I nod my agreement.

'Second. If he goes there, we follow him in, catching him and whoever else is involved simultaneously. Depending on the scale of what they're doing, upwards of a dozen people could be involved. There must be surgeons, nurses, anesthesiologists, and goodness knows who else is involved.

'A full surgical team?'

Yes. Then finally, if there's anyone on the operating table when we go in, we'll need a team there to take whatever life-saving measures may be required. This will be tricky to coordinate without word leaking out.'

'Unless you borrow the staff you need from a separate hospital and don't tell them where they're heading?'

'Good thinking, Sammy. I think I have the contacts to be able to do that.'

'What about the actual raid? Is this an FBI operation or SFPD?'

'You should confirm with your team first, but I think it would be better as an SFPD raid with FBI assistance. We've got a pretty small field office here and need some serious backup on this. Probably SWAT.'

'I'll talk to the sergeant and clear that. Why don't we meet back here at five?'

Back in SFPD at five, we've moved into a larger conference room and been joined by several other people. There's the sergeant's boss - Lieutenant Su Huang - head of the SFPD SWAT team. Head of the SFO FBI field office and Cataldo has brought the hospital Facility Manager along with him.

The Facility Manager has spread a full-scale schematic of the disused building on the table, and we're studying it in detail. Having agreed, it's an SFPD operation. It's the lieutenant who suggests the way the operation should go.

'Two points of entry. One through the closed-up entrance from the main building. Can you make that possible for us ahead of time?' She asks the Facilities Manager, who nods his agreement.

'Lead Agent Cataldo will lead this group. The medical team will follow the first team at a safe distance and be ready to deal with whatever we find there. The second entry will be through the loading docks at the rear. Sergeant, I want you to lead that one. You will have SWAT in support.'

'What's the timing on this, lieutenant?' I ask.

She looks at the sergeant, who tells us that he's receiving live information on an earpiece from the surveillance team on Zhan Wu, and at that moment, he tells us that Wu has switched vehicles at the Black Juggler and is now driving a black Chevrolet Tahoe with tinted glass.

'So you don't know who's inside the vehicle, do you?' I ask.

'Sorry, Sammy. Your girls might or might not be; we've no way of knowing. Anyway, we think his main lieutenant is traveling with him - Hou Jiang, and they're currently just north of Golden Gate Bridge heading our way.'

'Right,' says the lieutenant. 'We'd better all take up our places. If Wu enters the hospital, we go. If he doesn't, and we're sure, we still have to go. So be ready either way. I'm the operations commander. Stay in touch at all times, and nobody goes in without my authority. Am I clear?'

By the time everyone is in their positions, the sun has disappeared, and the street lighting is on. The rain has just started, and the temperatures dropped. One of the SWAT guys has given me a warm ski jacket with SWAT in large letters on the back. I pull it on over my Kevlar vest and feel toasty.

The sergeant and I are in a black 4x4 with two Ford F550 SWAT trucks behind us. We're parked out of sight, round the rear of the hospital, ready to follow Zhan Wu in.

We have a spotter on top of a high-rise apartment block across the way who confirms what the surveillance team is telling us. That Wu is heading our way.

The spotter follows Wu's Tahoe into the hospital yard and tells us when they have parked out of sight behind the loading bays.

We wait sufficient time for Wu to be inside the building before the Commander signals to proceed.

The sergeant and I hang back as the two teams of heavily armed SWAT officers make their way across the road, through the rear gates, and check the Tahoe is empty.

We're on their heels as they pass the vehicle and enter the building.

Inside, the corridor splits. One team goes left, the other right. I look at the sergeant, and he indicates we should do likewise. So, he goes one way, and I go the other, each following a SWAT team.

The building is gloomy inside, and I can taste the dust in the air. Even though the wing has been closed for years, there's still a lingering smell of anesthetic and disinfectant mixed in with the general decay.

I can hear the steady shuffling footsteps of the team in front of me.

The pale gray decor may have looked attractive in its day, but now with patches of dampness and mold, it's just plain depressing. Discarded medical detritus, cigarette packs, hypodermics, and bottles of all kinds, litter the floor. I don't think the people we're after are the only inhabitants of this place.

The team up ahead stops when the one in charge raises an arm. We're at a corner - a time to be careful. I stay tucked safely behind them.

When the leader has looked around the corner, they move on as silently as possible.

I notice that at some point, emergency lighting has come on. It's not much, but it helps.

When they come to double push-doors ahead, they enter just as a barrage of bullets takes them by surprise. I see one officer down, clutching his thigh while two others return their own deadly salvos, and a fourth goes to the injured man's aid, dragging him back through the double doors, followed by the other two members.

The one who assisted is tasked with taking the injured member back, leaving three of us.

The lead SWAT sergeant tells us to close our eyes and cover our ears, then he moves to the doors and pushes one open while throwing a flash bang through the gap.

When we hear the explosion, the two remaining members are through the door and moving quickly up the corridor. I'm a little slower off the mark, and by the time I catch up, they've already disarmed and secured two very disoriented men writhing around in obvious pain.

By now, we can hear shouting somewhere deeper in the building, so the three of us leave the men and work towards the sound, me staying at the rear as instructed.

Again, I feel foolish not having a weapon, but what can I do? I'm paying my penance.

Before anyone can react, someone up ahead pushes a heavy metal cylinder into the corridor. When I first see it, I think it's an oxygen tank, but when the two SWAT officers start choking and fall to their knees, I realize it's not. I don't know what it is, but as it stops rolling, I see a black skull and crossbones on a yellow background.

I don't stop to think. I act.

I pull my coat up over my mouth and nose, run past the two fallen officers and kick the cylinder with the flat of my foot as hard as possible. It starts to roll, so I kick it again. Now it's rolling back the way it came, and although I'm starting to cough, I turn back to help the two SWAT members.

They're already on the move, helping each other, staggering back the way we came.

When we get through the double doors, they collapse to the ground, loosening the clothing around their necks and breathing the damp, moldy air like it's nectar from the Gods.

It's clear they're not going any further, so if anyone is, it's me.

Seeing this for himself, the sergeant gives me his handgun and, with a forced grin, reminds me to turn off the safety.

Leaving them there, I go back through the double doors and along the corridor, past the now empty cylinder, until I reach another set of double doors. A large sign tells me that only surgical staff can proceed beyond this point, and an entry button to one side.

I pause and wait as I see the first team approaching me from the opposite direction, with Cataldo in the lead.

'Sounds like you've been having some trouble. We heard the gunfire and flash bang. Where's the rest of your team?'

'I'm all that's left, I'm afraid. I think everyone will be okay though.'

'Right,' says Cataldo, sidearm ready. 'Shall we see what we have in here?'

I punch the entry button, and the doors open to reveal a theater prep and scrub room with stainless steel washing tubs and taps. There are glass sliding doors on the far side of the room.

We make our way across, the rest of the team behind us.

As we look inside, it's hard to believe what we see. It's like something out of a science-fiction movie.

There are a dozen beds, with a child on each, most wired to various machines. I recognize the ventilators and ECG monitors but not the rest.

The children In the nearest five beds are different. They look as if they've just fallen asleep. I assume these are new arrivals that Zhan Wu has brought down from the Black Juggler.

Two nurses are moving back and forth between the beds, making minor adjustments to drips or monitors, and beyond the room, there's a brightly lit operating theater with an entire team of medical staff around an operating table.

There's an operation in progress, as we feared might be the case.

Cataldo asks the SWAT officers to check there's no further danger, and they go to do that. Leaving Cataldo and me watching helplessly.

We're not sanitized and in surgical scrubs, so we can only watch and wait until we get the all-clear back from SWAT.

The two nurses have seen us, but it seems they've too much to do to worry about us.

Five minutes later, SWAT give us the all-clear, and Cataldo radios for SFPD officers and the backup medical team to come forward.

When they arrive, the medical team undergoes a rigorous scrub-in process as they would typically do, and when they're ready, Cataldo taps on the window to the first room where the nurses are and signals for them to come out.

As they do, the medical team enters, and some of them immediately start checking the condition of the children.

The head surgeon does exactly as Cataldo had done a few minutes prior. He taps on the double doors to the operating theater and signals for those inside to come out.

One of the surgeons comes to the door, and there's a conversation I can barely make out. I think they're ensuring the new team knows what procedure is being carried out and where they are in the proceedings.

When they reach an understanding, the surgeon inside speaks to his team, and they head for the door. It's not a clean takeover, as some people have to stay to monitor the patient until their replacements are there. Still, after a few minutes, the new team is in control, and the former team is being taken away, escorted by SFPD officers.

There's nothing more Cataldo, or I can do, but we're strangely reluctant to leave. It's as if we think our presence is essential to the children in some way, but the reality is it's the survival of the children that's important to us.

Cataldo and I met in the hotel bar the previous evening for a few drinks. The mood should have been jubilant, but it wasn't. It was somber.

Speaking for me, I was shocked at the nature of the illegal operation we've just closed down. Surgeons, anesthesiologists, nurses - all professional people, most likely with day jobs in the medical world, probably routinely saving lives.

Yet, here they were. Deliberately placing children's lives at risk for profit.

Cataldo had seen it all before, but I don't think that made it easier for him.

Everyone is gathered in the lieutenant's conference room in SFPD on Tuesday morning for the operational debrief. It seems the atmosphere in the room mirrors what Cataldo and I felt the night before.

Even the donuts fail to lighten the spirits.

First to speak is the lieutenant, who introduces the lead surgeon of the team that we took in with us and asks him to give the update he had already given her earlier in the morning.

'Good morning, everyone. I want to start the update by personally thanking everyone involved in rescuing these unfortunate children.'

'Rescuing *some* of them,' I add.

'Yes. Sadly, we were unable to save five of them.'

'What was going on in there, Doc,' asks the sergeant.

'The five new arrivals are recovering well. They were merely sedated, and other than being malnourished, they will be fine.'

'And the others?'

'What was happening was beyond barbaric, Detective. The others in the recovery room were mostly in medically induced comas.'

'I thought that was only usually done for brain injuries?' I ask.

'Normally, yes. A brain injury alters the brain's metabolism, resulting in differential blood flow across the organ. In other words, some areas of the brain will have adequate blood supply, whereas others will likely not, and this can lead to permanent, or even fatal, damage.'

'So the coma helps?' asks Cataldo.

'Yes. It slows down all brain functions, slowing the demand for blood flow, allowing the brain time to heal.'

'So, less long-term damage?' I suggest.

'Exactly. The induced coma reduces the effects of swelling and protects the damaged areas. But, in the case of these poor children, the induced comas were merely being used to extend life while their organs were being progressively harvested.'

'Sorry, Doc. What do you mean progressively harvested?'

'This is a terrible metaphor, but think of the children as a vegetable garden. A full crop of peas in one day would be far too many for most families. Or the meal that day may demand carrots, but not spinach.'

'So, pick carrots, not the spinach, and keep the peas on ice. But have the spinach and peas ready for another time?' I finish.

'I did say it was a terrible metaphor. Most children had several organs removed and were artificially kept alive for further harvesting. The medical science used to achieve this is quite impressive, but how they used it is abhorrent.

Cataldo put it differently.

'This is the law of supply and demand. When an organ is needed, they look for a match in the children, and if they find one, they remove the organ and keep the child alive by any means so that the rest of the organs can be made available for someone else later.'

'Yes, that's exactly what I'm saying. One child has already lost both lungs, but rather than let her die and waste her remaining organs, they hooked her up with a machine that extracts blood from the neck, adds oxygen, and filters out carbon dioxide before returning it to her groin. Another child lost both kidneys and was being kept alive by extreme use of a radical kidney dialysis process. Yet another lost most of her gastro-intestinal tract and received intravenous nutrition and hydration to keep her alive.'

As the doctor wraps up his explanations, the room is even more gloomy and despondent.

I'm feeling it myself, but I can't imagine how those people in the room who have kids of their own are feeling.

The lieutenant thanks the doctor and escorts him from the room.

When they're gone, the sergeant asks me if the two children I've been looking for have been ID'd.

'Yes, they're both accounted for, but unfortunately, only one has survived.'

'Sorry to hear that, Detective.'

'Yeah, thanks. Anyway, better news for you folks. The lieutenant says that all the other children are Chinese and that two of them are the brother and sister your PI was searching for.'

'So, I've heard,' replies the sergeant. 'They're both having corrective surgery today, but should be okay.'

At this point, there's a natural break in conversation while we consider everything we've heard, top up our coffees or tackle the donuts, and wait for the lieutenant's return.

When she's back and once again sitting at the head of the table, we get what I feel is the obligatory motivational speech.

'Listen, everyone, I know what we discovered in the Pacific West yesterday was disturbing for everyone, but I want to remind you that we achieved much to be proud of. Today, we have eight children who are alive and have escaped unimaginable torture and pain.'

After giving time for us to digest her opening remark, she continues, aiming her following comment at Pat Cataldo.

'We should be equally proud that we worked together across organizational boundaries that have been difficult in the past, and much of that has been down to you, Lead Agent Cataldo. So, thank you. I look forward to hearing more about your T.E.N.S initiative when it works down the organization.'

With the speech out of the way, Cataldo asks the question on everyone's mind. 'So, how did Zhan Wu and his henchman - Hou Jiang, escape?'

It's one of the sergeants from the SWAT team who answers.

'When the shooting started, we think they made straight for a fire exit at the far side of the building, out of sight of the officers we left by the docking bays out back. We should have been prepared for that.'

'Operations like this never go without some hitches, Sergeant. You know that,' answers Cataldo before turning to the lieutenant. 'Do we know where they are now?'

'Yes. The surveillance team found them when they collected one of the tagged vehicles and drove straight to the Black Juggler. That is assuming the two of them stayed together.'

'So, shall we go get them, Lieutenant?' I ask.

'You've completed your mission here, Detective Greyfox. You can leave this to us.'

'If it's alright with you, Ma'am. I want to stay and help see this through.'

'As you wish. How about you, Lead Agent?'

'Thank you, Lieutenant, but in my case, I have to get back to Washington.'

The lieutenant offers her hand and repeats that she hopes to work with him again. Then after a brief farewell to me, he's gone.

Just after lunch, our three-vehicle convoy enters the Black Juggler estate through the vineyards, straight past the shop without stopping, and up into the foothills towards Qui Chang's residence.

Up ahead, a drone with a TSJ-mini cell phone blocker fitted has already been maneuvered onto the residence's roof, preventing early warning of our arrival. This only has an effective range of thirty feet, but it will be good enough for us.

As our vehicles slide to a halt on the dusty driveway, the accompanying SFPD officers spread around either side of the house while the lieutenant, sergeant, Ling Yú, and myself wait out front.

The lieutenant and the sergeant are standing off to one side, and she's whispering something to him. I suddenly feel as if indecision is creeping into the operation.

I move towards them and ask directly.

'Is there something wrong?'

The lieutenant and sergeant exchange glances, telling me I'm right.

'Lieutenant, I can see you're concerned with something, and if I'm putting my life on the line here, I think I deserve to know what it is?'

She gives it just another moment of thought, then opens up.

'You're quite right, Detective. Do you see the car parked in front of the house?'

'You mean the fancy Jaguar convertible?'

'Yes. Well, I know the owner.'

'And?'

Another glance between the two, but she's committed now with nowhere else to go.

'It belongs to a former District SFPD Supervisor. A former Supervisor who is now the Mayor of the City and County of San Fransisco.'

'Awkward.'

'Yes, Detective. To say the least. She's in her second term and extremely popular with her stance against police heavy-handedness, and our Chief of Police serves at her pleasure.'
'I can see why you're hesitating. What do you intend to do?'
'I'm going to do my duty, Detective. But, carefully.'

While we're having this conversation, each SFPD team has called in to say they're in position, so with firearms drawn and pointed to the ground and me feeling naked yet again, we start towards the front of the house.

Before we take even a couple of steps, the front door opens, and the Giant African American I met at the previous visit lowers his head and steps out onto the front porch., blocking the entire entryway.

The lieutenant shouts and tells him to put his hands on his head and step aside, but he doesn't move.

She repeats the instructions but in a louder voice and more urgent tone.

Still, the giant remains unwilling to move.

The sergeant holsters his sidearm and points a tazer toward the giant. It's his turn to call out.

'If you don't obey, you WILL be rendered unconscious!'

When the giant ignores this new threat, the sergeant fires, impaling the giant with steel prongs with fifty-thousand volts delivering pulses of twelve-hundred volts, nineteen times every second.

Having been through tazer training, I know that each pulse is like being sucker-punched repeatedly. It isn't just painful, which it is. It takes the legs out from under you. Anyone hit by one of these probes should fall to the ground in seconds, but the giant of a man we're facing looks down at the prongs embedded in his thigh, pulls the connection out, and throws it away.

I can see the shock on both the sergeant's and lieutenant's faces as, from behind me, Ling Yú takes a few steps forward, her sidearm holstered, speaking softly.

'Does your leg hurt?'

The giant turns towards her and replies with a simple nod.

'Would you like me to give you something for it?'

This seems to be a tricky proposition for the man, but when he thinks it through, he nods for a second time.

'Okay. Please wait where you are for a moment.'

Saying nothing, she indicates to the rest of us to back off and let her handle it as she moves back to one of the patrol cars and returns with what she wanted.

She walks straight up to the man with her hand in front of her. In it are two tablets. In her other hand, she's offering a bottle of water.

He reaches out, takes both, swallows the tablets, and hands her the water back.

'Why don't you keep it?'

This seems to please him.

'My name is Ling Yú. What's yours?'

For a moment, it looks like he's not going to answer, then he rummages in a pocket, pulls out a printed card, and hands it to her.

"Walter. Your name's Walter?'

The giant man smiles, a smile that would lighten up a darkened room. It's a smile that changes the whole complexion of the problem in front of us, and I realize for the first time what Ling's doing.

'Well, Walter. Do you like walks in the country and watching the birds and animals?'

Another big grin brightens up his face.

'How would you like to walk with me?' She asks, holding out her hand. "Let's see what we can find.'

This causes him to frown.

'You don't need to worry about Madam Chang. We'll explain to her later. I'm sure she won't mind.'

Slowly, innocence replaces the frown, and the giant man gently accepts her hand.

'Let's go this way, shall we?' she says, leading him toward the vineyards. 'We can explore together.'

I turn towards the lieutenant.

'That's one smart detective you've got there. I didn't see that coming.'

The lieutenant agrees, then again leads the way to the front door, still standing open, and shouts her warning out loud.

'SFPD armed officers are entering. If you have weapons throw them down and raise your hands above your heads.'

Inside, without the Giant leading us the way he did when I was last here, we find ourselves in a vast open-plan lounge. There's oak flooring, a stone-built log-burning fireplace, plenty of comfortable seating, and a dry bar against the far wall. There are half a dozen doors off the room, and together we start clearing them one at a time until, in the most distant room, we find a woman sitting on a bed, holding a child's hand.

From the immediate sense of deference, I realize this must be the Mayor. She looks up as we enter and is the first to speak.

'I'm so glad you're here, Lieutenant. As soon as I heard what this terrible Chinese woman has been doing up here, I just had to come and see for myself.'

'Yes, Madam Mayor. There certainly have been some terrible things happening here. We're here to arrest Madam Chang for the trafficking of underage children, but I must say I'm surprised to find you here.'

'Well, I'm sure you realize I have my sources, and as soon as I heard, I couldn't stop myself from coming. It seems I'm just in time to help rescue this young girl here.'

'That was extremely brave of you, Madam Mayor. I look forward to hearing more details from you later.'

'Of course, Lieutenant. Whatever I can do to help…..'

Before the Mayor can even finish, the young girl at her side springs up, rushes towards the lieutenant, and throws her arms around her legs.

Looking down at the terrified child, she gently removes her arms and passes her back to the sergeant before turning back to the mayor.

'I see you have your personal car with you, Madam Mayor. But perhaps it's best if you travel back to the city with me, and I'll have someone return your car to you later?'

'Excellent idea, Lieutenant. That will allow us to discuss how best to tidy up this messy situation.'

With that, the Mayor stands and follows the lieutenant, leaving the sergeant and myself with the girl.

Outside, we pass the young girl into the care of a female SFPD officer, while in the background, the dust rises as the lieutenant and the mayor head off down the driveway.

'What do you think the lieutenant will do?' I ask.

'I honestly don't know, Sammy. But I would trust her to try her best to do what's right.'

'Well, I don't envy her. She's got a political tiger by the tail there?'

At that moment, Ling Yú reappears from the vineyard with a sense of urgency.

'Walter has told me that Qui Chang is heading for a small private airstrip a few miles north of here at Calistoga. Time is difficult for Walter, but I would guess they left just before we arrived - around twenty minutes ago.'

'Where's Walter?'

'I've left him watching butterflies with a couple of officers happy to take a break. I've explained his condition to them, and they know how to manage him safely. When I left them, the girl we rescued had found him and was holding his hand and singing to him. I promised we would come back for him later.'

'Okay, let's go,' shouts the sergeant, jumping into one of the remaining SFPD vehicles. 'There's backup already on the way to the airstrip, but we should be able to get there first.'

According to the sat nav, the trip should take forty-five minutes; we make it in just under thirty-five. On the way, Ling Yú finds a number for security at the airstrip and calls to try and have them delay the departure of Chang's plane. Seemingly, security consists of one man who promises to see what he can do.

As our vehicle slews through the airstrip gates, I see a small plane on the runway and an altercation between three men on the single strip.

As we career across the grass, the men see us coming, and two of them break off and run in opposite directions. The sergeant shouts at me to check the plane as he and Ling Yú take off in pursuit. I suspect my lack of a firearm has something to do with his thinking.

I approach the third man, standing beside a tow truck parked across the airstrip.

'You must be security?'

'The one and only, Tom Chalmers is the name,' he replies, offering his hand.

As I shake, I congratulate him on his quick thinking.

'You certainly closed the airstrip effectively.'

'It's all I could think of.'

'Good job, Tom. Can you help me get the door open on this aircraft here?'

'Sure can. It's a Cessna Skyhawk, by the way. Two thousand and five prop job.'

After communicating with the pilot, the door is unlatched from the inside, and the stairs are folded down.

The pilot is first down, followed by the copilot.

I ask them how many people are inside. They tell me Madam Chang is on her own. I ask them to step to the side, then shout into the plane.

'Anytime you're ready, Madam Chang.'

I wait a few moments before shouting that she doesn't want to make me come and get her. That seems to work.

Two minutes later, she appears at the top of the stairs. She's wearing a black two-piece suit with the skirt cut rather inelegantly short for a woman of her years. Having said that, if I had her long slender legs, I might show them off as well.

However, the stairs are steep, and she probably reveals more than any lady should as she struggles to climb down and stand before me.

I turn her around, cuff her and pass her off to backup officers who have arrived just in time. They do the same with the pilot and copilot. I've no idea how involved they may be, but we can figure that out later.

Looking around, I see the sergeant and Ling Yú walking back with Zhan Wu and Hou Jiang in cuffs.

They're also taken by the SFPD officers, leaving the three of us to thank Tom Chalmers again.

'Looks like a wrap,' says the sergeant.

'Not yet,' replies Ling Yú. Can you drop me back at the Black Juggler? I've got a promise to keep.'

The sergeant and I drop off the 4x4 at SFPD headquarters and head to the nearest bar for a celebratory drink. It's an Irish bar called the Purple Shamrock, and we ask the proprietor which Irish drinks we should try.

He recommends a pint of Smithwick's Ale, and a shot of Jameson whisky.

The pub is dark, not just because we've come in from the light. More because the clientele like it that way. The only light of any note is above a dart board in the far corner, where four men sporting huge beards are playing.

A couple of old souls are sitting at the bar consoling half-empty glasses, but other than that, we have the place to ourselves.

The sergeant raises his ale and toasts me.

'Sláinte, Sammy. A pleasure working with you.'

'I prefer the fuller version. Sláinte is táinte.'

'Health and….?'

'Health and wealth. Something I'm a little short of right now.'

We sip the ale, allowing ourselves to unwind, until I ask again what the sergeant thinks will happen to the Mayor.

'Did you see the expression on the lieutenant's face when the girl ran towards her and hugged her legs?'

'Not really. I was looking at the girl.'

'Well, if you had, you would know how seriously the lieutenant intends to charge the mayor with everything she can come up with. I'm not saying politics won't get in the way, but she'll give it her best shot. You can be sure of that.'

'Why do you think Zhan Wu took all the girls down to the hospital but one?'

'I've been wondering the same thing myself.'

'Do you think they deliberately set the mayor up?'

'Could be. I reckon the mayor didn't find out what was happening through official channels.'

'You mean she was there for her own reasons?'

The sergeant shrugs at the suggestion before commenting.

'I think Qui Chang knew we were coming and invited her to the Black Juggler for a special treat.'

'You reckon the mayor is a pedophile?'

'Either that or she's involved in the organ-trafficking business. Maybe a sick relative or something started it off?'

'So, you think there was bad blood between them, and she deliberately set the mayor up.'

'Maybe.'

I think about it for a moment while I sip some ale.

'Sounds plausible. Perhaps the mayor was providing high-level cover and had come to think she was more important than she was?'

'Or was simply becoming greedy.'

'Do you think Qui Chang allowed the children to be abused at the winery?'

'Forensics will answer that, but I would say yes if you're asking for a guess. Perfect place. People coming and going all the time. Who would ever suspect such a thing?'

'And the organ selling?'

'Your guess is as good as mine, Sammy. If you remember, the doctor explained how sometimes the traffickers will wait for demand before they supply a child. I think the girls were being used at the winery until there was a more financially lucrative deal on the organ front.'

I think, at this point, we're both on overload. We clink our small glasses and down the Jameson in one swallow. It burns all the way down. I feel like my throat is on fire, then slowly, it eases into a spreading warmth.
'Same again?' asks the sergeant.

When he returns, I ask him about Ling Yú's fantastic performance with the gentle giant, and he explains that she has an elder brother with severe learning difficulties and other mental and physical disabilities.
'So, she recognized a kindred spirit?'
'Yeah. Just as well too. Did you see him pull the Tazer out? Bullets would have been next.'
'I hope you recognize her for that. She probably saved his life.'
'I will. Don't worry. How about you, Sammy? Have you now recovered all of the girls you were searching for?'
'Yes, all twelve are now accounted for, but four didn't make it.'
'But eight did, Sammy. That's what you need to focus on, and that's one hell of an achievement.'
'Why doesn't it feel like that?'
'No one likes to lose someone. It's in a detective's DNA. Unfortunately, that doesn't mean we're always successful. You have to take the rough with the smooth in this job.'
'I know. But the rough is just that….rough.'

Another clink of glasses, followed by two more burning throats. It doesn't seem so bad the second time around. I could get used to this.
'Are you going back to Homeland?'
'Right now. I honestly don't know.'
'Well, if you want my input. I don't know what Homeland needs, but you're a damn fine detective.'

***

HUGH MACNAB

AUTHOR DIRECT TO READER

Thank you for your purchase.

If you enjoyed the book and would like to find out what else is available, I would love to have you to visit my book store at

hughmacnab.com

If you find something you like, you can apply the following discount code to recieve 20% reduction on any book you choose.

Discount code : **Offer 20**

I am also interested in any feedbaclk you have on my books and would appreciate you letting me know your thoughts.

You can contact me at

Hugh@hughmacnab.com

D.S. Eli Ross series

A veteran Brooklyn homicide cop, a recovering addict, and a teenage boy with an IQ in the top one percent of the world hunt Serial Killers.

All available at Hughmacnab.com

A Crime thriller with a supernatural twist

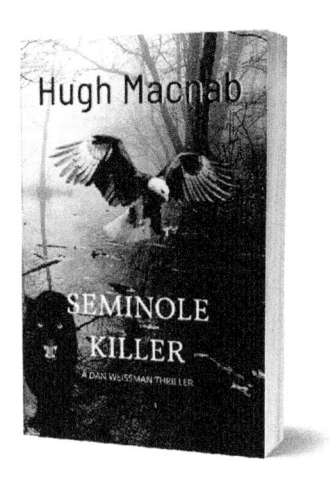

Seminole Killer

A dark flicking tongue appeared round the head of the axe, and small black lifeless eyes saw her for the first time.

Sergeant Dan Weissman thought he had left chasing the worst serial killers behind when he left New York. Instead, he is now searching for someone terrifying beyond words. A killer who leaves everything at the crime scenes a Detective needs - yet still remains puzzling and illusive.

Psychologist Luisa del Roy moves to Florida for a new beginning, little realizing that she has a long-standing debt to pay - an ancient debt incurred by forces beyond her understanding.

* * *

Tommy Blue Johns angers his Grandfather by casting aside the traditional ways of his people, yet now as a reporter, he becomes once more ensnared not only in uncovering the truth behind the new casino being built on ancient burial grounds but also in saving his people from an Evil which threatens from beyond the grave itself.

Available at Hughmacnab.com

SELF HELP BOOKS

These books will not only help you understand why you feel, think, and behave the way you do when you are at your worst but will also explain the most likely cause for all of this - and it may surprise you.

The books also include access to nine half-hour videos that will help you overcome your symptoms using a simple step-by-step process. These videos, combined with the book, form the three-week recovery program.

No program will work for everyone, but over 1200 people have successfully used these programs.

The programs start from the premise that perhaps there's really not very much wrong - and that's likely to be so different from how you feel.

All available at Hughmacnab.com

Printed in Great Britain
by Amazon